C000174312

PRIMEVAL

FIRE AND WATER

Also available in the *Primeval* series:

SHADOW OF THE JAGUAR
By Steven Savile

THE LOST ISLAND
By Paul Kearney

EXTINCTION EVENT
By Dan Abnett

PRIMEVAL

FIRE AND WATER

SIMON GUERRIER

TITAN BOOKS

Primeval: Fire and Water
ISBN: 9781845766955

Published by
Titan Books
A division of
Titan Publishing Group Ltd
144 Southwark St
London
SE1 0UP

First edition April 2009
10 9 8 7 6 5 4 3 2 1

Visit our website: www.titanbooks.com

Did you enjoy this book? We love to hear from our readers.
Please email us at readerfeedback@titanemail.com or write to us at
Reader Feedback at the above address.

To receive advance information, news, competitions, and exclusive Titan offers online, please register as a member by clicking the "sign up" button on our website: www.titanbooks.com

A CIP catalogue record for this title is available from the British Library.

Printed and bound in the UK by CPI Group UK Ltd.

For the famlee
You asked for it.

ONE

"*Batsha sengathi yizibhanxa* — they only eat us if we're stupid."

Jace stood perfectly still on the edge of the dirt-track road, the brick-red earth solid under his heavy boots. Long experience had taught him how to keep still, to exert only the barest effort under the hot, dry sun.

"*Ewe*," — the isiXhosa word for 'yes'. Beside him, Ellie slammed shut the door of their 4x4. She hefted the .375 calibre rifle in her lean and muscular arms as she surveyed the open land around them.

"This lot," she added, "were *really* stupid."

In front of their 4x4 stood another all-terrain vehicle; a more plush and comfortable model, the kind fitted out especially for tourists. One of the passenger doors stood open, as if its occupants might return at any moment. It was parked beside a battered, wooden sign at the edge of the road which warned visitors — in no uncertain terms — to stay inside their cars.

The people in the car had clearly ignored the warning. The sun beat down on the gore and scuff-marks that littered the dirt in front of the sign. Jace and Ellie were upwind of the blood but still tasted its putrid tang in the back of their throats, nature's stomach-turning way of expressing horror.

They stayed away from the scuff-marks, knowing that all kinds of creatures could be hidden in amongst the dense acacia trees that grew just behind the sign, their thorns as long and sharp as needles.

Anything could be attracted by this terrible stink of death.

Instead, the two rangers stood waiting, listening, watching. Squinting their eyes against the glare they combed the vast expanse of game park that sprawled off in all directions. Sun-bleached blond grass and bushland shimmered under the cloudless sky. Tangles of trees and rocky outcrops speckled the landscape, occasional bald patches exposing the iron-rich red soil.

The air sat still and silent, heavy with anticipation.

Jace let his eyes pick slowly over every tiny detail, straining to spot any movement. He'd been doing this job for nearly a decade and yet still his mind played tricks on him, conjured life out of shadows, patterns of rock, or the lightest breeze ruffling the grass. Coming out here day after day for so many years, he realised his eyesight didn't get sharper; his instincts didn't build up. He could never hope to know this land as well as the animals that lived here.

This is their territory; you see them when they let you.

When they didn't deign to grant an audience to lumbering, noisy humans in their lumbering, noisy SUVs, the native species could sink unseen into the grass and bush, invisible as ghosts. The hippos, elephants, zebra and giraffe, even the impala and warthogs, were more at home here, more in command than any human being ever would be.

Yet these stupid tourists got out of their car to take pictures by the warning sign, he thought ruefully. *No wonder they were such easy prey.*

"Leopards or lions, you reckon?" His voice broke into the unsettling quiet.

Ellie rolled her eyes at him.

"With the size and body mass to drag 'em all away," she said, "gotta be lions."

"Yeah," he agreed. "Figured."

Lions don't normally eat people, thought Jace. Well, they didn't in this park anyway. It wasn't good for business.

The new management wanted this incident and the others like it cleaned up long before there could be any enquiry. They had to provide a coda — instant closure — to the news story when it broke.

Yes, they'd say, *lions killed a family. But those lions have been destroyed.*

It didn't matter that the lions had just done what lions do. The new management had ideas that differed from the old guard of gamekeepers like Jace and Ellie. This wasn't the animals' territory, into which humans intruded. This was, they said, a business, and the animals were assets for attracting tourist revenue. Lions eating customers was little different to rats infesting a hotel; they just needed to be dealt with, swiftly and severely. Humans would impose their order, their rules, upon the wildlife.

They would enact revenge.

Yeah, it was stupid. But what choice did he and Ellie have? The management had already sacked a whole bunch of the old guard, replaced them with cheaper, less experienced gamekeepers who had no interest in the wildlife, and acted more like security guards or mercenaries. People with whom he had nothing in common, lacking even basic tracking skills, who made more problems than they solved for the game park.

So here they were — just the two of them, no backup but a second rifle each. And all they could do was follow this trail of gore and see where it led them. See if they could spot the perpetrators somewhere in the vicinity, find out if there was anything left of the victims.

And they had to do all that without getting eaten themselves.

"Come on, then," Ellie muttered, as if reading his mind, and she started forward. Jace followed, keeping his distance so that he could cover her if something leapt out.

Well, *maybe*, if he was quick enough.

The acacia trees rasped against the tough fabric of their uniforms. Jace held his rifle high, keeping his hands and exposed forearms clear of the thorns. It was an easy trail to follow, the tangled scrub trampled and bloody where the bodies had been hauled through by their attacker. There were occasional trophies hanging from the needle-like karroo thorns: strips of brightly coloured fabric that had once been a person's clothes. And then, as they ventured deeper into the undergrowth, there were scraps of flesh.

"Jeez," Jace said, disgust in his voice. "They're gonna be a mess."

"Yeah," Ellie replied, nodding soberly, "but at least they were dead up this far." She glanced back the way they'd come, at the jagged scuff marks in the ground. "They were struggling back there. Here, they weren't struggling. Reckon it's better that way."

Jace swallowed slowly, less at the thought of how the people had died than at Ellie's superior tracking ability. It always impressed him.

As they continued on their way, he found it difficult to look at anything else but the taut and capable woman moving along in front of him. At times she seemed almost like a wild cat herself. He remembered that night a year or so ago, when their associate Mac, a bit drunk, had refused to take no for an answer. She'd punched him so hard the fat white letch had lost two of his teeth.

Mac had loved that, and he'd told everyone he met. Even used it to explain why management had laid him off. *How could they keep me when Ellie's more of a man than I am?* Though that didn't explain all the others who got laid off at the same time.

Funny, Jace thought, *so few of the old-timers left, the park has become a different place.* Maybe that was what had spooked the animals. They picked up on stuff people didn't notice, odours, vibrations in the air. Perhaps they didn't like the scent of the new regime. He didn't understand the politics that were involved, but he knew this new lot stank to high heaven.

He was about to say as much when Ellie stopped dead in her tracks, about six metres ahead of him.

Jace froze instinctively, eyes flicking left and right, barely breathing. He felt a fat pearl of sweat track down through the dust that caked his face.

Lions. Two females and a male blended into the blond grass ahead of them. Short legs, long bodies, the male's tawny mane reaching back well past his shoulders. He was about two metres long and no more than four years old, judging by the light speckling of his nose. All three stood poised and wary, their back haunches trembling with lithe and terrible power as they readied themselves to pounce.

But they weren't watching the two gamekeepers. And as Jace very, very slowly raised his rifle, he saw they bore no marks of a kill. Their jaws weren't bloody and — from their posture and the shape of their flanks — he guessed they hadn't eaten in days. Lions would go half a week without food.

No, they'd been drawn by the smell of the blood. They, too, had tracked the real killer.

They were staring at it now.

Jace peered ahead, past Ellie, into the dense bush, looking for anything that represented a competing predator — a mane or tail or paw. So he only saw the thing when it actually moved. His first thought was that they'd brought the wrong cartridges, that they needed something that would take down an elephant. Maybe the .470 or .500 Nitro with the kick that could knock you on to your back.

The creature was at least six metres long — the length of the three lions combined and then some — and maybe twice the height of a man.

He blinked, trying to make sense of it. Tan-coloured, glimmering skin like a snake's. It stepped forward on long powerful legs, two skinny forelimbs reaching outward like human arms.

In horror, Jace realised it was ignoring the lions and was edging slowly towards Ellie, pushing easily through the thorny bush until it stood over her. Her usual poise and quick thinking seemed to have abandoned her as she stood gawping up at the terrible creature, paralysed by fear and disbelief.

Pure adrenalin pumping through his veins, Jace raised his rifle, targeting the creature in its huge and dark left eye.

Head low and submissive like a naughty dog, it towered over Ellie, sniffing the air around her.

Arm steady, Jace adjusted his aim as it moved, waiting for the right moment. The creature's wide mouth parted so that it seemed to smile. The bloody pulp of human remains hung from its long, sharp teeth.

"Yeah," Ellie breathed. She seemed to understand its intent, yet was too utterly stunned by its existence to react.

"Get down!" Jace yelled.

He pulled back on the trigger.

The rifle punched hard into his shoulder. Time seemed to slow down as he saw the black speck of the bullet streak fast into the creature, just as it reacted to the noise. The bullet punched the tough bone of the creature's forehead... but didn't break it.

The creature took a few steps backwards, stunned just for an instant. Jace let out the breath he'd not been conscious he was holding, and made to fire again.

But he was too late.

His brain struggled to catch up as the tan-coloured blur smashed through Ellie's fragile body, knocking her aside like a rag doll, and launched itself at him.

He squeezed hard on the trigger, felt the gun kick into his shoulder again, unbalancing him, and sending him backwards into the ground. A moment later there was an explosion of pain, followed by a weird calm that somehow didn't make sense.

Lying there in the hot soil he tried to breathe, and found that his lungs weren't working. He couldn't move or feel his limbs, and felt somehow unbalanced. With tremendous effort he raised his head just a tiny fraction to look down on his own body.

And just had time to see the creature nosing through his exposed, dismembered guts.

TWO

A tall blonde woman stood waiting in Arrivals at Johannesburg Airport. She bore an A4 card on which she had written in firm, precise letters, 'Lester'.

James Lester and Danny Quinn fought their way through the crowd of newly landed passengers towards her.

Danny had assumed that gamekeepers would be seasoned, serious types, with deep-etched scars and stories. But this woman was young, tanned and, he thought, beautiful — dressed in a khaki vest, shorts and a sturdy pair of boots. For the first time since Lester had marched into his office brandishing plane tickets, visas and a curt order to "get packing", Danny reflected that this assignment might actually be fun...

He walked over, one arm outstretched, the other carrying his bag.

"Hi," he said brightly. "I'm Danny, and that's Lester over there," he gestured at the immaculately dressed figure moving towards them at a more refined pace. "You must be from the park."

The woman didn't smile or even make eye contact — instead she just tucked the card into her satchel.

"I'm Sophie," she said; she had a South African accent and her voice was curt and dismissive.

"Nice to meet you," Danny said, trying to appear undaunted. Sophie glanced over at him, shrugged, and continued to sort out her bag.

He would win this woman over whatever it took.

"We've kept you waiting," Lester said as he arrived. He didn't extend his hand, just fussed testily with his cuff links. "Trouble with your customs," he went on, his impatient tone implying that it had been Sophie's fault. "In an astonishing display of complete incompetence, they refused to let us bring through our vital equipment. Seemed to think we were planning a hostile takeover."

"Equipment,'" Danny echoed. The airport authorities had — strangely enough — baulked at allowing two British Government officials to bring a vast arsenal of guns into the country without giving any good reason.

In fact he and Lester had only brought minimal kit: one handheld anomaly location detector, two tranquilliser pistols, two tranquilliser rifles, a G36 sniper rifle with the added grenade launcher, a Mossberg 500 pump-action shotgun, the Beretta Cougar that Danny had adopted since joining the ARC, and the old Glock 17 he'd never quite given back to the police force.

Only the essentials, yet it had all been impounded.

Lester's name-dropping — and increasingly angry sarcasm — had only annoyed the security people, and at one point Danny thought they might both be arrested or put on the first plane back to London.

In the end Lester had been forced to concede defeat and leave the guns behind, though he had been on his mobile ever since, pulling strings, trying to ensure that South African Customs regretted landing on the wrong side of James Lester.

It was all part of the plan, and it seemed to be working a little too well.

Back at the ARC, Lester had proposed that Danny would be playing the good cop out here. He had done so with a slight wince, as if it were a radical change from the norm. Danny still couldn't be sure if he'd been joking. Lester had an unsettling way of making you feel he was several steps ahead of you.

"We can make up the time on the road," Sophie said curtly as she turned on her heel, leading them both through the bedlam. Danny ran to keep up with her, while Lester ignored them both, marching along at his usual pace.

As they emerged from the air-conditioned cocoon of the airport, the atmosphere outside slammed into them, hot and heavy. Instantly Danny felt the sweat drip from him as he followed his guide up the stairs and then over the walkway into the car park. What must he look like, he wondered, straight off a plane after eleven hours in the air without stopping to comb his hair? He had on his usual leather jacket, a polo shirt and jeans while Lester wore a pale tan, tailored linen suit and elegant silk tie. Somehow he still managed to look slick and fresh, despite the long flight. It probably helped that Lester had upgraded to Business Class, while Danny had been forced to fold his long frame into an Economy seat.

Sophie paid the ticket machine, received the card that would let them leave the car park, then led them up to the next level. Danny dropped back to walk beside Lester.

"Can't take her eyes off us, can she?" Danny muttered. Lester smiled thinly.

"She's a professional. Knows not to ask any questions. Better for all parties this way."

"Here," Sophie called back to them as she reached a battered old SUV, rust curling round its edges. She heaved open the wide hatch at the back and moved around to the driver's-side door, while he and Lester tossed in what little luggage they had brought. Just an overnight change of clothes, the kit for a quick stopover to assess the situation. Not anything like their usual kit.

By the time Danny had got his luggage safely stowed, Lester had already taken the front passenger seat beside Sophie. Danny sighed and folded himself into the back, his long legs stretched behind Lester's seat, the rest of him behind Sophie. His body protested at being jammed into yet another small space so soon after the flight.

"How long is it to the park?" he asked, already feeling restless and fidgety.

"About two hours," Lester told him before Sophie could answer.

"Depends how fast we go," she said. She cranked the car into first gear and soon they were out of the anonymous, concrete world of the airport and speeding through Johannesburg itself.

Danny watched out the window, content to sit back, take in the sights and sounds of this — to him — new country. As in any big city, there was plenty going on. Vast glass and aluminium skyscrapers springing up, garish, barely legible posters announcing concerts and comedy clubs and selling everything from perfume to cars. He smiled, watching the people just going about their lives: carrying shopping bags, holding hands, yammering into mobile phones. Just like at home in London, only different.

Every now and again there was a glimpse of distant mountains, of the huge world beyond the city. Then they were lost, hidden behind yet more urban sprawl.

He tried to spot the legacy of apartheid in the streets themselves, his only real knowledge of the country and its complex politics having come from old TV news. Everything seemed pretty jumbled and as multicultural as it was at home.

It took a moment to recognise the difference between rich and poor, because the poor seemed to take such pride in their appearance. That was something he wouldn't have seen in London, or in most cities he'd visited; a defiant, hurt-but-healing pride. This was a place of great hope and possibility.

Once he recognised it, he could see the great gulf that existed there, segregation inspired not by colour but by cash. He'd done some reading on the plane, in between his futile attempts to sleep, and the guidebook had warned of a country without welfare — where it was all too easy to fall from grace. And this was a nation with far too many guns.

They stopped at a traffic light — or 'robot', as he'd learnt from his book. Sophie pulled up the handbrake and sat back in her seat. Danny peered round, getting his bearings, and watched as a weary old minivan studiously ignored the queue. It drove down to the right of them, well out into the oncoming lane. It was crowded with people, all black, all dressed smartly for work. No one else seemed to notice when the vehicle overstepped the red light and pushed forward into the traffic, streaming left and right, cutting a precarious path through to the other side.

He was certain there was going to be a collision, yet somehow, impossibly, the stream of cars swept round it. No one beeped or shouted. The drivers all seemed to be looking completely the other way. But Danny's heart was in his mouth.

"Did you see that?" he gasped.

"What?" Lester said. He was busy on his BlackBerry.

"Cab," said Sophie flatly. "Got their own rules, them."

"But that was *idiotic*!" Danny protested. "They could have all been killed."

"Yeah," Sophie replied, though her accent made it sound like "Yoh". "But they weren't." She just shrugged.

Then the robot turned green, but unlike in London, no one seemed in any rush to put his or her foot down. The cars in front of them laboured, the drivers releasing their handbrakes and pushing off sedately. Danny had never seen anything like it; it was as if they all just *assumed* some loon would jump the lights.

In some ways it made for a more relaxed drive than he would have experienced back home. Everyone was better behaved because they expected some nit to do something stupid.

Even so, he sat in a knot of tension as they made their way out of the city. He'd never been a very good passenger, never liked to surrender control to anyone. But this was beyond anything he could have expected.

They climbed the crest of a hill and were suddenly out in the countryside. Danny gasped at the great expanse of scrubby land stretching out in front of them as they headed north.

"It's so... big." He gaped. "It's like the horizon is further away than it is at home."

Lester tutted, lifting his head from the small screen he had clutched in his hand.

"Really, Quinn. You know that isn't possible."

"But he's right," Sophie said in a sudden burst of conversation. "Don't know how you people live in England. So small. An' always raining."

"That's a bit of a cultural cliché," Lester retorted.

"We were lucky to get off the ground at Heathrow," Danny reminded him, keen to stick up for Sophie. "Been storms all this past week."

"That's a recent development," Lester muttered, returning to his BlackBerry. "Extremes of weather are an indicator of climate change. I'm sure Sophie's seen similar changes here."

"No," she said. "It's *always* like this here. Apart from when it isn't."

Danny laughed. But she looked deadly serious.

They drove on in silence, and as they got further from the city he wondered what it might be like to call this vast landscape home, somewhere so untouched by humans that it seemed unlikely that you could ever feel like you really belonged here.

"Is that a mine?" Lester asked, snapping Danny out of his reverie. He looked up to where Lester pointed. A huge, ugly factory squatted in the landscape.

"Platinum," Sophie explained. "Not so pretty as a gold mine. And a gold mine isn't pretty."

"You've got to exploit the potential of your resources," Lester replied in clipped tones. "Encourage the entrepreneurs. It's good for the economy."

"Whose economy?" Sophie snapped. "The mine by the game park is British."

So, Danny thought, this was where their cover story came into play. He and Lester were in South Africa to look into the strange deaths at the game park, but they were doing so under the pretence of being concerned about the British-run oil mine that loomed just next door. Rather than being seen as hunters, they were assessors of health and safety, insurance men, that sort of thing. What better excuse to be sniffing around, asking tricky questions, than to say that they were protecting large sums of money?

Like all the best lies, the story contained a fair amount of truth. Lester's superiors were keen that the oil operation should not be compromised by an anomaly. The mine might just play a major part in solving Britain's energy needs, they said, presumably with many more mines to follow.

Danny suspected that Lester was hoping to impress certain high-ranking officials by sorting all this out. That was why he was here in person, on safari in a rusting old SUV. For something to get him out from behind his comfortable desk, there would have to be the potential to score some serious brownie points, perhaps even a promotion.

"The consortium," Lester replied smoothly, word-perfect on his brief, "is an equal mix of British *and* South African interests. The day-to-day grunt work is mostly done by a British team, but profits are split fifty-fifty. Otherwise, do you think your government would let us be here at all?"

"They'll do anything you tell 'em if you say you'll make them rich," Sophie replied hotly, refusing to give in to Lester's cold logic.

"To be fair," Danny put in, the contents of the brief coming back to him, "it's more like seventy-thirty in your favour. We covered the costs of set-up, and that eats into our share."

"Yes, thank you, Quinn," Lester said, and he sighed wearily, ungrateful for the back-up. "I'm sure our hostess doesn't need to hear your opinions."

Danny bristled at this, but tried to convince himself it was just Lester being in character. The idea was to have them slightly at odds, to make them seem less of a team, and thus less of a threat. Not that Lester could ever exactly be described as a team player.

Though on the ARC team for a relatively short time, Danny had observed how Abby and Connor worked when investigating creature sightings. They weren't like policemen, all formal and in control. They bickered and goofed around, and didn't wear anything like a recognisable uniform. On a police beat civilians always wanted someone official to take charge. But if you'd just seen a T-rex ransacking your bins, you wouldn't say so on the record — not unless you wanted to be carted away to the asylum. So by not wearing a uniform, being a bit clumsy, they seemed to help witnesses to come forward and say, "It sounds crazy, but —"

Danny liked to think that Abby and Connor might have planned it that way, but suspected it was just a happy accident. This new game he was playing was all about lucky chances.

For as long as their luck holds out anyway, he thought ruefully. *Our luck*, he corrected.

He himself had only just filled a dead man's shoes. Since Nick Cutter had died — and Stephen Hart before him — there was a sense at the ARC that they all lived on borrowed time. He remembered Jenny's warning as she'd walked away from it all, not two weeks earlier. People died doing this job.

He looked up to see Lester scowling at him in the rearview mirror. Sophie seemed to have noticed the scowl, too. Danny realised it must have looked like he was biting his tongue, holding back on telling Lester where he could stick his advice.

"What?" he said irritably, playing it up.

Then he went back to gazing out of the window, drinking in the incredible landscape. The pale road snaked between huge, blocky rock formations like a series of ancient weathered castles. Danny knew there was probably a simple scientific reason for these things and yet that didn't explain their inherent majesty, how they seemed to speak of such vast scale and time. They effortlessly dwarfed such puny things as all of human history.

When he glanced back into the car, he caught the reflection of

Sophie's eyes flicking away from him again. He pretended he hadn't seen her watching, and bent forward to admire the view from her side of the car. But his grin wasn't all about the majestic land before them.

Gotcha, he thought.

He decided to push his luck.

"So you think our mining operation caused what happened in the park?" he asked her.

The car swerved as Sophie twisted her head round to look at him, her expression seeming to register shock.

Lester's sharp intake of breath made her turn back around, take firm hold of the steering wheel, and lurch them back into their lane.

"What do you mean?" she said now, and she seemed to be trying to sound casual.

"I, uh," Danny said, stalling for time. He wasn't sure *what* he meant. How to pursue this without blowing their cover, or bringing up the topic of prehistoric creatures?

God, this wasn't in the briefing!

"I've seen it on the television," he said quickly. "Animals are more sensitive to what's happening around them, aren't they? Stuff people don't hear or see. So maybe the lions hear the noise of the mining, and it makes them go wild." He hoped he didn't sound like an idiot.

She concentrated on the driving, but he could see that her cheeks were flushed. Was she cross with him, he wondered, or with herself for letting slip her guard?

"You don't agree?" he persisted.

She snorted. "That the mine made the lions go wild?"

"They're already wild animals," Lester said with exaggerated patience. "What Mr Quinn was trying to say, in his own clumsy way, is that it might have prompted them to strike out."

"Yeah," said Danny, riled by this. "That's what I meant. I'm not stupid."

"Nor am I," Sophie countered. "And you know as well as I do, lions didn't do this."

Her words hung in the air for a little too long.

"What makes you say that?" Lester asked pleasantly. "Surely there's no reason to think otherwise, is there?"

"Ha!" Sophie said. "I *know* it isn't the lions. I've seen what happened to the bodies. I've seen the tracks in the ground. Sure, someone's tried covering it up. Telling us it's nothing to worry about. But you two didn't come all the way from London just 'cause a lion has killed some tourists."

"So what do you think jumped on these people?" Danny asked.

Lester cleared his throat.

"Hmm," Sophie began. "Tracks made me think it was an ostrich or something," she said. "But it'd have to be a big one. Runs on two feet, anyhow. Big. Quick. And a carnivore."

"And is there an animal like that in the park?" Danny asked.

"Nah," Sophie said. "Only..."

"Only?" Danny pressed, leaning forward. He could see that look in her eye, that need to share her reading of the facts, no matter how ridiculous or impossible. The same look he saw in everyone else he'd ever met who'd come into contact with the anomalies' creatures.

"Only," she continued, "maybe some kind of giant lizard. Like they got on Komodo. Don't think the Komodo ones run on two legs, though. Should probably check that out."

Good, Danny thought. She was keeping it within the realm of the conceivable. Which made it easier for him to support her.

"And you think whatever it is has been introduced to the park recently?"

"Yeah," she said. "And you two think it's a risk to your precious mine. Puts your insurance up or something. Or you think someone's trying to mess things up on purpose." Lester and Danny said nothing, which Sophie took as confirmation. "Whatever it is," she added, "it's got to be pretty tough."

"The autopsies didn't make for much fun reading," Danny agreed. He was more familiar with bullet and knife wounds than with maimed and eaten corpses.

"It's not that," Sophie said. "That's what you expect when an animal gets you. But what about the other animals, eh? This thing is on their turf. Why don't they scare it off, or just kill it outright? If it's on its own that shouldn't be too hard."

"You've not found the remains of any animals who have tried?" Lester asked, peering imperiously out of the car, not bothering to make eye contact.

"Not yet," Sophie said carefully. "Park's a big place. Chances are we'd only see bodies if they were near the road. If this thing kills them, they'll be dragged off somewhere out of sight, so it can eat them in peace. And if they're wounded, they'll go find somewhere quiet anyway. To lick their wounds or die."

"So you wouldn't know?" Lester said, his voice vaguely accusing.

"We'd know eventually," she told him. "Tracking takes time. This thing sticks around though — goes on unopposed — all the territories will change. We'll just watch the other animals and see which areas they avoid."

"How long will that take?" Danny asked, feeling his heart sink. He'd hoped the park rangers would have already isolated the creature, so he and Lester would just need to neutralise it, and send it back to its own epoch. But it sounded as if they might be in South Africa for at least a few days. He'd not brought enough underwear for any longer.

Sophie shrugged.

"Spring's the breeding season. All the boys get hot-blooded, so they're more likely to fight for their favourite spaces. And you want to take down or steer clear of an aggressor if you're raising young."

"Spring," Danny said, his heart sinking. "But over here that's not for another five months."

THREE

Velociraptors, noted Captain Becker, *really* do *hate the rain just as much as human beings.*

From his safe vantage point in the living room of a flat above a newsagent, he watched six of them sheltering underneath the bus stop across the street. They were a little shorter than humans, skinny, vicious and grey, and had made short work of the bloody pork loins he'd got his men to hang there. Becker watched the raptors shove and bite and kick each other. They were cross that they'd run out of food and because they didn't all fit under the shelter.

It didn't help that floodwater kept surging over their feet and ankles.

"Think we should put them out of their misery?" he said — and he didn't get a horrified response. Becker looked round, and found no Connor. A couple of soldiers loitered in the doorway of the small living room. Lieutenant Jamie Weavers sat slumped in an armchair, his black uniform and body armour making a strange contrast to the issue of *Heat* magazine in his hands. A small child — the son of the woman whose home this was — sat to one side of him, gawping at Weavers' various guns.

A tray of tea things sat on the low table to one side. The plate that had earlier overflowed with Jaffa Cakes and Bourbons now lay empty but for a few crumbs. Which explained, Becker thought, where Connor had disappeared off to. Both Connor and Abby were sulking because this was *his* plan, not theirs. But as Becker had explained to them — while they rolled their eyes and pulled faces — this was all about tactics.

So far it had been raining for three days. At times it would die down to a drizzle with a grey wetness clogging the air. Most of the time, though, it came clattering down, thick, consistent, and bruising. The drains in many parts of the country couldn't cope with the volume of water and their roads were now fast-flowing rivers.

Stinking black and brown water surged through Maidenhead's suburbs and shopping centres, smashing walls and windows as it went. And then, as if the damage hadn't caused trouble enough already, an anomaly had opened up right in the midst of it. The late Professor Cutter had suggested that bad weather might exacerbate the anomalies — though they'd never found any concrete proof. To Becker, it was just an example of the old army principle: *It never rained, but it poured.*

Connor had called the Met Office, but they didn't think anything unusual of the rain. Well, they said, it was heavier than usual for the time of year, but it had a natural cause. The United Kingdom apparently sat on a sort of 'weather crossroads' between the North Pole and the Tropics, between the Atlantic Ocean and the great continent of Europe. It only took a warm current of air running down one side of the country and a cold current on the other, and massive black storm clouds whirled up in between.

Connor and Abby had been keen to point out that though raptors were warm-blooded, being desert dwellers they wouldn't normally venture out into a storm. They'd argued possibilities all the way from London, but Becker had his own ideas. Connor said the raptors would mainly kill prey for themselves, but there was nothing out in this downpour. The creatures would be cross and hungry and the runaway river had disrupted litterbins and sewers, disgorging foul-smelling filth all through the town. Becker understood the simple economics of scavenging from his own tours of duty. If you were hungry and thought there'd be food you could grab easily, you didn't mind getting wet.

The trick was to think like a lizard, with a worldview that didn't include things like sniper rifles. The bus stop stood in relatively open space, with little cover for an ambush. The raptors would gauge the fresh meat hanging there as a treat rather than a trap... and once they'd got themselves under cover from the rain, they wouldn't move until they had to.

They were, thought Becker as he regarded them coolly from his safe position, creatures of instinct. Like several Anomaly Research Centre staff, they acted without considering the consequences. Becker was a soldier — and a good one. He knew how to scope out situations, assess different possible interventions, gauge their chances of success and their cost in resources and men.

There were three options open to him. He could use his safe position to pick off the raptors with a single grenade — a messy, inelegant solution that would earn him little favour with Abby and Connor. He could take them out one-by-one using tranquilliser darts, but he suspected the group would scatter after the first of them was hit.

What is *the collective noun for raptors*, he wondered. *A brace? A brood? A terror?*

Or he could place himself in the most danger and face the things head on. Challenge them, poke them, get them to notice him so they would chase out into the rain. And then see which of them was fastest...

"Weavers!" he barked.

"Sorry, Captain," Jamie said quickly, struggling to extract himself from the depths of the chair. "Sir!"

"Get Abby and Connor up here."

Becker found himself smiling at the prospect of telling them his plan. It was foolhardy, dangerous, and put the lives of the creatures above those of himself and his men. But he'd show them he was more than just a jumped-up bodyguard, that he played the same game as them.

"Um," Jamie said.

Becker felt a familiar sense of dread.

"What have they gone and done this time?"

"They, uh, took a speedboat off about twenty minutes ago, Captain."

"What?" Becker snapped. "Which idiot authorised that?"

"Um," Jamie said again, scratching his forehead with his rolled up magazine. "They said you did."

Becker swore under his breath. "Fine. We'll show them we can do this without them. I need two cars and another driver."

Jamie gaped at him.

Becker grinned.

"Good man. Well volunteered."

***

"With weather like this, it's no wonder people are beginning to see... strange things, but I think we can assume, Debbie, that what you saw swimming down the High Street was a badger, or something like that, and not the Loch Ness Monster..." The voice from the speaker paused, then continued. "Next we've got a text from Joe, who's stuck in traffic in Winnersh. Apparently there's about three feet of water under the railway bridge and —"

A small, slim hand reached out and turned off the radio.

"Hey," Connor Temple called over the roar of the engine and the lashing rain. "They might have mentioned us."

Abby Maitland shook her head wearily — or perhaps she was just trying to shake her sopping fringe out of her eyes. They were whooshing down Maidenhead's narrow High Street in a speedboat they'd pinched from the army. As a result of several days of rain, the lower end of the High Street was now a fast-moving torrent of foul-smelling water and debris. Behind the spot where Abby crouched, their boat's sludgy grey wake slapped against the shop windows of McDonald's and Dixons.

Connor saw she was staring at him, her head on one side, her lips parted ever so slightly. Connor let his own head tilt over, losing himself in her eyes. One day he'd find the right moment to tell her —

"You're such an idiot, Connor," she called out over the noise of the boat. "Why would *we* get mentioned?"

"Well," Connor admitted, moving back from her, "I don't know exactly. But Jenny's not around any more to make sure we're not."

"Her team's still with us. They're the ones telling people to stay in their homes because of burst sewage pipes and stuff."

"That's not a cover story though, is it?" Connor responded, wrinkling his nose. "And it stinks worse being at the front of the boat. Can't we swap, and I'll drive for a bit?"

She nodded reluctantly, and he reached for the control in her hands. It didn't look too difficult — a lever on the back of the boat that attached to the great fin of a rudder. You pushed the lever in one direction and the boat nosed in the other. Even he couldn't get that wrong.

"Connor!"

Abby yanked the lever out of his hand and pulled them hard around the tree that stood in their way. In fact, there were trees and telephone boxes at irregular intervals all the way down the High Street.

"Ow," he said, rubbing his fingerless-gloved hands together as if he had been stung. Abby steered them neatly between the obstacles, frowning in concentration.

"It's really just Mario Kart, isn't it?" he said. "Like steering past the crabs."

"Sort of." There was suddenly a wicked gleam in her eye. "Have you beaten my high score yet?'

"Yeah, like ages ago," he told her, for the first time glad that he and his Wii had been evicted from her flat, because she wouldn't be able to check.

"Come on," she said. "You're meant to be searching for whatever scared the raptors out into the rain. You're facing the wrong way."

Huffing, he shuffled back round to face the front again. His knee hit the radio, knocking it backwards over the edge of the boat. Connor pounced, caught it, lifted it up to show Abby with a wide grin on his face. Then they bumped hard against a great wave of water and Connor found himself sprawled helplessly on top of her.

There was silence. No sound of the engine. Just the lash of the rain on his back, and the splash and plop of the water around them. The warmth of her body inside her army-issue waders, pressing hard against him. Connor lay stunned and sore and soaked to the skin.

But really this was okay...

"Get," she said, "off."

"Uh, yeah." He disentangled himself from her, being extra careful where he placed his hands. Abby sat up crossly.

"You've done something to the motor. You'd better be able to get it working."

"And I, uh, I think I dropped the radio over the side."

"Connor!"

"What? You wouldn't let me listen to it anyway!"

"Yeah, but it wasn't ours. You'll have to explain it to Becker."

"Oh, I wouldn't want to do that. It might distract him from his mouse trap."

"You're scared of him," she teased.

"Me? Never! He's just, you know, quite serious about all his army stuff. Got to wonder about anyone with such a thing for guns. What's he compensating for, eh?" There had been a time when he had been quite excited about the prospect of carrying a gun, actually. But somehow, since Cutter had died, he hadn't felt quite the same way about things.

"He means well," Abby said. "And those guns have come in quite useful. You should give him a break."

Connor considered that for a moment, looking out across the flooded High Street. Then he found himself facing something altogether more important.

"Abby?" he said gently.

"Yes, Connor."

"Actually, I think we *should* have brought Becker with us. Look."

He pointed carefully across the water to the NatWest Bank, some way upriver from them. An ornate old clock high above the entrance gave the time as a little past seven. A breeze seethed through the rain as the night came on. Yet Connor felt chilled for another reason entirely.

A railing broke the surface of the water that was running in front of the bank. Debris had got trapped between the railing and the wall. And in amongst the stinking mulch and litter were two impossibly enormous crocodiles.

Crocodilians, to be precise. Their snouts were as long as Connor was tall, jagged teeth showing all the way down.

"*Deinosuchus*," he murmured. "That's quite bad." He peered down the street and then back behind them, as though hoping to find something in the running water.

"I don't believe it," Abby said with a giggle in her voice, a crooked grin on her impish face.

Connor turned back to peer at the giant crocs. What could she find so amusing? These things, he knew, ate other dinosaurs — even the bigger, scary ones. They weren't really what you wanted to happen across when you were only armed with tranquilliser pistols.

They should back away now, he thought silently; get reinforcements, come back another time. Yeah, he'd even apologise to Becker. After all, the giant crocs weren't going anywhere. They lay in the shallow, black water almost perfectly still, one on top of the other...

"Um, Abby," he said at last. "Are they doing what I *think* they're doing?"

FOUR

Shadows reached long across the ground. The sky remained huge and blue above them, yet without the pressing vibrancy of before.

Weird, Danny thought, glued to the window. *In this vast, empty wilderness, even the dusk feels different.*

They crested a low rise and looked out over a long, shallow valley that stretched for five miles or more ahead of them. Sophie raised a hand from the steering wheel to point off to the horizon, where an ugly dark blob of smoke belched into the sky.

"That's the oil mine," she told them without any attempt to hide the accusation in her tone. "Can you see the Union Jack?"

Danny squinted, then realised she was joking. Again, he thought he glimpsed her watching him in the mirror, and smiling. But in an instant her eyes were on the road again, and he couldn't be sure.

"The game park is just the far side of it?" Lester asked.

"About another twenty minutes." Sophie nodded. "Be dark by the time we get there."

"That's not really 'next door' to it," Lester observed. "I think we're wasting our time out here, Quinn."

"It's near enough," Sophie countered anxiously. "And there's nothing else out here. Our mystery creature gets through the fence, that's the next thing in its way."

"How would it get through the fence?" Danny asked. "We're not talking

Steve McQueen on a motorbike, are we? You think it'd just charge through?"

Sophie grinned at him wickedly.

"Depends how much it wants out."

"But the fence is electrified," Lester said.

"Kill a man without much problem," Sophie told him. "Kill an elephant if it hangs about. But this thing of yours..." her smile faded. "It's an unknown quantity, yeah?" Her eyes flicked to Lester, then to Danny in the mirror, as if checking their reactions.

Danny shrugged at her, but felt uneasy. This woman was a hunter, a tracker, and she was hard upon their trail. It was going to be damn difficult to stop her from following what they got up to, to stop her getting involved.

On the other hand, she knew the country and the rest of the wildlife. She was smart and understood the danger. She was *exactly* what he needed. Someone not afraid to get her hands dirty — unlike Lester, who he imagined would leave all the action man stuff to him. Truth be told, Danny was looking forward to the chase, after being cooped up in planes and cars.

That, he told himself, was all this feeling was.

They were on a long, straight road now, scrubby bushland on either side of them. A tall wire fence followed the roadside on their right, enclosing acres and acres of emptiness that reached as far as the vast reddy hillside a few miles beyond, its outline stark in the lengthening shadows. The fence was twice the height of a man, and an additional barbed wire section on top angled sharply out at forty-five degrees, making the thing impossible to climb. The same sign appeared at regular intervals: a black stick figure on a yellow background being vividly electrocuted.

It took Danny a moment to realise why such empty landscape would be so fiercely guarded.

"This is all the park," he said.

"We're coming round the perimeter, yeah," Sophie acknowledged.

He sat forward, eagerly scanning the emptiness for signs of life. Ahead, the road stretched on to the horizon. Yeah, the park was big. He began to understand what more than 500 square kilometres actually meant. And how hard it was going to be to find one escaped dinosaur somewhere deep within it. Why this might take them months. Lester wouldn't keep them out here that long, would he?

Sophie turned right, following a dirt track. The SUV bumped and bucked easily over the coarse terrain; the road might not be tarmacked, but it had been maintained. They kept on for perhaps another mile and then came to a series of sentry posts. A man in a dark green, army-like uniform stepped forward to intercept them, one of the modern Winchester Model 70s cradled in his hands.

The gun was, Danny noted, made from black resin, not wood — cheaper and longer lasting but not quite as cool. He'd learnt about guns in the police force. The new Model 70, he recalled, had controlled round push feeds, though he couldn't remember exactly what those were. But this was a serious, no-nonsense gun for dealing with huge and lethal beasts.

Sophie coasted to a stop in front of the man with the gun and pressed the button to lower her window. He came over and broke into a gap-toothed smile. He had a small head with high cheekbones, all perched on a long, skinny neck. His dark skin shone with sweat as if he had been varnished. He and Sophie exchanged pleasantries in a language full of strange sound effects — clicks with the tongue and at the back of the throat. The man poked his head right into the car to get a better look at Lester and Danny, but he seemed more curious than suspicious. As if the Englishmen had landed from the moon.

"Hi," Danny said, grinning awkwardly. The man gazed at him with wide, keen eyes, and Danny felt his grin falter.

And then Sophie swatted the man away with what might have been a swear word. Laughing, he lifted the barrier to let them through. As she put her foot down, he called out to her, suggesting something rude that didn't need to be translated. Sophie just shook her head and pressed the button to raise the window.

"Friend of yours?" Danny asked.

"Ted's all right," she responded. "But he's on duty tonight. Pissed he's gonna miss out on the drinks."

"Drinks?" Lester said. "What drinks?"

"To celebrate your arrival," she answered scornfully.

Dusk was coming on quickly as they drove deep into the game park. Danny's eyes picked over the details of bristly shrubs and grasses as they whooshed by and he soon found that he couldn't concentrate on anything that close up to the car. Even as he shifted his gaze, there was just so *much* to keep his eyes on in the middle-distance. A tree branch that might be a giraffe. A shadow that might be a lion. Sophie was braking just as Danny saw a pattern in the long grass ahead of them that might be a —

"Zebra!" he exclaimed.

The car stopped abruptly, jolting them in their seats. Three zebras mooched slowly across the road in front of them, one turning its head back to stare balefully at the vehicle.

Danny realised he was grinning like a kid.

"I saw them first," he said. "How many points is that?"

"Have a million," Lester said blandly.

"Great! I'm winning."

"You've still got all the Big Five to go," Sophie told him as the car started on again.

"Big Five?" he asked.

"Lion, elephant, buffalo, leopard, rhinoceros... We tell the tourists they're the rarest to spot, but that's not really how they got the name. Truth is, they're the most valuable kills."

A little later they just made out in the dwindling light a small herd of elephants crossing a grassy plain. They were such strange creatures, huge and round yet moving rather gracefully on their tree-trunk feet. Nothing like the carnivorous creatures Danny had encountered through the ARC. He couldn't understand how anyone could wish harm on these gentle beings. It would make you *less* of a man to shoot one.

As they crossed a trickle of river, he thought he spotted a crocodile — though it could just have been a log floating by the bank. But night was drawing in now and it became more and more torturous to pick out detail in the dusk. Sophie clicked on the car's blinding headlights. White light seared deep into the roadside bush, conjuring lurid, twisting shadows as they drove quickly by.

Without warning they turned off the main dirt road onto one that was narrower, more windy and bumpy; plunging deep into the heart of darkness. Danny's skin prickled with goose flesh at the strange magic of the place; he could feel the wild pressing in around them, and suddenly he felt apprehensive.

Up ahead there appeared a warm glow from some kind of building. Fully forty-five minutes after they had passed through the gate, the road wound lazily round the structure, allowing Danny to appraise it. Less a log cabin than a log complex, a series of interconnected one-storey buildings all raised up from the ground on stilts. They didn't look particularly well defended.

Danny peered at Lester, and sensed his distaste at the building's lack of a five-star rating.

They emerged into a clearing around the back, a simple car park next to the lodge. Sophie brought the SUV round to fit neatly between two other battered vehicles already parked up by the entrance. The full beams swept across the uneven ground.

The lights glared red in the eyes of a pride of lions.

Sleek and beautiful and undeniably deadly, seven of the creatures stalked the edge of the car park, their back legs in the bush. Sophie stopped the car but left the engine running and sat there, watching them coolly. The lions shifted uneasily on their feet, eyeing the newly arrived intruder and its edible cargo. Danny felt a cold bead of sweat trickle down the side of his face.

"There must be a hole in your fence," Lester said, nerves making his sarcasm sound less cutting than usual.

"No fence round the lodge," Sophie told him. "Waste of time. Animals rarely come anywhere near us. Don't like our music and the noise we make."

They sat, watching the lions watch them impassively.

"Maybe that's the problem," Danny said. "There isn't any music."

They all looked up to the lodge. Light glared from the windows and the open front door. No sound came from within — no sign of life at all.

"Stay here," Sophie said, turning off the engine.

"If you insist," Lester said.

"I'll come with you," Danny volunteered. Sophie turned around to look him up and down.

"You ever fought a lion?" she asked.

"Uh," he said. "No."

She considered. And then her eyes lit up with a grin.

"Me neither," she said. "Come on."

Slowly, gently, they opened their car doors and let in the hot, sweaty night air. Danny struggled to get his long, tired legs out and onto the ground. He stood gingerly, pins and needles in his feet, while Sophie made her way calmly round to the hatch at the back of the car. Seven lions watched them both with interest, but made no move. Only one had a mane, and some of them seemed smaller. They might have been teens rather than full adults.

Even so, the family group clearly wasn't to be messed with.

Sophie eased open the back of the SUV and reached in for a rifle. Danny joined her, trying to broadcast the same waves of assurance and cool. He took the gun from her — a bolt action Winchester Model 70 like the one belonging to Ted, the gamekeeper at the gate. It was heavy, and he checked it over quickly, familiarising himself with its features. It carried a massive .458 calibre cartridge.

"This enough to stop them?" he asked.

Behind him he heard one of the lions murmur with irritation.

"Hope so," Sophie said.

"We normally use a tranquilliser."

"All right," Sophie said. She snatched back the rifle and handed him a feeble looking dart gun.

"Great," he said, turning slowly towards the animals, rubbish gun at the ready. But the creatures weren't even looking in his direction.

"This is no fun," he said. "Don't I look like a good meal?"

"Richer pickings in the lodge," Sophie replied as she closed the back of the car. She carried the Winchester she'd taken from him, plus the khaki satchel that must be her handbag. Turning, she headed for the stairs.

He followed her slowly up to the lodge. The bush all around them bristled with life; things creaking and twittering and breathing. But the lodge remained eerily silent. And there was an acrid tang in the air; one Danny knew from many a call-out as a policeman.

The unmistakeable stink of blood.

Sophie must have noticed it, too, and she stepped quickly up onto the raised platform running around the lodge. The wood creaked loudly under her weight, and they both glanced back cautiously and saw one of the lions behind them become suddenly alert. It stood up tall, straining forward as though about to pounce.

"Don't worry about her," Sophie said, turning back to him. "They're all cowards, really."

Danny nodded, but he wasn't entirely convinced. He joined her on the platform, and they edged carefully towards the open door. Sophie slowly pushed it wide.

"Hell," she breathed as light streamed out from inside.

The hallway beyond wasn't much like a hotel reception — it looked more like the front porch of a teeming, ramshackle family home. Jackets swamped the coat hooks to his left, and there were crates of empty bottles, a stack of crudely split logs presumably for a fire, and — oddly — an old wooden rocking horse.

There were books and papers all over the floor where a bookcase had fallen. A bare hand and arm protruded from under the bookcase, the chunky, golden watch on the wrist smeared with blood and grime.

"Oh, God," Danny said. And he tensed as a door slammed loudly behind them.

"I'm not going to be left out there on my own," Lester said as he stepped into the room behind them. "I was starting to feel like a tin of Whiskers —" He stopped, seeing the mess and the body. "Oh," he said. And then, "I should have a gun, too."

Sophie ignored him as she crouched down beside the exposed arm and felt for a pulse. She looked up, shook her head, a chilling emptiness in her eyes.

"They didn't want us 'cause they've already eaten," Danny said.

"Wasn't a lion that did this," Sophie said quietly, getting to her feet. "They're just waiting for their turn."

A chill ran through Danny.

"But if they're waiting," he said, "whatever killed him must still be here."

"Yeah," Sophie agreed. "The mess room and kitchen are down the hall. The bedrooms all lead off that. You can go first."

"But you've got the gun," Danny said.

"So I'll cover you," she said.

Danny turned to Lester, who just shrugged at him. "What the hell — what can possibly go wrong?" he sighed, and started down the hallway.

Beyond the hallway, through a door, there was a wide-open space, a mess room not unlike the canteen at the ARC. But it had been ransacked. The sofa and chairs had been upturned, the large dining table cracked in two. And two bodies in army-green uniforms lay strewn under and on top of the furniture, their limbs wrenched at impossible angles. It was less like they'd been attacked than as if a whirlwind had torn through.

Sophie quickly went over to them, confirming one at a time that her colleagues were dead, without saying a word. Danny stood where he was, not wanting to get in her way, and watching for any sign of the creature that had caused such carnage.

An odd stench mingled with the tang of blood. It took Danny a moment to spot the broken glass behind the table. The park rangers had been planning a boozy welcome for him and Lester when whatever it was had killed them.

"So much for the party," he said.

"Wasn't going to be a party," Sophie said quietly. "Just a few drinks."

"Who do we need to call?" Lester asked, exerting authority and practicality with a single question. He went over to the telephone that was mounted on the wall.

"Ted will be on Sentry Two," Sophie told him. "But tell him to hold back."

Lester turned.

"Hold back?"

"The killer's still around here somewhere..." Danny told him.

"...And we need to find it," Sophie finished.

Lester stood with the phone in one hand, his other one reaching for the speed-dial button that would call Sentry Two. He stood perfectly still, gazing through a side door into what seemed to be the kitchen. Slowly, the hand that had been reaching for the speed-dial button pointed at what he saw.

"Oh —" Danny began, raising his dart gun.

Sophie stepped forward into his line of sight to see what Lester had found.

Beyond her came a terrible, primal roar. And then the creature was on them.

FIVE

Sarah Page sat beneath the five large screens of the anomaly detection device and wished someone was around to make her some tea. She didn't really want the tea; it would just give her an excuse to strike up a conversation, to kill a bit of time.

But the huge main operations room of the Anomaly Research Centre remained eerily quiet. She'd once relished being left on her own to work. Then an anomaly had opened at the British Museum and her life had changed forever. Now everyone else was off on exciting adventures, leaving Sarah to watch the screens and call people if anything happened. So far, since Abby, Connor and Becker had raced off to Maidenhead, nothing had.

Sarah leaned back to put her feet up on the little platform that held the Anomaly Detection Device's keyboard, and leafed through the notes she had written up on some of the ARC's most recent cases. Only days ago — just a couple of feet from where she sat — Jenny Lewis had almost frozen to death while infected with a virulent fungus. The extreme cold had played havoc with the ADD and the team's other equipment. So while the technical guys had tried to fix the glitches, Sarah had started writing up notes in longhand. It felt good to rely on a thick notebook and retractable pencil, the kit she'd used on so many digs, because sand and water and laptops really didn't mix.

She wrote slowly, carefully, gathering her thoughts before entrusting them to paper. On a computer she would just batter away, knowing she could shunt the order and meaning of her words once she'd got them down. Writing it out longhand, she first had to get the story clear in her mind, the sequence of incidents and reactions.

The anomalies were suddenly starting to appear more frequently, all around the world. She had read about Peru and Siberia, and ever since then more and more had manifested. Their small, embattled, secret gang was struggling to fight back the tide. Sarah had thought her role was going to be as an archivist or researcher, explaining the history humanity shared with the anomalies and the creatures. She had been tasked with finding proof of early encounters, ferreting it out in ancient stories, myths, and religions. But now, as she prepared to put her thoughts to paper, she realised her real role.

To discover a way for them to survive through to the future.

The ARC needed to change how it worked fundamentally, or they were all going to die. And in an instant, she knew what they needed to do. Just for an instant, it all seemed so clear, if she could *just* write it down.

She wrote carefully into her precious notebook: *The solution can only be —*

And then her mobile rang.

"Hi Sarah," Abby whispered into her phone, cradling it to her ear with both hands, in the hope that the rain wouldn't get to it. "We're in a bit of trouble." Water bashed against her wrists and hands, cold tendrils dripping down her sleeves. She told herself — not for the first time today — that a long bath awaited her later, if her brother had left any hot water.

She was in the front of the boat, watching over Connor's shoulder as the Deinosuchus couple continued with their coupling. Crocodilians weren't really her speciality, but she suspected they didn't go in for post-coital cuddling and cups of tea. Any moment now they'd disengage, after which they'd both be hungry. And conveniently placed just upstream, they'd see two stranded, defenceless human beings.

Connor sat bent over the speedboat's engine, trying to get it working. But he probably hadn't done it much good when he'd lifted off the plastic cover and exposed all the workings to the rain.

"What do you need?" Sarah asked from her warm, dry office.

"Have you heard from Becker?"

"Um, isn't he with you?"

"We sort of got separated," Abby said hurriedly. "And now we can't reach him."

"You and Connor ran off again, didn't you? He *is* there for your protection, you know."

"Yeah," Abby said, so loud that Connor boggled at her. "But you know what he's like," she said more carefully. "We find a creature, and he starts to shoot at it."

"Usually it's so it doesn't eat you," Sarah argued.

"Well, yes. And he may have a point. You see, we're in sort of a situation with two giant crocodiles who are about to realise they're peckish."

"Giant crocodiles? You mean a Sarcosuchus?"

"Um, Connor thinks they're Deinosuchus. But he's not got his laptop."

Connor looked up from his work.

"I don't need to look them up any more," he protested. "I know my dinosaurs."

"Connor *knows* they're Deinosuchus," Abby said down the phone. On the other end of the line, she could hear Sarah tocking away on the keyboard.

"Puts the anomaly as Late Cretaceous," she said at last. "Except the raptors would come from Late Cretaceous Asia while the Deinosuchus would be Late Cretaceous North America. So you might have two anomalies."

"I know," Abby said through gritted teeth. "We really need to get hold of Becker."

"I can't reach him either. He must be busy with the Velociraptors. They *were* what you all got sent out to deal with in the first place. I can't help it if you don't stick together."

"Sarah!"

"I've got him on redial. The moment he pokes his head out of the water, I'll tell him where you are."

"Right," said Abby. "We're —"

"At one end of Maidenhead High Street," Sarah told her calmly. "I triangulated your signal just now using GPS. In fact —" For a moment there was a clatter of quick typing. "— I've got you on CCTV. Yes, I think I can see Connor's bum."

Abby leaned forward in her seat, towards where Connor was kneeling with his back to her. She twisted slowly round, scanning the High Street until she spotted the camera mounted on the side of a building.

Instinctively she waved, and the camera twitched left and right in acknowledgement.

"So where's the —" Sarah began cheerily, and then Abby heard her exhale. The camera had rotated, and she was watching the crocodilians.

"I guess you can see what they're up to."

"Yeah," Sarah said. "Um, not something you see every day. Do you think I should record it?"

"Sarah!"

"All right! I'll keep trying Becker."

The engine screamed in protest as Becker put his foot down. A plume of thick amber sand sprayed out high behind his armoured car and with a lurch he started forward, bringing the vehicle around in a wide arc. The car bounced and bucked over the hot, dry ground. If he could only keep on moving he might avoid getting bogged down.

The plain inclined steeply upwards towards open woodland, perhaps a mile away. Unruly foliage marked the edge of a wide, shallow river, flat like a mirage. Between Becker and the trees the anomaly twinkled brightly in the sun, leading back to the Maidenhead monsoon.

The six raptors stood between him and the anomaly.

They had taken the bait, and followed the vehicles he and Weavers had driven through into this hot summer in the past. If it weren't for the ravenous creatures bearing down on him, Becker might have considered staying longer — the weather was certainly better than back at home.

But the raptors weren't watching *him* any longer.

Steam coiled from his soaking clothes as he leaned out of the window to see how Weavers was getting on. They had both got caught in the loose sand as the lower part of the plain became desert. Weavers was fighting with his gears and pedals, while all the time watching the raptors. His armoured car was sinking imperceptibly, its front wheels dragging the rest of it down. The raptors had seen the distress he was in and trotted idly towards him, almost as if they meant to help out.

Becker spun his own car around and raced towards Jamie.

Roused by the sudden movement, the raptors started running towards the prone car.

With one hand on the steering wheel Becker reached for his prized SIG .229, which he kept in the pouch at his thigh. But then his conscience got the better of him and he grabbed the tranquilliser gun from the seat beside him. Left hand still on the wheel of the car, he aimed the gun out of the window with his right. A split second to aim, he pulled back on the trigger and *shunk!* — he shot one of the raptors in the back of the neck. It dropped, mid-stride, into the sand — to sleep for roughly an hour.

Its comrades didn't even glance round.

Dammit, Becker thought. He cranked the armoured car into fifth and hurled himself at them. They leapt nimbly out of his way as he sped through, dropping back into formation in his wake.

Still with his foot down he leant his head out of the window and yelled at the top of his voice.

"I can't stop! You'll have to run to me!"

For a moment it didn't look like Jamie had understood. But no, he was just gathering his senses. Then his car door was open and he began running for his life. In his arms he cradled his HK G36 — standard issue, without the grenade launcher.

The raptors spotted him out in the open and redoubled their efforts.

Becker was almost there now. He put the car back into second, the engine wheezing as it slowed right down. The captain had been trained in emergency driving, but the usual bootleg turn wouldn't work on the sand; he'd just have to drive in a loop and take the raptors head on.

He leaned over to the passenger door and yanked at the handle. The door opened wide and then slammed shut again. Becker reconsidered the idea and pressed the button on his right. The window in the passenger door rolled down smoothly with an electric buzz.

Slowing down even further, he turned the car.

"Jump!" he shouted. All he could do was keep his foot on the gas.

A sudden drag on the side of the car and Jamie's front half was through the window. His arms flailed about as he tried to find purchase, smacking Becker in the head.

"'Scuse me, sir," he said awkwardly as he clung on to the passenger seat. His legs billowed out of the car window, cracking against armoured side panels. He swore at the sharp pain.

"Get yourself comfortable," Becker told him sternly. "We've got to get through this lot yet."

He couldn't steer too severely because of the sand, but a wider arc gave the raptors more time to catch them up. That's why he'd wanted two cars in the first place — so the creatures wouldn't just be chasing a single target.

There they were, in his peripheral vision, as he brought the car around. Five furious, scaly beasts, intent on making him and Jamie their supper. He reached for his tranquilliser gun again, fired blind in their general direction, and caught one of them in the knee. It stumbled and fell into the dirt, but the other raptors ignored it.

"Use a proper gun!" Weavers muttered, clinging to the seat. But Becker ignored him as he crunched through the gears. The vehicle struggled in the mud. And the bloody raptors were gaining.

The anomaly gleamed at them from above the edge of the river, broken glass glinting in the sky, reflecting on the water's surface. They had a hundred metres, maybe a bit more...

The pieces of the anomaly were starting to rotate a little slower; the brilliant light wasn't gleaming quite so brightly. It was starting to fade — and if it closed, the two soldiers would be trapped a hundred million years from home.

Becker had his foot flat on the pedal, but the car wasn't built to be nippy. It growled as he forced it hard up the slope. He just prayed it wouldn't conk out with the effort.

The raptors had almost reached them. In his mirror he glimpsed mad, hungry eyes.

Weavers screamed in pain, his face suddenly pale.

"Hold on!" Becker ordered. He whipped the pistol from the strap on his leg and shot the raptor without a moment's hesitation.

"Thank you," Weavers croaked, exhausted, his face grimacing in pain. "It's taken a chunk right off my leg."

"We're almost there!"

The armoured car shook as something large leapt onto its roof. A claw appeared in front of Becker, on the far side of the windshield, hooking itself round the wipers. He realised what the creature was reaching for just as a huge, toothy mouth poked into his open window. Becker shot once, and the raptor toppled off into the sand.

Three left.

And forty metres...

Thirty...

Becker could see right through the fading anomaly now, to the trees that stood behind it. Any second now it would wink out of existence.

"Sir," Weavers said in a small voice.

"Almost there," Becker insisted.

"Yeah," Weavers acknowledged. "But they'll just come through with us again, won't they?"

Becker looked quickly at the man next to him. Blood drooled from his nose and lips. And his legs no longer smacked against the outside of the car.

"Hold on," Becker insisted.

"Tell Janine —"

And then, *thwip*, Weavers was gone. He didn't cry out, didn't make a sound. Looking in the mirror, Becker's stomach turned in horror as he saw the three remaining raptors tearing what was left of Jamie apart.

There was nothing he could do.

His survival instinct kicked in as he pressed on up the hill and through the anomaly. That awful sparkling, magnetic sensation, like going through a cheese grater, and then he was back in the grey and rain.

Safe.

"Lock it," he barked at the soldier working the tripod on which sat the strange sci-fi bazooka Connor had constructed. The anomaly locking mechanism burbled with power, ready to seal the way through so that the raptors couldn't follow him.

But before the soldier could fully activate the mechanism, the anomaly disappeared.

Becker sat forward, his forehead on the back of his hands as they gripped the wheel. They were slick with sweat. He stayed there, getting his breath back, listening to the slop and plop of the never-ending rain, knowing this moment couldn't last. He'd have to explain about Jamie Weavers. There'd be family who had to be told. The team would need to get back to London, anyway, and be ready for the next call from the ADD.

He just had to keep on fighting.

He sat up and wiped the sweat from his eyes. Men were running towards him, slushing through the floodwater. And his earpiece pinged to tell him someone had left him a message.

"Now I can't get hold of Sarah either," Abby said, and she sighed audibly. "I think we're on our own." She put her phone away in the pocket of her waders and batted Connor's booted foot away from her face. Connor wasn't a great respecter of people's personal space.

Or, at least, of *hers*.

She didn't like to examine her feelings for him too closely, but she *did* like to have his attention. And Connor was ignoring her, lying on his front watching the Deinosuchus couple through his field binoculars. The two giant crocodilians had made no move to pursue them, so for now the boat was moored to a lamppost and they bobbed leisurely above the brackish water, conducting decidedly voyeuristic observations.

"I think they're finished," Connor said quietly. "They're just not doing anything."

"Maybe they're exhausted."

"Mmm," Connor mused, wriggling round to face her. "But also, all that rubbish wedged around them. I don't think that's right."

"You think he should have taken her somewhere nicer?"

He grinned.

"Like a nightclub or something?" he suggested. "It's more that it's not just any old rubbish." He handed her the binoculars. "It's got lots of bits of fast food, tree branches, berries and flowers..."

Abby adjusted the focus and picked out the two incredible creatures floating together in the dark water. The rubbish bobbing all around them *was* very specific. No traffic cones, no planks of wood, none of the other crude artefacts the flood had gathered up.

"You think it's some kind of nest or something?" she asked.

"It makes sense," Connor said. "They live in the water, but they breed in the shallows or on land."

"But if they've only just mated, why would they be so quick to settle down? Abby asked.

"Don't know," Connor admitted. "Maybe they're the romantics of the Cretaceous set. And how does a bloke let the ladies know he's found the perfect spot? What would you want if you were a lady crocodile?"

"I'd like flowers and a nice dinner," Abby told him. "With you in a suit."

"Exactly," Connor said — oblivious to her hinting — "and that gives me an idea..."

"No, wait," Sarah said into her phone. "They're on the move again. Heading away from the Deinosuchus... I think they're going into one of the shops."

"Right," Becker said, and he sounded tired. "I'll get over there now."

"Are you sure you're all right?" she asked.

"I'm fine," he said curtly. "Just another day at the office."

And he rang off.

Sarah stared at her phone for a moment, worried. Becker sounded exhausted and angry to have lost one of his men. But he refused to admit it. He liked to maintain an air of cool efficiency, the old-school kind of army officer standing tall and unruffled against any enemy. He probably ironed his socks. Yet he was also young, and nobody could ever really get used to the things the ARC had to deal with.

Again she saw the team as Lester must have seen them: amateurs, bluffing their way as best they could, yet inevitably getting ground down. While waiting for Becker's call, she'd been reading up on some of the ARC's older exploits. The anomalies overturned so many basic assumptions about science and history, and thanks to her years as an academic, she saw radical papers and post-doctoral theses in every line she read. She could easily envision herself as unofficial archivist — not that Lester would let her publish anything, even internally. He wanted the anomalies contained and kept secret. The government thought they could control them.

That mindset was why they kept losing ground. If she could just get him to see reason —

Sarah turned, sensing movement behind her, but there was no one in the labs. Lester's office overlooked the ADD, and she peered up at the window, but saw nothing. She must have imagined it.

Still, she couldn't shake the sensation.

"Hello?" she said, getting to her feet. Why this nervous feeling? The ARC was one of the most secure buildings in the entire country — even the Palace of Westminster did fewer scans and checks. And why shouldn't there be ARC staff working in the evening? In fact, wasn't it *more* strange that the place seemed to be so empty?

You're being silly, she told herself as she walked over to the swing doors that separated the main room from the labs and offices. Before she could reach out to the door, it opened out at her.

Sarah leapt back, yelping in surprise as masked soldiers rushed at her.

"Who are you?" she demanded, but before she could say anything more, a soldier grabbed her arm. She fought to escape as he pulled her close. His body armour pressed hard into her flesh.

"Let me go!" she demanded, terrified.

She felt a prickle at her throat, twisted round to see the soldier withdrawing a syringe.

"What...?"

The room began to swim around her.

She was unconscious before she hit the floor.

SIX

The dinosaur charged at them.

Sophie raised her rifle but the creature's tail sent her flying into the wall. Lester dived out of the way, arcing over some upturned chairs. Sophie's gun lay out of reach in the middle of the room.

Danny took a step forward and shot at the creature with his tranquilliser gun, aiming at its head. He could already see that he'd misjudged the shot, and underestimated just how quickly this thing could move.

The dart punched into the creature's flank. It stumbled slightly in its stride... And kept coming.

Danny worked quickly to load a second dart into the gun. His brain was racing, trying to think of something that might help.

From what little he was beginning to understand about the creatures they encountered, he saw that it was a theropod – it ran on two legs, a great long tail behind it and three-toed feet. Its twitchy, quick movements were like those of a small bird. Even as he aimed the gun, Danny's quick mind processed the details so he could describe it to Connor later.

Maybe six or seven metres from nose to tail, and tall enough to lick the ceiling. Um...

Blood oozed from the wound in the creature's side, where the dart had punctured its skin. It turned to face him and roared angrily, its teeth and chin were spattered with blood and gore — clearly not its own. It wasn't a vegetarian. So perhaps Danny shouldn't have been so quick to get its attention.

"Uh," Danny said, and he gaped. He was the only one with a gun now. He had to keep the thing away from Sophie and Lester.

"Can't we talk about this?" he said.

The creature's roar was met by an echo from outside — from the pride of lions. The dinosaur hesitated, considering the sound.

Danny fired again, but the creature was already on the move, ducking its head low as it charged.

The dart smacked into the wall.

He took a couple of steps back, wishing he hadn't declined Sophie's rifle, now lying on the floor. As the dinosaur launched itself with a roar, he knew he didn't have the time to aim.

A chair smashed hard into the creature's head, knocking it off course and straight into the wall next to Danny. He ducked under the huge tail as it followed the creature round and slapped hard where his head had just been.

"Everyone out of here!" Lester ordered, panting from the effort of throwing the chair. The three of them raced back out into the hallway as the dinosaur clambered to its feet. The Winchester rifle lay behind them, on the floor in the middle of the mess room.

Danny skidded to a stop and ran back to close the door behind them. But the latch of the door didn't quite meet the plate. The door wouldn't stay shut by itself. So with the dinosaur heading towards him again, he slammed the door and pressed himself against it at an angle, his feet wedged between the wall and floor behind him.

Thwapp!

The force of the impact threw him back against the wall. The door swung open and the dinosaur poked out its long head, gnashing at him. Prone on the floor, Danny looked up into its slavering, drooling teeth.

It didn't half have bad breath.

"All right," he said hoarsely. "We can call it a draw."

The creature lunged forward to bite him.

Danny turned his face away instinctively — just in time to see four lions charging down the corridor. They hurled themselves at the dinosaur, slashing at it with huge claws, knocking it back into the debris of the mess room.

Lying vulnerable on the floor, he watched incredulous as the creature fell back from the onslaught, surprised and hurt and outnumbered. Then it reached nimbly forward and bit through one lion's throat. The lion gargled and spat in agony, pawing ineffectually as it was lifted from the floor by its bloody, open neck. The dinosaur twirled like a dancer, letting the lion go mid arc so the huge cat sailed across the room and smashed into the upturned sofa. The creature roared with satisfaction and launched itself at the three remaining lions.

Gingerly Danny eased himself off the floor and reached up to close the door on the pitched battle. The whole lodge shook as something slammed into the wall just beside the door. The roaring, rasping, seething cries did not die away.

"Just leave them to it, shall we?" he said, and he reached for the upturned bookcase with the body underneath it.

"Good idea," Lester agreed. Danny might have been surprised to find that his superior had stayed behind, but Lester looked keen to help. They lifted the bookcase so that it wedged against the door and kept it closed. "Perhaps a nearby hotel...?" Lester suggested wryly.

"What is that thing?" Sophie asked, her tanned face white with shock. She stared at the remains of the man they had just exposed, a man she must have known and worked with.

"I'm sorry," Danny said. "There's nothing we can do for him now."

"It isn't possible," Sophie protested in a quiet voice, her tough bravado seeming to have fallen away. Danny recognised the look in her eyes. It was the look of someone who had seen prehistoric creatures invading their modern world, the fear and wonder as their sureties collapsed. He wanted to find some way to reassure her. But they were on a mission, and he guessed Sophie's defiant nature wouldn't welcome his gesture, no matter how well meant.

"We can discuss that when we get to the hotel," Lester said, his clipped tones invading Danny's thoughts. He looked around and winced, as if this was all too wretchedly inconvenient.

Sophie glared at him. "We're not going anywhere," she told him flatly, nodding her head towards the door that led out into the night. In the darkness, they could just make out three more lions prowling round the platform. One poked its nose in through the door and sniffed at them — as if, thought Danny, deciding which of them it would dine on first.

"Ah," he said. "We're a bit stuck."

"It's the cubs," Sophie explained. "Kept safe while the adults go to work. But the kids don't know to be wary of us, either. We won't make it to the car."

"We can't stay here," Danny said.

Again from behind the closed door came an almighty crash and the roar of a lion giving as good at it had received.

"We need a position we can properly defend," Lester agreed.

Danny looked around. The hallway only offered the room where the dinosaur still fought the lions.

"We could get out onto the roof," Sophie suggested. "There's a panel somewhere up here."

They scanned the ceiling, and Lester located a narrow hatch.

"I'll give you a leg up." Danny interlocked his fingers so that his hands made a kind of stirrup. Sophie didn't hesitate, placing one booted foot into the stirrup and then pushing herself up by pressing down on his shoulders. Danny exhaled, surprised by her weight. The thick sole of her boot cut into his skin. She smelt of soap and sweat.

"It's not opening," she told them as she fussed with the panel, involuntarily kicking downward as she did so.

"Take your time," he said, and he grimaced. "Don't mind me."

Sophie cursed under her breath as she fought with whatever mechanism held the hatch in place.

"It looks like it might be on hinges to your left," Lester offered, standing to one side.

"I can see that!" she snapped. Angrily, she punched at the panel with a firm left hook. The hatch clicked, swinging neatly up and open.

"Brillia—" Danny began before Sophie smacked him in the jaw with the foot he had been holding. She wriggled, eel-like, through the tiny opening in the roof. Through the pain he admired the graceful movement of her long, bare legs as she drew them up after her. And then the hatch slammed shut.

"Hey!" he shouted.

They heard frantic skittering from above, which might have been her trying to reopen the hatch.

"Sophie? Sophie!"

"It's stuck!" she called back to them. "I think it's wedged itself."

"Come on," Danny said to Lester. "You'll have to get up there. See what you can do."

Lester sighed and did his best to accept Danny's leg up while retaining some semblance of dignity. He seemed lighter than Sophie had been, his polished brown brogue smaller than her boot. Danny found he had to compensate when Lester leaned too far in all directions, whereas Sophie had kept her balance like a gymnast.

"It's not budging," the man muttered from above him. "You've only bent the pin."

"Give it more power," Danny snapped at him. "You're going to have to smack it."

"Do shut up, Quinn."

He felt Lester's body tense as he brought the punch around. Of course, all the ARC staff had learnt some unarmed combat. Danny had even heard wild tales of Lester taking down some escaped future predator without even breaking a sweat. He looked up to see the man's knuckles crack sharply into the edge of the hatch.

It lifted, just a fraction, then clicked shut again.

Lester lowered his hand, the knuckles grazed and raw.

"You're not sitting on it, are you?" he called up to Sophie.

There was no response.

He took a breath and punched again, this time without effect. He punched again, even harder, and only succeeded in drawing blood. It stained the cuff of his pale suit.

Lester swore viciously.

"It's no good," Danny said, grunting from the effort. "We'll have to think of something else."

"You'd better think of it quickly," Lester said as he clambered down to the ground again. "Once that creature polishes off the lions, it's going to come looking for dessert."

Danny nodded, and walked back down the hallway.

"For God's sake Quinn, don't be an idiot."

"Can't help it," Danny called back. "Born this way." And he budged the bookcase out of the way of the door.

Up on the roof, Sophie sat hugging her knees, her cell phone in one hand. She had called Ted at the gatepost, and he had assured her he would get people over as soon as he could. Sophie hadn't told him all she'd seen, just that there were lions in the lodge. There didn't seem to be any point — they'd never believe her until they'd seen it for themselves.

What had she got herself caught up in? She'd been told this would be simple. Just bring the men to the lodge, and the rest would be taken care of.

The building shook beneath her as the remaining lions battled with the... whatever it might be.

No, she told herself, she knew exactly what it was. She'd guessed as much from the tracks it had left. The three-clawed toes matched the imprints they had found in the mud. That thing was a dinosaur... Real and alive and rampaging through her game park.

And the two British guys hadn't seemed surprised.

She cursed to herself. Then leaned forward and struggled to get her fingertips round the edges of the hatch. A tear escaped her eye and slid down her grubby cheek. She realised couldn't let these men be killed. If nothing else, she needed answers.

SEVEN

Connor pulled from his pocket what looked to Abby like a snazzy new mobile phone. He held it up above his head, aiming at the sensor for the automatic doors that let customers into Boots. The shop was closed, its lights off, tall shelves of beauty products looming in the darkness on the far side of the glass.

He pressed the enter key and the device buzzed for a moment. Then the glass doors of Boots sighed quietly open, letting the stinking grey water from outside slosh into the six-inch deep pool already in the shop.

"Oh," Connor said sheepishly, looking at the mess and then back at Abby. "Didn't think of that." They stepped quickly though, and Connor clicked the button on his device once more. The river washing in behind them was cut off by the closing doors.

"Are you meant to have that thing?" Abby asked him.

"This?" Connor said. "No one even knows about it."

"Come on." Abby tugged his sleeve. "We don't want to be found here." She headed down the central aisle, every possible shade of lipstick laid out on her left. The next section of shelves offered an assortment of brightly coloured sponges and shampoo.

Connor grabbed one of the baskets from the stack by the door and ran to catch up. His feet splashed through the shallow pool of water, echoing loudly round the otherwise silent shop.

What a relief, Abby thought, *to get out from under the rain.*

"You know they shot looters in New Orleans?" Connor said cheerfully. "I read this thing on the net."

"Yeah," she responded. "But we're with the government, aren't we? And anyway, this is Maidenhead. They won't shoot us. They'll just ask awkward questions."

"Right," Connor said. "Here we go."

He stopped at the rack of men's toiletries. Under-arm sprays and roll-ons, aftershave gels and ointments, all arranged in neat rows. There was something much stockier, Abby decided, more mechanical and metallic about the packaging than on the same stuff for girls. Like you weren't buying something that just made you smell nice, but something more like a gadget.

Boys really like their clever toys, she decided.

Connor reached for an aerosol in the centre of the display, tugged off the cap and sprayed a tiny breath of fine white particles into the air just in front of him. He sniffed, tentatively at first and took in a proper lungful. Then he realised Abby was watching him, arms folded, one eyebrow raised.

"What?"

She reached past him to scoop her arms around a whole row of products. Connor dashed in quickly with his basket, to catch them as they tumbled off the shelf.

"That enough?" she asked him.

"They did look like they've got a lot of armpit. Maybe we should raid the women's shelves, as well. But it's the lady Deinosuchus we want to attract and —" His mischievous grin suddenly faded. "Or maybe this is enough."

Abby followed his gaze over the tops of aisles of toothpaste, toiletries, and plasters. At the back of the shop, behind the desk where clerks processed people's photos, a tall grey shadow lurked. It stood upright, on tiptoe, maybe six foot, all alert and listening. Yellow lizard eyes blinked back at them from the darkness.

"Velociraptor," Abby said quietly.

"Yeah," Connor agreed, his voice going up an octave.

There were long, prickly spikes up its spine and peeking over the top of its head, like a Mohican haircut. Livid blue markings showed around its eyes, like it was wearing war paint. Its wide, open mouth showed a row of razor-sharp teeth. All in all, not the most gentle looking of creatures.

"Must have found a way in through the back," Abby whispered. "Come in to get out of the rain."

"Yeah."

She glanced quickly back round to the shelves on the far side of the shop, displaying deals on drinks, crisps and sandwiches.

"It hasn't ransacked the food in here," she observed.

"Probably doesn't recognise chocolate bars and things wrapped in plastic," Connor said, edging up the aisle towards the exit.

The Velociraptor continued to stare at them both with yellow, beady eyes.

"I meant," Abby said, taking very slow steps through the shallow water, "that it's probably hungry."

"Yeah," Connor acknowledged. "I was just trying not to think about that."

"Okay," she said. "Just don't do anything to make it —"

Connor's basket, overflowing with toiletries, smacked into the aisle beside him. Lipsticks clattered from the shelves, splashing into the water round his feet.

She and Connor looked back to the Velociraptor, still unmoving in the photo-processing lab. Abby realised she was holding her breath and let out a long sigh.

That was the moment the dinosaur came leaping over the desk and across the aisles towards them.

Becker steered his speedboat onto the A308, glancing at the map displayed on the anomaly detector in his free hand, its screen bright in the gathering dark. A red dot showed his own position, marking his way to the turning for the High Street on his right. Two dots, green and blue, marked Abby and Connor's positions, just a thumb's width away.

As he steered onto the High Street, the boat suddenly picked up speed, riding the crest of water coming down from Castle Hill.

His keen eyes picked out movement up ahead, in the darkness of a shop. There was a distinct clamour coming from inside. Tucking away the detector, Becker reached for his SIG .229.

Something was happening in Boots.

Becker brought the boat in for a closer look. Ten metres ahead of him the glass doors of the shop slid open. It had the effect of a break in the riverbank, and he was suddenly caught right in the midst of a current veering through the door. He leant his whole weight against the rudder, trying to steer back into the main course of water. But the boat wasn't having any of it, and he found himself hurtling towards the open doors...

At the last second he remembered the driving technique for getting a car out of a skid. You didn't try to break away, you steered *into* the spin. He yanked the rudder towards him, heaving the boat sharply left, lifting its nose right out of the water. The engine sputtered, the rotor blades trying to find something to push against.

For a split second he sat perfectly still as the river rushed round underneath him. Then the rotor blades caught again, and Becker shot forward into the shop.

He barely had time to blink before Abby, Connor, and a basket laden with toiletries hurled themselves over the bow of the boat to land at his feet. Behind them, the onrushing water toppled aisles and aisles of shelving. And a Velociraptor leapt nimbly from one to another, hurtling straight for Becker.

He dug the rotor down into the water, lifting the front of the boat. It hit the creature hard, knocking it back into the water. The boat bucked and bumped as it rode over the top of the raptor. Becker glanced back, to see it thrashing angrily in their wake.

The shelves had all been toppled, and they and their contents now bobbed on the surface of what looked like a dirty indoor swimming pool. As the water reached a level with the outside, the current quickly died off. The raptor kicked and shrieked its way out into the river of the High Street.

"Better get after it," Becker said as he piloted the boat back out into the lashing rain.

Abby and Connor scrambled up on to their knees, both red-faced, both looking exhausted and amazed.

"We're going to have to have a chat," Becker told them, "about not wandering off."

"You wouldn't listen!" Connor protested. "I said the raptors didn't like the rain!"

"Which we used to our advantage," Becker replied. But given how things had gone on the other side of the anomaly, he didn't feel like elaborating.

"We've got bigger things to worry about than raptors," Abby cut in impatiently. "Much bigger."

"There could be another anomaly," Connor began. "Because —"

But before he could continue they heard a great roar from downstream — and a squeak of terror.

"Oh," Connor said, sadly. "I think that raptor found the two Deinosuchus."

"The two what?" Becker said.

"Think giant crocodiles," Abby explained.

"Ah," Becker responded with a sigh. "Back to square one." And he cranked the engine on the speedboat.

EIGHT

Two lions remained, both bloodied but unbowed. They circled in different directions around the scratched and battered theropod, keeping just beyond its reach.

Danny stepped calmly into the mess room. The lions continued to stalk the dinosaur, recognising it as the greater threat. The Winchester rifle lay in the middle of the floor, the creature and the lions circling around it. Flinching at the smell of blood and animal sweat, Danny made his way round the side of the room, past the bloodied, open carcass of a lion, giving the creatures as much space as he could. The theropod swished its head round in his direction and seethed through jagged teeth.

He dodged back, barely escaping a vicious swipe, and one of the lions darted forward, trying to clamp its jaws around the creature's neck. The dinosaur skipped around like a boxer, kicking the lion as it passed, sending it sprawling right at Danny. For an instant Danny thought he was done for. But it seemed the lion had no interest in him, and lithely leapt back at the theropod. After the initial surprise and bombast of the first attack, it seemed as if the two remaining lions were well-matched against the creature.

Danny needed to break the stalemate.

Taking a deep breath, he picked up one of the upturned chairs and hurled it across the room. It sailed past the creatures and smashed through the window beyond. Glass splashed and tinkled from the frame, and a breath of cool air teased into the mess room. Through the sweat of fear and adrenalin, he hadn't realised quite how hot the lodge had been.

The theropod raised itself up tall, so that the top of its head brushed the ceiling. It sniffed at the cool air and its eyes narrowed. Then it turned back to the lions.

"Nice work, Quinn," Lester called sarcastically from the far side of the room. "I hope you have a Plan B."

Danny grimaced, and continued around the perimeter of the room until he reached the broken window. Cool air licked around him pleasantly. He wanted to stand there, close his eyes, surrender to that breeze. Instead, he steeled himself for what he was about to do.

I shouldn't be scared, I should be pissed off, he said to himself. Danny recalled the cramped flight, his knees up against the seat in front of him for all eleven hours. They'd not brought the right equipment, they'd not been fully briefed, and now a dodgy clasp on a loft hatch had left him to fight three bloodthirsty predators single-handed. He had been sure leaving the police force and joining the ARC would open up a world of possibilities and answers. Yet it just seemed to offer ever more complex frustrations and insanity.

He squared his jaw, feeling the rage welling up in him.

"Oi," he shouted at the dinosaur. "You, ugly mug! Call yourself a T-rex?"

The dinosaur bobbed its head round to regard him curiously. Danny had expected the lions to choose that moment to pounce but they, too, turned to look at the source of the unexpected noise.

"You can't even take on a couple of jumped-up pussy cats!" he yelled at the top of his lungs.

"What are you *doing*?" he heard Lester hiss from the far side of the room. And, really, the man had a point. But Danny had started this now, and there was no going back.

"Why haven't you finished them off?" he bellowed. "They're just two dumb cats. What are you, *chicken*?"

The dinosaur regarded him coolly, still motionless, towering over him.

Danny grinned up at it.

And then he was sprawling forward, diving for his life. Some sixth sense had seen the dinosaur tense, just before it pounced. A blur of brown coming at him fast, and then Danny was smacking hard into the floor. He twisted around, and just saw the whip of the creature's long tail vanish through the broken window.

It took most of the window frame with it.

The two lions sighed with exhaustion. Then they looked up at Danny, strewn there, completely defenceless, the Winchester rifle still well out of his reach. There was no way he could get to his feet before they were on him. So he smirked wickedly, just like he imagined James Dean or Brando would have done.

"Go on then," he told them. "After him."

There was a roaring outside, as the young lions encountered the embattled theropod. That decided things. The elder felines bounded out through the broken window, the night outside punctured by their own gleeful roaring.

Danny slumped against the floor, exhausted. "Exactly as I planned."

"So that was Plan B," Lester commented, standing in the doorway, arms crossed, and making no move to come over.

"Yeah," he said, and he sighed. "Figured the thing was just as cornered as we were. Just needed to be shown a way out."

"Hm," Lester muttered. He collected the rifle from the floor and walked cautiously up to the great hole that had once been a window.

"I wouldn't get too close," Danny told him as he got wearily to his feet.

"You don't say," Lester said. "Well, we can't possibly stay here now."

"You want to go home already?"

"No. We've got a job to do. But we can't stay here." He waved generally at the mess room — the mess of upturned furniture, dead lions, and dead people.

"Maybe we can find somewhere with a pool."

Of course, the hatch in the roof opened relatively easily when it wasn't a matter of life or death. Sophie reached her legs down to put one boot on Danny's shoulder, then half jumped, half wriggled back to the floor.

"Saw them run off," she said. "Whatever you did, well done."

"Thanks," he said. They stood there gazing at each other, both amazed to be alive. And something had changed about her, too. Like maybe he'd broken through the wall of her resistance.

"What happened with the hatch?" Lester asked pointedly.

The light switched off behind her eyes and she was back to the tough cookie who had picked them up from the airport.

"I must have knocked it as I got my feet out. It's all rusted on top from the sun. But look —" She showed him raw, scratched hands — "I tried to get it open."

"I see," Lester said, but he didn't sound entirely convinced.

Danny grinned at her.

"It's okay. If you wanted to kill us, there are easier ways."

"I guess so," she said, and again he thought he saw that strange resistance in her, that need not to like him.

Maybe she'd had bad experiences with men in jeans and leather jackets, he surmised. Maybe there was something else. He had a policeman's instinct for spotting someone who was withholding information. And he knew she wouldn't tell him anything if he pushed her too hard. Best to lay off, get busy with something else, let her learn to trust him.

"There's a lot to sort out in there," he said. "Can we call up some of your lot? That bloke we met on the gate. Get them to give us a hand."

"Already did," she said. "Rang them on my cell up there. Be here in maybe half an hour. Maybe a bit more. The guys who were meant to be on duty..." She glanced down at the body lying in the hallway. "Well, they were in here."

"I'm sorry," Danny told her.

"Yeah," she said, not lifting her eyes to him.

"Well," Lester said. "Might as well get started then."

They cleared the broken chairs and furniture, and the detritus from the window, then, heaving the heavy bodies between them, they laid the park rangers side by side. There were three of them: two men, one woman — two black, one white.

"Who were they?" Danny asked quietly.

"Last of the old guard," Sophie said simply. He'd meant what were their names, what were the details of their lives, but he didn't press her.

Even Lester removed his jacket and rolled up his sleeves, mucking in with the grisly chores without a word of protest. He and Danny dragged the two dead lions through the hallway and out into the open, a hot and wearying job. Blood spattered Lester's shirtfront and his trousers, but if he noticed, he didn't say anything.

Eventually, Sophie led them into the long kitchen and found them ice-cold beers. She had to root around for a bottle opener, but finally she found one. They drank in silence, exhausted. Danny had knocked back half the bottle before Sophie spoke again.

"Danny," she said — the first time that she'd used his name — "that was a dinosaur." There was an accusing tone in her voice.

He looked to Lester, who put his beer bottle down on the table.

"We don't know that," he said smoothly, with the practice of a lifetime politico.

"But it looked like one," Danny said, playing the good cop again. "Have you seen anything like that before around here?"

"Of course not," Sophie said, shaking her head. "What kind of idiot do you take me for? It's... I was going to say it isn't possible. But it was here. It tried to *kill* us."

"It was cornered," Danny said. They couldn't pretend anything after Sophie had seen the creature — and after what it had done to her friends. "The lions have probably been on its trail for ages," he continued. "It's not like it was on their turf."

Sophie stared at him. "You're blaming this on the lions?" she asked him incredulously.

"No," Danny said, surprised by her anger. "I'm just saying it was cornered."

"It killed three rangers. And then two lions. It would have happily trampled us. And it didn't flinch when you shot a dart into it, either. It's not some poor victim."

"That's not what I meant —"

"It's an intruder," Lester said firmly, taking control of the exchange. "It's a threat to your game park and the precious species you have living here. It needs to be dealt with."

Danny started to add something, then thought better of it.

Sophie drank back the last of her beer and then got to her feet. But she didn't seem to want to go back to where the bodies lay.

"We'll go out after it at first light," Lester said, suddenly playing the good cop. "Your colleagues will be here soon. Maybe you should call again..."

She whirled on him.

"They wouldn't just desert me," she told him. "If they're not here there's a reason."

"Sophie," Danny said. "The creature could have attacked them, too."

"Maybe," she conceded, "but we work shifts, some people will be at home."

"Then they need to be called in," Lester insisted.

"I know that!" Sophie snapped at him. "Ted will be calling them now. You guys don't think we know how to run things here, do you?"

Lester didn't say anything.

"We're just trying to help," Danny told her carefully.

She glared at him again, but he held her gaze until her features softened.

"Yeah," she said. "But all this, you know? It's hard. We should be doing something."

"What can we do?" Danny asked her. "We're here to help."

Sophie looked from one to the other of them.

"Really?" she said.

"Really," Danny told her. "Scouts' honour. If I'd been a scout."

"All right," she said, "there's one thing we can do."

"This is madness," Lester protested. He was dressed in borrowed khakis, a strange contrast to his usual immaculate suits.

"Shouldn't we at least wait till morning?" Danny asked. "At least then we'll be able to see."

Sophie stepped down from the platform onto the coarse earth of the car park and turned back to face them. She had her own rifle in her hands, plus two others on her back and a savage hunting knife in a scabbard on her thigh.

"Trail will be cold in the morning," she told them gruffly. "The animals lay low in the sun — that's why we haven't been able to find them. We want to catch these things up, we have to go after them now."

She marched over to her SUV and slung the guns inside.

"Come on," she said. "You said you were here to help."

"Well —" Lester began.

"All right," Danny said, still keen to win her over. He jumped down from the platform and joined her at the car. "Didn't have anything else to be doing anyway, and it's not like I'm going to be able to sleep."

"Quinn, you're not serious," Lester said. "You know as well as I do —"

"You can stay here if you want to," Danny told him. "until Sophie's mates turn up. But until then, you'll be on your own."

Lester considered for half a second.

"Fine," he said angrily, climbing down from the platform. He glared at Danny, who had already got into the front passenger seat, and seethed as he climbed in the back. Sophie was already revving the engine as he slammed the door.

"Okay," she said, spinning the car back in a wide arc and then pushing it into first. "This thing leaves a wide wake behind it. Tracks and trampled bush. And both it and the lions were bleeding. So even you guys should see the trail."

"Now hang on just a moment —" Lester began.

"Hey," Danny told him. "We're here to help."

Sophie put her foot down and they surged off into the night.

NINE

"All right," Becker said into his earpiece. "See you in a moment." He looked up at Abby and Connor. "Everyone's ready downstream." The way he said it made it sound like this had all been his idea.

"Good," Connor said impatiently. He felt that familiar tight knot in his stomach, a mix of terror and excitement. It would be good just to get moving again, after sitting in the rain. His clothes felt cold and heavy, sticking to his skin in all of the wrong places. He turned to Abby, playing it cool.

"All set?"

"You really think this is going to work?" she asked him, wide-eyed.

"Hey! Of course it's going to work. It's always worked before, hasn't it?"

"Connor, we haven't *done* this before."

"Yeah, but we've done loads of stuff like it." He shrugged heroically — at least he hoped it looked that way. "We're like professionals now. And the artificial pheromones in these cans give us our best shot."

"*Like* professionals," Becker echoed, not looking up at them as he checked over the speedboat's engine. "That bodes well."

"You don't have to do this," Connor told him. "We can manage by ourselves."

"Can we?" Abby asked.

Connor turned to her. "Yeah. I think so."

"All the same," Becker said, clicking the heavy plastic cover back into place, "I'd better come along, just to see how the experts do it."

"All right," Connor conceded, not sure how much the man was joking. "So, you're going to steer us round —"

"Yeah," Abby said. "He knows."

"Right," Connor replied. "And Abby, you're going to —"

"I know that, too."

"Well then." Connor said. He looked downstream towards the two giant Deinosuchus, still skulking in the dirty water. He might have imagined it, but the large male seemed to blink at him, as if he knew what was coming.

"Um," Connor said, not looking at his two compatriots. "Do you *really* think that this is going to work?'

"Only one way to find out," Becker answered, pulling hard on the starter. The engine let out a triumphant roar and the speedboat shot towards the giant crocodiles.

Spray whipped at Connor's face as they sped ever faster forward. He tried not to think about what terrible diseases the water might contain. Just his luck to survive the combined might of the Late Cretaceous only to be brought down by cholera. He glanced at Abby, poised beside him, the basket of deodorants resting on her knees. She flashed a quick smile at him, then returned her attention to the two giant crocodilians up ahead.

They were right in the middle of the stream now, dashing across the water. The whole bottom of the boat buzzed with vibrations he could feel all through his body, even in his teeth.

Ahead of them, the giant crocodiles stirred and broke apart from their strange embrace. They must have been able to feel the vibration of the boat speeding towards them and see the three small humans that sat aboard like so much fast food. Their fat, bulb-like snouts would give them a brilliant sense of smell because the nostrils were kept well apart. Connor had a sudden horror of how he might smell to the creatures: the crocodile equivalent of a burger and fries.

The creatures were enormous. Just the head and shoulders of the male that reached out of the water were the height of a man. They moved slowly, deliberately, like nervous swimmers.

As the boat swerved towards them, the male snapped his jaws right at Connor's head. Connor fell back, letting out a squawk of horror, and would have been plucked from the boat had Becker not steered hard to the right. Instead, Connor got a lungful of the creature's stale, meaty breath. He gagged, fighting back the reflex need to vomit.

He reached for two cans of deodorant.

"Think you need this, mate," he told the Deinosuchus. And he sprayed two long bursts of deodorant out over the back of the boat.

There came a strange croak from the dank water behind the male, and the female lurched around. Water crashed in all directions as she pushed off from what had probably been their nest. She let out a second terrible croak and began to paddle after the speedboat. Within moments she'd passed her fatter, slower mate, who struggled to keep up.

"It's working!" Abby cried, joining Connor with the spraying. His aerosols began to sputter. He shook them, sprayed again, but he'd already emptied the lot. For a moment he was going to drop them over the side of the boat into the water, all cool like Han Solo. But Abby wouldn't approve of that so, feeling superior, Connor dropped the empty cans onto the buzzing floor of the boat. They rolled away from him as he reached for another two cans.

"Careful where you're pointing those things," Becker snapped, knelt beneath their outstretched arms as he steered the boat deftly down the river. Connor had sort of been spraying him right in the face.

"Sorry!"

"I'm out!" Abby said, dropping her aerosols just as Connor had done, and reaching for two more.

Connor's arms ached at being out-stretched for so long. Becker didn't dare pull too far ahead, or the deodorant spray would dissipate, and their targets would lose interest. But that didn't seem to be a problem. The two crocodilians were having no trouble swimming in the speedboat's wake. Meanwhile, the waves created by the boat and the creatures slammed into shops and buildings on both sides of the High Street.

The female reached her fat-nosed, enormous head right out of the water to exclaim another croak.

"I think she fancies me!" Connor said, and he laughed, dropping his empties and grabbing another pair.

"It's the Lynx effect!" Abby agreed, giggling.

"Hang on!" Becker shouted, hauling on the rudder with all his weight. The boat twisted hard about to the right, hurling Connor and Abby to the left. Connor instinctively grabbed Abby's sleeve, stopping her from falling overboard. The basket of deodorants bounced, smashing into the back of his hand and drawing blood.

"Ow!" he said pointedly in Becker's direction.

"The route ahead was blocked," Becker explained through gritted teeth, struggling to see past Abby and Connor.

Looking over the back of the boat, Connor saw the Deinosuchus couple emerge from the right, fighting with the water to veer after them. He picked up another can and began spraying its contents. The stronger current swept past, carrying all sorts of rubbish to some unknown destination.

"How much of a distance have we got on them?" Becker asked.

"Maybe fifty metres," Abby responded, retrieving her arm from Connor and grabbing for a can of her own.

"Good," Becker said, "because there's a roundabout ahead."

Connor and Abby both turned, but too late. The speedboat slammed into a fast-moving river cutting across their path, left to right. Abby clutched onto Connor as they both fell forward, scattering the contents of the basket around the boat. Connor just had a moment to realise that they'd mixed up all their full aerosols with the empties, and then the front of the boat smacked hard into something.

There was a horrifying crunch — possibly of Connor's bones, he thought — and then a terrible silence but for the trickling water.

Behind their prone, battered bodies, Connor heard Becker swear. He twisted round to see the soldier busy poking around at the engine. The speedboat had hit the central, concrete island of the junction and was drifting awkwardly backwards the wrong way around the roundabout.

"Uh, guys?" Abby said, pointing a finger back towards the street from which they'd come, where two giant figures were streaking through the water towards them, thrilled at the sight of their suddenly helpless prey.

"You've got to get it working!" Connor urged Becker.

"Yeah," Becker said. "I'd figured that out." He swore again, unable to get his fingers at whatever bit had gone wrong. He pulled the pistol from the pouch at his thigh and fired warning shots to the side of each of the crocodiles. The bullets hit the water and the crocodiles didn't even slow. Becker snorted, and smacked the speedboat's engine with his gun.

It puttered, and then roared back into life.

He immediately clicked the casing back into place. Then he pushed the rudder hard away from him and the boat struggled to twist round in the current. The two crocodilians paddled easily into the water that was sloshing around the roundabout, and were quickly just a body-length away. The female took an agile stroke forward and could have bitten easily into the back of the craft. Instead she twisted round to kick back at the male, to keep him away from what she clearly regarded as *her* prey.

"Right," Becker said, with the boat more or less pointing the right way. He'd hardly let his pressure off the rudder, so when the current picked them up again, the engine stopped protesting, and they were suddenly gathering speed, lurching high above the water, skipping away from their huge pursuers.

"Ha ha!" Connor laughed triumphantly, getting a mouthful of rain and spray.

Becker weaved them neatly through the debris bobbing in the water. On their right they passed a sharp turning blocked off by the wreckage, and he steered them round. Connor had to admit that the man knew what he was doing. He just wouldn't admit it very loudly.

"We're well ahead of them now," he said.

"We can't get too far," Abby reminded him, as she found a full can and began spraying again. "We *want* them to chase after us."

"Oh, yeah," Connor said, reaching for the aerosols that were rolling around the floor. The first one he tried turned out to be empty, but soon he had a long trail of mist streaming out behind them. The female Deinosuchus reached her head high out of the water to inhale it, and let out a happy croak. Then she crashed back down, creating huge waves on either side of her, and kept on with her pursuit. Tagging behind her came the hapless male.

"I really think she likes you," Abby teased, nudging Connor in the ribs.

"Yeah, well," he said modestly, "it's got to be the trousers. Girls love a man in stripes."

"Do they now?"

"Oh, yeah. It's well known."

"Um," Becker said from the back of the speedboat. "We're going to have a problem."

He nodded downstream. The road sloped ahead of them, and then levelled out just before it entered the wide and swollen river cutting across their path. Narrow islands poked out of the water all along the waterway, and Connor couldn't quite tell if they'd been there before, or had been created by the flood. This was where all of the debris was going, and as they looked ahead, every path was crowded with junk and rubbish. Once they entered the main channel, they would lose all their speed.

More importantly, there were no soldiers waiting for them, which had kind of been the plan. If they could find somewhere safe to lead the creatures... Becker reached for his handheld anomaly detector but he needed to keep control of the boat's rudder. Abby leant forward to help, tapping the keys with her nimble fingers. She shook her head.

"I can't get a signal on my earpiece either," he said.

"Think that's a phone mast floating over there," Abby said, pointing. "Looks like we're on our own."

"They must have hit a snag," Becker said.

"Maybe if we took a turning?" Abby suggested.

"It's too shallow everywhere except for this main avenue," Becker replied.

Out of the main centre of Maidenhead, there was more surface area for the water to escape, so it wasn't as deep and quick as on the High Street.

"So what do we do?" she asked.

Becker remained tight-lipped. He flicked at the overhanging comma of hair just above his eye.

"Need a bit of faith," he said. "My men will be here."

The slope of the hill was steep enough for the giant crocodiles to surf. They crested the waves and came down on their huge, thick bodies, so that it almost looked like they were enjoying themselves.

Connor glanced round, desperate for anything that might help them. The aerosols in his hands were giving up the ghost. He was about to drop them when he had a better idea. Stretching his right arm out he brought it back quickly, like a cricket throw. The aerosol sailed up and over in a graceful arc towards the female Deinosuchus. He realised he'd misjudged the shot, that it was going to land too short. But the female ploughed forward, opened her enormous jaws and swallowed the thing whole.

Abby stared at him.

"We shoot it, and then it explodes," Connor explained. "Just like at the end of *Jaws*."

"Connor!" Abby wailed. "That won't do any good."

"I was joking," Connor said. "I just thought, you know, it might help put them off. There's nothing else we can use."

"He's right," Becker agreed. "Give them everything you've got!"

So Abby and Connor took turns flinging the aerosols at the pursuing creatures. Full or empty, it didn't matter. The Deinosuchus couple were steadily gaining on them. Cans thumped and bumped on their long snouts or nearby. Abby was a pretty good shot.

They were fast running out of cans, and options. Connor glanced at the front of the boat. They were almost onto the flooded river and the sudden quashing of their speed. Maybe if they all dived into the water and went in different directions, *one* of them might survive...

He glanced back at Abby. She had that determined look on her face he had come to love. Even now, she just got on with the job at hand. No time for panic or fear. He was just about to reach out to her when something caught his eye.

Upriver of them, some distance behind the crocodilians, a group of speedboats emerged from a side street. They chased down towards the river at top speed, in pursuit of the pursuers. The boats were laden with men in the same black uniform as Becker.

"They're here!" Connor shouted. He waved frantically at the soldiers' boats.

"Good thinking," Becker said, mostly to himself. "There's no strong position down here, and they'd have had to fire over the tops of our heads."

The Deinosuchus male noticed something haring down behind him. He turned his head to see the enemy just as the soldiers fired. Volleys of tranquilliser darts rained down on the creature's face. He shook his long, fat-nosed head, swiping many of them right out of the air. His thick skin resisted all but the best-angled shots, but some of them struck home. The male let out a croak of frustration, three tranquilliser needles poking from his skin.

He sank back into the water and began to lose speed as another volley followed.

But the female hadn't been hit at all, and she was fast gaining on her prey. Connor and Abby were completely out of aerosols, and they could only watch helplessly as she got closer.

They both jolted as the speedboat hit what felt like gravel underneath them. The engine chugged and coughed, and rather than pushing quickly forward they just drifted to one side. They were on the flat of the flooded river now, idling along. Connor gasped at the sudden stink all around them, from all the rubbish their own current had borne here before them. A couple of traffic cones bobbed in the thick water, which seemed to have taken on the consistency of custard.

The female Deinosuchus actually slowed, and seemed unsure of venturing into the disgusting stream. She sculled at the edge, drawing in breath through her enormous nostrils. Her mate floated unconscious past her, but she didn't seem to notice him.

The soldiers let off another volley of tranquilliser darts, aiming right at her face. She seemed to gaze craftily at Connor and blinked a double set of eyelids. Then she ducked down into the water — and disappeared. Tranquilliser needles plopped uselessly onto the surface where her head had been.

Connor instinctively leant out over the side of the speedboat to try to spot her under the surface. Abby grabbed his arm and pulled him back. They sat in silence, watching the current undulating all around them, searching for any sign of where she'd gone.

The soldiers' boats chugged slowly forward to the place where the female had been. They cut their engines and drifted in silence as well. Becker nodded to his men, but didn't say a word. All eyes were on the water, trying to cover all the angles.

Connor found he was having trouble breathing. His heart pounded in his chest.

The body of the slumbering male Deinosuchus bumped against their speedboat, and spun slowly off in another direction. The creature huffed contentedly in his sleep, oblivious to the excitement and tension.

Long minutes passed. The rain continued to patter down on them, making Connor conscious of the cold.

He sighed. The female could have swum off *anywhere* by now, gone looking for easier pickings. They might as well regroup their forces and go looking for her again later. Hey, he might even have time for a change of clothes or a mug of tea.

He turned to Becker, ready to suggest this. But the look in Becker's eyes made him reconsider. He looked away, down, and saw something glint behind the soldier's booted feet. It took him a moment to realise what it was. Then to realise that he was grinning.

Connor reached forward. Becker and Abby both turned to see what he was doing but remained silent. He extracted his prize, then revealed it with a dramatic flourish.

"Oh," Abby said, clamping her hands hard over her mouth.

Becker leaned around to face the soldiers' boats, waving his hand and making a couple of quick but deliberate signals that they clearly understood.

Then he turned to Connor and nodded. Connor nodded back, fighting off the urge to grin again, or pull a face. He didn't acknowledge Abby, knowing he'd only laugh. Instead he raised his arm, popped the cap of the last remaining aerosol with his thumb and pressed down on the tab.

Nothing happened.

Connor wavered. He tried again, and nothing happened.

His arm felt suddenly very heavy. He lowered it, scrutinising the outside of the aerosol as if he might spot the answer. All eyes burrowed into him, and he could feel their prickling heat.

Then he shook the aerosol hard, raised it high above his head again and didn't even look as he pressed down on the tab.

The aerosol hissed.

He dared to look now. Pale, sweet-smelling mist fell lightly on his face. His nose itched at the acrid smell and he had to blink his eyes. All around him the water undulated softly. The rain battered down, but all else was silent. He directed the aerosol across the water, towards one boat of soldiers, and pressed the tab again. Cool spray sighed across the water.

With a roar the female Deinosuchus shot out of the water and hurled herself at him. Connor fell back, landing on top of Abby and Becker, resulting in a writhing mass of limbs. The massive crocodilian glided through the air, its claws out and its long tail dragging. The huge jaws opened wide and Connor looked up into her dark throat. She exhaled a terrible stench of decayed meat mixed with aerosol deodorant.

He thought he was going to vomit.

He threw the aerosol and it chinked off her front teeth, rebounded on to her tongue, and was swallowed in an instant. But she didn't pause, and Connor braced himself for the impact. At least it would be quick...

Then the Deinosuchus closed her huge jaws and dropped heavily into the water. Her long face and neck was beaded with maybe twenty or thirty glinting tranquilliser needles. Connor blinked, amazed.

And took the full brunt of the tidal wave.

Abby found Connor huddled on the back step of one of the army trucks, underneath two blankets. She squeezed into the space beside him, handed him a mug of soup and sipped at her own. The soldiers had a special recipe — tomato soup from tins beefed up with peppers, chillies, and garlic to get you on your toes. It ravaged the back of her throat and made her eyes water, but it also fought off the cold.

"Becker says we have to pay for the deodorants," she said. "He claims he's trying to get hold of the shop's manager now. I told him it's nearly midnight, but he says it's only right."

She laughed, but Connor didn't say anything. They sipped their soup and watched the soldiers using thick ropes and plenty of tarpaulin to lug two unconscious Deinosuchus towards a huge container lorry. After they had captured the creatures, Connor's anomaly detector had picked up the last vestiges of an anomaly close by where they had first seen the giant crocodiles, but it had closed before they had had a chance to lock it. There had been some serious argument and phone calls about what to do next, before someone decided they'd have to store the creatures at the facility just outside of London. Oliver Leek had set the place up for his secret army of monsters. It had been empty since then, but it would be ideal.

The ARC would look after — and study — the Deinosuchus couple. If the team could understand the anomalies, even learn how to control them, then one day they could be sent home.

Some people thought they should just be sent through any anomaly that was roughly in the right period, but Cutter had always insisted that even the right period might be millions of years out for the individual creatures, which could cause all manner of disruption to the already mangled timelines.

Sombre at the thought of their departed friend, Abby watched the scientists fussing around the giant bodies, plucking tranquilliser needles from their weathered faces, ensuring they were comfortable but would remain sleeping for the journey. She felt wet and cold and weary, but still wanted to join in.

A thought struck her as she watched the giant female.

"What if she's pregnant?"

Connor's morose face contorted into a grin.

"She should cut down on eating deodorants, if she is."

"We could have one born in captivity," Abby pressed. "That would be a first."

"So would finishing a day at work without being covered in gubbins."

Abby leaned over to him and took a deliberate sniff.

"You smell."

"Yeah?" he said.

"Yeah."

"A nice smell?"

"Hmm," she sniffed him again. "It's okay. Sort of a mix of a rubbish tip and a huge great crocodilian."

"That's better than most days, isn't it?"

"I guess." She reached round for the edge of his blankets, wrapping them round her own shoulder so they were snuggled up together. "Connor —"

"Oh, hell," he said, and reached for the pocket of his damp, stripy trousers. His mobile buzzed in his hand as he withdrew it. He glanced at Abby, rolling his eyes apologetically. She bit her lip in frustration, but resisted the urge to grab the phone and fling it off into the dark.

"Danny?" Connor said cheerily into the phone. "Yeah, we're fine. Nothing we can't handle. How are you two getting on?"

TEN

The SUV bumped and bucked over the scrubby ground — the car's suspension had clearly seen better days. Danny narrowed his eyes, trying to spot the tracks that Sophie claimed she was following.

The full beams cut a bright path through the looming darkness, but all he could make out were rocks and bits of tree as they clattered past.

"Definitely a theropod," he said into his phone. "Stiffened tail, three-fingered hands with a large first claw, three-toed feet..."

"Smaller than a Tyrannosaur," Lester put in from the seat behind him.

Danny glanced at Sophie, but she seemed too busy with the driving to pay attention to their strange conversation. Or she had already accepted that her two passengers did this all the time. He suspected there would be lots of questions later.

"Um," Connor said on the other end of the line.

He sounds pretty miserable, Danny thought. *Maybe he's still sulking because* he *hadn't got to come on this trip.*

"We've just had a run-round with a whole lot of Velociraptors," Connor told him. "They're easy to identify because they —"

"It wasn't a raptor," Danny interrupted. "I've seen them in pictures. This thing was twice as big, maybe seven metres long. You got your laptop with you?"

"I don't need my laptop," Connor told him, "I've had to learn this stuff.

It sounds like an avian theropod, could be a Megalosaurid such as Eustreptospondylus, though they were quite rare."

"A what? Connor, I still have trouble pronouncing amonaly."

"*Anomaly*."

"Yeah, that's kind of my point."

"All right, it's yoo-*strep*-toe-spon-dilus. Sort of as it's spelt. Means 'well-curved vertebra'. Got named in the 1960s. But, get this: the only fossil we've got of it was found in the nineteenth century by the bloke who came up with the word 'dinosaur'."

Danny sighed. "And this is going to help me find it *how*?"

"Oh, yeah, sorry. Well, if it *is* Eustreptospondylus then it's mid-Jurassic. Callovian stage, I think. I've got a poster at the ARC with the stages all in different colours."

"Connor..." Danny muttered. He leant forward, peering out into the dark, unable to distinguish any specific features under the vast canopy of stars.

"One theory is that they swam between the little islands of what's now Oxford city centre. That's where Richard Owen discovered its remains. So if that's what attacked you, I'd look for a river or lake. It's sort of what it will think is home."

"Good," Danny said. "That's the sort of information I can use. Hope the girls are looking after you." And before Connor could protest, he clicked off the phone. "Best guess is that it's a *yoo-strep-toe*-something-or-other," he told Sophie and Lester, "and it likes living by the water."

Sophie nodded. "The lake is up ahead of us. There's a good observation platform there where you can usually see the other animals who like water. I'd almost pity this monster if the locals are about."

"More lions?" Danny asked.

"Worse. Something that kills more people every year than any other animal in Africa."

"Some kind of snake?"

Sophie smiled thinly, still focused on her driving.

"We set the same riddle for the tourists, and none of them ever puzzle it out."

"So what is it?" Lester prompted. Danny could tell he didn't like playing this game.

"Wait and see." She didn't seem to care what Lester liked.

They drove in silence for a while, Lester with his lips pursed, arms folded in the back, Danny scanning out of the windscreen for any sign of movement.

"We should have brought more guns," Lester said at last.

"You guys are exterminators, huh?" Sophie asked. "You said you only used tranquillisers."

"I used to be a policeman," Danny told her.

"That's how you got caught up in this?" Sophie asked. "Investigating. Asking stupid questions."

"Not quite," Danny said.

"We did try to put you off the scent," Lester muttered.

"Too pig-stubborn," Danny said, and he grinned in the gloom. "Always been my problem. But the idea is not to kill these creatures — we try to get them home. They come through these sort of holes in time."

"Anomalies," Sophie said.

"Er, yeah."

"What do you know about them?" Lester said, sitting forward.

She smiled, and put her foot down and the SUV growled up a short, steep slope. They'd rejoined the dust road and the journey felt much smoother.

"Only what Danny said just now on the phone. So, holes in time. These monsters come through, and you lot chase them back, right?"

Danny shrugged.

"Basically, yeah. We try not to hurt them or let them hurt us. I guess you do the same thing here. Stop the animals doing too much damage to each other."

She snorted in response.

"We let nature do what nature does. It can be pretty rough, but we can't get involved. It has to play that way, like it always has done."

"But surely your responsibility is to the well-being of the animals, conserving the ecosystem and stuff," Danny said.

"We let them do what they've always done. Chase each other around, eat each other, leave the old and sick to die... You can't do anything else for them. Mostly our job is stopping tourists getting in between them. We need the money they bring in, but people are one hell of a nuisance."

"Oh."

"What were you expecting? You've seen what your creatures are like, you think ours would be any different?"

He was silent for a moment, absorbing the bleak idea of nature red in tooth and claw, with mankind just a small distraction that sometimes got in the way. He realised with a jolt that they were at the heart of the savage wilderness now. The only rule was that of survival. He'd just been being naïve and sentimental. It went with his good-cop image, but hardly made him look the expert. He needed Sophie to respect him if she was going to tell him anything.

He still sensed that she was holding something back; that she held some kind of answer — even though he didn't yet know the question.

"Well," he said finally, "we can at least get our creature off your back, can't we? Have you or your colleagues seen anything like a great big hole in the atmosphere? Looks like broken glass hanging in the air."

"No one's reported anything like that."

"We do have equipment for tracking the things," Lester said, "but your customs people impounded it." It was his turn to sound accusing.

"There are things we can do, though," Danny said. "The anomalies have strong magnetic properties."

"So compasses go crazy when you're getting close," Sophie surmised. She tapped the dashboard. "Got a compass here and it doesn't seem to be affected."

"And they also resonate at 87.6 Megahertz, so you can pick them up on the radio."

"But you'd need radios in different places to triangulate the signal."

"Yeah," Danny admitted, "but you can do it."

"Or you could get someone from your organisation to insist that we need our equipment," Lester said testily from behind them. His voice shook when the vehicle bounced.

"That *would* make things simpler," Danny said. "There's a screen with a little map."

Sophie tilted her head to one side, long blonde hair falling away to expose her slender neck.

"Seems like cheating," she said.

Lester snorted.

"Far more sporting to come out in the dark with no idea what's out here, with no one knowing where we are. In fact, I'm surprised we're even in the car. Shouldn't we just get out and walk?"

The one word that defined Lester was expedient, Danny noted. His whole *modus operandi* was sorting things out with the least fuss and nonsense. Being torn apart by a dinosaur out in this wild darkness would just lack the grace and style to which he aspired.

Sophie's eyes were laughing as she followed the dust road.

"What?" Danny asked her.

"I wasn't going to tell you till I had to, but we find a space up here to park and then we go ahead on foot."

There was a groan from the back seat.

They could hear but not see the water as they climbed out of the car. It lapped and trickled somewhere to their right. With the full beams now off, the only light came from the stars, glittering brilliantly in the expansive sky. It took a moment for their eyes to adjust, and when they did it became clear that the world around them was bathed in an eerie silver light.

They had stopped in an oblong clearing just off the dusty road. It must be some kind of car park on the trail, though there were no other vehicles around. Danny was surprised to see deep wedges in the ground — suggesting the path of one heavy vehicle, rather than several tourist cars.

"Has some kind of lorry been this way?" he asked Sophie as he joined her at the back of the SUV.

She handed him a Winchester rifle. This time he didn't say no.

"What makes you say that?"

"The tracks." She followed his gaze, and then just shook her head. "Ah, well," he said. "I'll leave it to the experts."

Sophie gathered up the rest of the equipment, checking the ammunition and the one torch she had.

Danny peered up at the incredible explosion of pin-pricks filling the sky, amazed at how different it looked from any night sky in England. He knew how to spot a handful of the most familiar constellations in the northern hemisphere, but didn't recognise anything here. That realisation brought back to him how far he was from home.

"It's getting chilly now," Lester said, slamming the passenger door shut. He winced at the noise he had made. Sophie scowled at him.

"Here," she snapped, handing him a Winchester Model 70 just like Danny's. "Know how to use it?"

Lester looked peculiar in his borrowed khakis, but he handled the gun like a pro. He raised an eyebrow at Sophie.

"Ready when you are."

She carried the one torch so Danny and Lester followed behind as she led them onto a dusty boardwalk. A tall wire fence bordered their path, leading them safely through thick bush and tall grass. The lap of the water became steadily louder and after a few minutes they reached a simple wooden structure with a sloping roof that was held up by four struts.

Sophie clicked off the torch as they entered. Danny and Lester's first footsteps echoed loudly on the wooden floor, and they both stepped more gingerly, joining her at a bench that sat before a single, long window.

There was no glass in the window. It looked out over a short drop onto the wide, slowly undulating lake. Starlight speckled the surface of the water, glinting and shimmering peacefully. A couple of scrawny birds sat on the surface some way out, seemingly asleep. Danny scanned the edges of the lake for any movement in the reeds. His eyes worked round every twig and stone, as best they could in the starlit darkness, but he could see nothing.

Sophie pointed out across the water. She offered the binoculars to Lester, who swiftly took them.

Danny strained to see what she had indicated. There was a strange dark patch out there on the water, something like a shadow.

A few moments later, Lester emerged from behind the binoculars. Wordlessly, he passed them to Danny, who pressed the twin tubes over his eyes. At first he couldn't make it out properly: something long, thin and dark was resting on the water's surface. The starlight caught on something at one end of the shadow.

An eye, he thought. Perhaps it was a snake of some kind, but stretched out taught across the water.

The thing shifted, shallow waves rippling out, making a wide oval-shape around the creature, and spelling out its bulky figure. At once Danny realised what he was looking at — the uppermost couple of inches of a hippopotamus, lurking in the water. As soon as he knew what he was looking for, he quickly spotted more: a whole family of huge, squat hippos, all almost entirely submerged.

He lowered the binoculars.

"They're not happy," Sophie whispered. "I think you might be right — there's something else here."

They stayed on the bench, watching the dark patches in the water intently, sharing the binoculars between them. The hippos did seem to be agitated, they clustered in the water a few metres in from a bald patch on the bank. Danny began to make sense of the markings in the mud, the heavy, round footprints of the creatures. The bald area must be a shallow entrance to the water, easy access for pudgy creatures with stumpy little legs.

And easy access to the water for anything else, as well.

Something lurked in the dark shadow of long grass just beyond the entrance to the lake. The grass wavered back and forth slowly, but not in time with the light breeze. And then a long, lizard nose poked out into the open and took a careful sniff.

One of the hippos waded a little way towards the new creature, a bulbous head emerging from the water. The hippo yawned, its head splitting almost in half to reveal a great expanse of flesh inside and grey, uneven tusks. Danny guessed that this wasn't actually a yawn, but some kind of warning.

Another one stepped up beside the first and performed an even more impressive yawn. The long, lizard nose retreated back into the grass. Moments later, there came the sound of the same angry roar Danny had heard before.

Without warning the great theropod tore out of the long grass, hurled itself down the short, bald riverbank and leaped on top of one of the two hippos. Its clawed feet struck deep into its flesh.

Danny turned to see Sophie's reaction to the violence unfolding before them, but her expression was as impassive as ever.

The hippos snapped at the creature, but the nimble dinosaur had already turned tail and run back up onto the bank. It tried to swipe one of the hippos with its tail, but the hippo had bulk on its side and took the full brunt of the impact without flinching. Instead, the dinosaur staggered, lost its step, but righted itself quickly. It seemed to hesitate, unsure now whether to run away or face its prey once again.

The two hippos heaved their heavy grey bodies out of the water. Behind them, more of the beasts poked their heads from the water, yawning their support.

"Come on," Sophie said, getting quickly to her feet. Danny and Lester exchanged glances, but she was the one with the torch, so they didn't have much choice but to follow her. They jogged to catch up as she made her way briskly across the car park, ignoring the SUV and heading for the road.

"You can't go after that thing on foot," Lester insisted.

"I just want to make sure it doesn't kill any more of the local population," she said over her shoulder, not slowing down. "We don't need to get too close. I take a shot, the hippos can finish it off."

"What about the lions that were pursuing it?" Danny pointed out, rushing to catch up with her. "Where have they got to?"

"They know better than to come onto hippo territory. Trust me. We'll be fine so long as we keep our distance."

Up ahead awful, brutal squawks and growls reached their ears as the fight kicked off again.

Sophie's torch swept the rust-coloured, dusty road in front of them. Again Danny noted the deep-laid tracks where some vehicle had come this way. The tracks still preserved the thick treads of the tyres — it really couldn't be anything other than a lorry or transporter, maybe two at a pinch. As he turned this information around in his mind a wild thought occurred to him — someone might have brought the dinosaur into the park on purpose. Perhaps it was some kind of corporate sabotage, someone seeing more value in all this land than wasting it on the wildlife.

Sophie glanced around at him, a strange look on her face. It seemed to Danny that she tried to maintain a veneer that she didn't like them muscling in on her turf. But something in the way she looked at him now, the sweat beading on her brow despite the coolness of the air...

"It's not just the creature, is it?" he said to her. "There's something else happening here."

Sophie looked surprised, startled like a petty crook Danny had just caught pilfering. Even in the meagre, silvery starlight he could see the slight blush in her cheeks. She stopped in her tracks, lowering the torch.

"You have to understand what we're up against. I can't talk about it now. But when we're done here..."

She turned away and continued leading them on. Lester glared at Danny but he only shrugged. Whatever it was, it would have to wait.

They came to a rough T-junction. Across the road, a sign fashioned out of a split log showed an arrow pointing right to a picture of a lake, and an arrow pointing left to some kind of refreshments. Beneath the directions — in capital letters — was a warning, "STAY IN YOUR CAR!"

Danny and Lester joined Sophie where she had halted at the junction leading to the right. She kept just behind the turning, and was staring straight ahead. Danny couldn't see anything up towards the lake, but the noise of the fight between the hippos and dinosaur had grown even more ferocious.

He noticed that the heavy-set tyre tracks had vanished — the large vehicle had clearly taken the left fork. He felt a little disappointed — it had probably just gone to stock up the soft drinks and chocolate, after all. So much for his conspiracy theory. *But something about it had agitated her*, he recalled.

"Okay." She gestured to them, and began to venture forward in the direction of the fighting. She held the torch low, so that the light fell only a little way ahead of her feet. Lester and Danny flanked either side of her, both ready with their rifles.

Danny knew from his days on the force that you should never go out into the field unprepared, let alone with a weapon you didn't know how to use.

There were all kinds of superstitions about handling weapons — beliefs held by men who'd survived when their compatriots had not. He knew full well that he was breaking all the rules. But they couldn't go back now.

The stench of blood carried on the breeze, which blew from the dark and noisy fight somewhere up ahead.

Sophie stopped again.

The road rose slightly up ahead of them, a pale ribbon in the darkness, then dropped steeply down. Some distance beyond, the starlight glittered in the water of the lake, so they had to be close to the fighting, though the rise in the road made it impossible to judge exactly *how* close.

She took a step forward, bending her knees, keeping low. She put the torch down on the ground, gripped her rifle with both hands, aiming out in front of her. Danny and Lester followed suit, crouching as they walked, scanning the darkness ahead of them, ready to fire. The torch behind them cast three long shadows out into the road ahead of them.

Suddenly the sounds of combat ceased.

Something moved quickly in the darkness and the theropod let out an almighty roar of rage. As quickly as it appeared, it was gone again. The mayhem resumed. Sophie turned to Danny and Lester, raising the palm of one hand, signalling them to stay put.

The two men stood in the middle of the road while she made her way to one side, her shoulder almost brushing against the needle-sharp thorns of the acacia. Crouching down so that her knees almost touched the earth, she took careful steps in the direction of the fighting. Her shadow merged with the bushes, so that only Danny and Lester's remained, filling the road right up to the rise.

She looked back at them, and in the faint glow, her expression appeared stern. Danny smiled reassuringly, ready with his gun. But Sophie didn't smile back, and he glanced around behind him to see if she was looking past him, at something else. But the torch lay bright in the middle of the road, blinding him.

He turned to look at Sophie again, and saw that she had ventured a few steps further, to the point that her blonde hair was the most visible part of her. She leaned out, peeking over the top of the rise at the battle going on. Movement appeared from time to time in the darkness, swishing and slashing in time to the growls and roars of weary creatures locked in battle.

She raised her gun.

Danny held his breath. He watched her body stiffen as she lined up the shot.

The gun barked loud in the night air. A great cry came from the far side of the rise, followed by the thudding of feet and heavy *splosh*es of hippos scurrying back into the water. She must have brought the dinosaur down, startling its opponents.

But no.

Danny watched in horror as a long, scaly head appeared over the rise, jaw hanging open, displaying awful, bloody teeth. The creature tottered forward, its body and neck a gruesome mass of jagged cuts and slashes. The lions and hippos had done it terrible damage, but still it kept coming.

It reared up on its two powerful legs, more than twice the height of Sophie. Then it made for her.

A gunshot cracked loudly, right by Danny. Lester quickly fired again. They both marched forward, firing with each step. Sophie sank back into the bush, also shooting rapidly.

The creature didn't run, rather it moved unevenly as the onslaught smacked into its damaged body. Blood oozed from the multiple wounds, but it kept on coming into the hail of bullets. It was dying — it *had* to be — but it meant to drag Sophie down with it.

Reaching where she cowered into the bush at the side of the road, it stood over her, dripping blood and gore, enjoying a delicious moment of anticipation. Danny and Lester were almost on her, too, shooting up at the creature's face and neck. It twisted its head back and forth, dancing round the bullets, and let out a long roar. Then it looked directly at Danny.

He stared into the deadly, yellow eyes of the prehistoric creature, knowing he was powerless to escape it. The creature stood poised over Sophie's defenceless form, tiny by comparison. Then its expression changed.

Danny *felt* rather than heard something behind them. Before he could turn around, a shadow loomed beside him and Lester. Without pausing to think, Danny threw himself at Lester so that they both tumbled off the road. His gun went off, smacking hard into his upper arms. For a moment he fell through the air, something whooshing just past his feet. Then they crashed into the painfully hard and spiky acacia, needles stabbing through their clothes and skin.

He scrambled around in time to see another creature, the size and weight of the theropod, running on all fours as it launched itself at the battered dinosaur. The theropod fell backwards with a yelp of surprise and both creatures tumbled down behind the rise.

"That was rather convenient," Lester said, lying stunned in the acacia where he'd broken Danny's dive.

Danny didn't stop to help him up. He ran to Sophie, who was already getting to her feet. She was wide-eyed and breathless, but shook off his attention. They both hurried down the road to see the two dinosaurs locked together in battle on the edge of the water. The hippos yawned and growled from well within the lake, like an audience cheering on a match between two wrestlers.

The vast, dog-like newcomer seemed just a little smaller than the theropod that writhed underneath it. *No, not dog-like*, Danny realised. *More like a crocodile, but with longer legs that lifted its flat body high above the ground.* It grappled expertly with the theropod, tearing at its long neck with sharp, serrated teeth. The theropod flailed and squawked, but weakened as it was, it seemed utterly powerless against this new threat.

Danny lowered his gun and reached instead for the mobile phone in his pocket. He'd got a souped-up model when he joined the ARC, which apparently had an extra million megapixels, and something that compensated for the darkness. Quickly he clicked the camera function and took a blurred snap of the brawling creatures.

"Well, shoot it then," Lester said, joining them. "You know, with a gun?" His face was badly scratched and bloody, but there was fire in his eyes.

Sophie raised her rifle and aimed. The crocodile-like creature turned from the dying theropod, whose legs still twitched and quivered feebly, to stare defiantly back at her. Then it stepped nimbly back, grabbed one of its victim's thick ankles in its teeth, and with startling strength dragged its prey roughly off into the bush.

The hippos in the lake continued to yawn, and one moved forward, its flabby head emerging from the water. They might have surrendered their ground to the two dinosaurs, but they wouldn't let the three humans have it.

"We need to fall back," Lester said firmly.

"Yeah," Sophie lowered her rifle, "nothing more we can do."

They turned, making their way quickly back towards the car. The torch lay in pieces in the middle of the road where the second creature had smashed it. Small bits of glass and metal reflected the grey starlight.

Another second, Danny thought, *and that would have been me and Lester.*

ELEVEN

Emergency vehicles lined the washed-out roads as they made their way into central London. Policemen, firemen and soldiers worked together in the rain, constructing lines of sandbags. They all looked worn and weary; it had just gone one in the morning and they would be toiling all through the night.

Connor and Abby sat up in the front of the military truck, sharing the not-quite-double-width seat next to the driver. Connor sat in the middle, and had to lean hard against Abby to keep his right knee from getting in the way of the gear-stick. He didn't mind, for all he might be squashed and uncomfortable in his damp clothes. Abby had fallen asleep on his shoulder, and he sat there, his arm around her, sharing her warmth and the blanket, actually quite content with life.

Tall skyscrapers gleamed wetly on either side of them. The street-lights changed from white to dull orange as they drove into an older district.

London sometimes seemed to Connor like a whole load of very different towns and villages all squashed up together — cross a road or turn a corner and you were in a different world. He liked the buzz and bustle of all these different cultures colliding, the rich melting pot of London life, so it felt especially eerie to drive on roads that were empty but for emergency vehicles. The city on the far side of the windshield seemed so grim and foreboding, like something out of a sci-fi movie, or as if they were at war.

Abby mumbled in her sleep, opened her eyes to look at Connor just for a moment, then curled up against his shoulder again. Funny how just having her close could make it all seem better.

Soon enough they were pulling through the imposing gates of the ARC headquarters. Rain washed down the sides of the wonky grey egg-shaped building. Their driver eased into a space, bringing the truck to a halt as gently as he could.

Ben scribbled his mileage into a small notebook that was tied to the dashboard with string, then sighed and yanked open his door. The rain crashed down loudly, cold droplets spattering into their cabin.

"Thanks for the —" Connor called just as he slammed the door. "— lift," he added in the sudden quiet.

Abby shifted, extracting herself muzzily from his arm and the blanket.

"Hey," she said.

"Hey, we're gonna have to run for it."

"Yeah."

Connor wished he'd not changed out of his waders earlier, even though they'd been half full of the River Thames. The concrete floor of the ARC car park sat maybe an inch or two underwater.

He jumped down from the army truck right behind Abby, and immediately cold water sloshed over his trainers.

"Ack!" he said with horror.

Abby wrinkled her nose.

"Come on," she said, taking his arm. "There'll be tea and toast in the canteen."

Together they dashed through the rain to the main entrance of the building, guarded by black-uniformed soldiers with the scary-looking rifles Becker seemed so proud of.

"Hi!" Abby said brightly, rummaging through her pockets for her pass.

Connor whipped his own pass deftly from his back pocket and ran it through the reader. Then he let the machine scan his fingertips and retinas.

The screen by the pass ran graphics of blue circles on grey squares, then showed a photo of his face, looking a bit surprised and goofy where he'd not been ready when they snapped it. In a blocky typeface the screen also said:

Connor Temple
432-7891-632-8544 CT
Dept 432-MT
Access denied

Connor pressed his shoulder against the door but it didn't budge. He checked the screen and only now took in the word "denied".

"Oh, great," he said to Abby, glancing over his shoulder at the heavily armed soldiers just a couple of metres behind them. "This happens to me at cash machines, as well."

He rubbed at the shiny chip in the middle of his pass then tried swiping it again. The screen quivered, then showed the same gawping photo and information.

Access denied.

"But I'm access-all-zones!" he told the screen. He checked the card just to make sure. Yes, that was what was written under his number and department. He showed the screen the card.

"Let me." Abby said, and she swiped her own matching card. The screen pinged and the door clicked open. Abby smiled winningly at Connor.

"I'm just special."

He muttered as he followed her inside, cross that whenever anything went wrong, it always went wrong for *him*. And because he was so busy muttering he walked slap into her back.

"Ow," he said as he twisted to avoid the impact. "You should watch where you're going." He looked up. Black-uniformed soldiers waited for them in the entrance hall, guns raised.

"Um," Connor said. "We work here, yeah?"

Becker stepped forward.

"Abby," he said, "can I have a word?"

"Sure," she said.

She took a couple of steps towards him and Becker grabbed her arm, yanking her out of the way of the line of armed soldiers, now all pointing their rifles at Connor.

Connor put his hands out in front of him, showing that he carried nothing but his fingerless gloves.

"What?" Abby said, struggling to free herself from Becker's grip.

"Look, there's been some kind of mistake," Connor said. "My pass probably just got wet or something..."

A soldier stepped forward towards him, brandishing a pair of handcuffs.

"Your access had been revoked pending a formal investigation into recent activity."

"This is mad," Connor protested as he let them snap the cuffs round his wrists.

"But he hasn't done anything!" he heard Abby shouting. "There has to have been a mistake!"

"I'm sorry," Becker said. "I have to follow my orders. We'll get this sorted out."

"No!" Abby wailed.

Numbly, Connor let them lead him away.

TWELVE

They drove in silence back to the lodge, following the slow dust road rather than cutting through the scrubby bush. Danny sat in the back seat this time, fiddling with his phone. He sent the photo he'd taken back to Sarah at the ARC. A message back explained that Sarah wasn't on duty — Danny supposed it was a bit late at night. Instead, someone called Anna would try to identify the creature that he'd seen.

There were lights on and other cars in the car park when they arrived back, and as they emerged wearily from the SUV they were met with plenty of activity.

Ted, the tall ranger who'd guarded the gate, came over and shook Sophie by the hand. They had a complicated, three-part handshake, but performed it quickly, without fuss. They spoke briefly in the clicking, articulate language they'd used before and then Danny and Lester followed them inside.

The bodies had been removed as had much of the broken furniture, and a plastic sheet had been secured over the broken window in the mess room, the breeze outside jostling against it. A handful of men and women in the same army-green fatigues scrubbed at bloodstains. They acknowledged Sophie with nods or a few words in the clicking language.

They completely ignored Danny and Lester.

Watching them, Danny felt instinctively that Sophie and Ted didn't fit in with the rest of this lot. He could read the pattern just in how they stood in the room. The other gamekeepers exchanged furtive, knowing glances when they thought no one else was watching. They either suspected Sophie of something, or were up to something themselves.

Sophie came over to him and Lester. She stood tall, made the effort to seem in command, but her eyes betrayed her exhaustion.

"There's not much left to be done here," she told them. "You might as well both get to bed."

"We want to help," Danny insisted. "Just tell us what we can do."

"Keep out of the way," Sophie replied. He looked for the smile he had seen earlier, but she didn't seem to be joking.

"All right," he said. "But I do a mean breakfast in bed."

She stared at him. Hell, had he gone too far? Perhaps being stood in the room where her colleagues had died wasn't the best place for levity. But again he detected that conflict in her, that effort not to smile or respond.

"Come on," Lester said, butting in. "Just show us where we are."

She motioned, and Ted led them through the kitchen and down a passageway with doors on either side. The last one on the left had been assigned to them. Two low, simple beds sat on either side of the room, with barely enough space to walk down between them. A sink with a single tap nestled dolefully in the corner.

"It's a lot like the Savoy," Lester said dryly, dumping his bag on one of the beds. Ted didn't respond, and made to leave them to it.

"Wait!" Lester moved to stop him. "What about washing facilities?" Ted thumbed back along down the corridor as he walked away.

Lester grimaced, and unzipped his case, pulled out a wash bag and put a beige towel round his neck.

"I suppose I'd better investigate."

While he was gone, Danny went through his own bag, digging out his change of clothes for the next day, finding his toothbrush and toothpaste. He flicked idly through the guidebook he'd been reading on the plane, then just sat on his bed, the events of the day running through his brain.

When Lester came back, shaking his head at the state of the bathroom, Danny headed down the corridor for his turn. As he washed his hands he noticed a remarkable creature sheltering on the ledge of the window. Not quite as tall as the width of his hand, it was pale brown and spindly, a bit like a stick insect. He didn't get any closer, but scrutinised the thing with care. Its peculiar posture, its forelimbs hooked together gave him the clue to its identity. It was a praying mantis. He couldn't remember if they were poisonous, but figured he wouldn't find out.

He could hear the gamekeepers still busy putting the mess room back together as he made his way back to his room. Lester was sat on his bed, eyes closed and his dusty shoes discarded in the middle of the floor. Danny sat down opposite him, unsure what to say. Lester, his eyes still closed, reached a hand into his bag and withdrew a bottle of whisky, handing it across.

Danny grinned.

"What else have you got?"

"Some perfume for my wife, but you can't have that."

Danny twisted the top of the bottle, cracking the seal. He took a quick swig, and then another, the hot liquid burning the back of his throat. It occurred to him that he hadn't eaten anything since the aeroplane. *Well, it'll have to be a liquid dinner then*, he thought.

His eyes feeling bloated and red, he handed the bottle back to Lester, who took a couple of swigs himself. Then he flicked his eyes at the open door, and Danny lent an arm out and batted it closed.

"Well," Lester said in a low whisper.

"Not a great first day," Danny said.

"What do you make of our hostess?"

"She's got something she wants to tell us, but doesn't know quite how. I tried to work the charm. Might be useful to us."

Lester raised an eyebrow. Then he spoke.

"She was well out of the way when that thing attacked, left both of us in its path. Perhaps it's just the instincts of a ranger on her home ground, but I got the feeling that she moved to the edge of the road because she knew what was coming."

Danny considered.

"Hell of a thing to have set up," he said. "She nearly didn't make it herself."

Nonetheless, Danny felt the skin on his forearms prickle with goose-flesh. Something had been bugging him about that, too, but it didn't make any sense. Why would Sophie wish harm on them? How could she have known about that creature? And if she had planned any part of what had happened, why had she put herself so much in danger? Despite the reserve she showed them, the tough act she tried to keep going, he'd seen something in her eyes. Like maybe she thought he wasn't such an idiot.

"We're missing something," he told Lester. "We have to be."

And on cue his mobile buzzed — it was Anna at the ARC. Now that he heard her voice, he thought he could remember her: pretty, red hair. One of the tech girls, helped with the science stuff, filled out the late shift. She didn't have a boyfriend — why would he know something like that?

Danny listened for a while then thanked her and clicked off the phone.

"Connor was right," he said. "The theropod was yoo-strep-toe... whatever it was. Callovian stage, mid-Jurassic."

"So what's the problem?"

"The creature that jumped on it was a Postosuchus. Early sort of crocodilian thing. Tall, narrow jaws like a T-rex that gives it a really strong bite. Back and head have got thick armour plating, plus a whole load of other special features."

"I see. Well, we don't try to catch it and send it home. We'll just have to bring this one down."

"Yeah, but dealing with it's not the problem. There's a lot of debate about the early crocodilians, she said, when they split from the archosaurs and stuff. But Postosuchus is mid-to-late Triassic, maybe fifty or sixty million years before that theropod."

"Oh."

"Yeah," Danny said, "so we're dealing with at least two different anomalies."

THIRTEEN

Abby tore down the main corridor of the ARC labs and offices, catching up with Becker as he pushed through the double doors and walked into the main operations room. Despite it being the middle of the night, technical staff attended the strange machines in various states of disarray on the high tables. Jonny, who liked eighties music, was working on one of Connor's gadgets; Manpreet had her tongue out as she connected tiny pieces of something together. Anna was working at one of the desks by the ADD, just in front of the curving walkway leading around to Lester's office.

Everywhere she looked there were black-uniformed soldiers brandishing guns and looking surly. They guarded the artefact and the tall hanger doors, watching and waiting, ready. Abby's stomach clenched in horror.

"You've taken over!" she yelled at Becker. "The moment Lester is out of the country, you've pulled off a coup!"

Becker turned to face her, his expression stern. She marched right up to him, caught him by surprise and poked him in the sternum hard enough that he had to take a step back to regain his balance. He reached his hands out to her shoulders, but she shrugged him off.

"I'm not going to go along with it," she told him.

"Abby," he said, "I've got my orders."

"Oh, *orders.* Well that makes all the difference. Lock up who you like!" Becker flinched at this and turned to look round at his men.

God, she thought, *he's embarrassed 'cause I'm shouting. Like* I'm *the one who's lost the plot.*

"Becker," she said, stamping down on her anger, "Connor's one of the good guys. What happened to your sense of loyalty?"

He blanched at her, and looked stung.

"I —" he began.

"Captain Becker understands loyalty very well," a plummy voice said from up above them. Abby wheeled round. On the balcony of Lester's office, looking out over the room, stood a tall, well-groomed man in a tailored pin-stripe suit, silver lines on black. His hair and beard were shaved close to his skin, giving him a practical, no-nonsense look. He leant his forearms on the railing of the balcony, revealing chunky silver cuff links.

"Who *the hell* are you?" Abby demanded.

"A friend, I hope," the man said amiably. He smiled, stepped back from the railing, then made his way calmly down the slope to join them. He walked with a definite swagger, the movement showing off the taut muscles that hid under his suit. Despite his expensive clothes and posh accent, he had the air of a gangster.

Abby glanced around the room at the soldiers, the technicians, certain all of them were part of this mad conspiracy. She had fought all kinds of creatures and people, but at this moment, in her own headquarters, she'd never felt so trapped.

"My name is Tom Samuels," the man said, extending a large and muscular hand as he made his way towards her. Abby ignored it.

Unfazed, he carried on.

"I've come over from the Home Office to help out. It's all above board. In fact, I'm an old sparring partner of Jim Lester's. We even boarded at the same school." He smiled, showing perfect teeth.

"You've arrested Connor," Abby replied, struggling to keep her cool.

"I'm rather afraid we have," Samuels agreed. He nodded to Becker. "Interrogate him, Captain. Leave no stone unturned."

Becker glanced at Abby, then back at Samuels.

"Sir, Abby was with him the whole evening. Surely that means —" But he tailed off as he saw the expression on Samuels' face.

Samuels kept smiling but his eyes, which had been warm and friendly a moment before, now glittered like ice.

"Sir," Becker persevered. "I'd personally vouch for Connor."

"Captain Becker," Samuels said, "the young lady questioned your sense of loyalty. I trust I won't have to do the same?"

Becker stood smartly at attention. "No, sir."

"I gave you an order, and I expect you to follow it."

"Yes, sir." Becker clicked his heels and marched out, studiously avoiding Abby's eyes as he passed her.

Her throat was dry, and she felt completely helpless.

"You can't do this." Somehow, she didn't believe her own words.

He raised one eyebrow.

"We'll stop you," she told him. "*Somehow* we'll stop you."

He toyed with the chunky Rolex on his wrist, as if he wanted her to notice his expensive taste. Then he looked up at her and spoke.

"Abby," he said, "I appreciate that this is a bit of a surprise. But you're wasting your time on Connor."

"*He hasn't done anything*," she insisted.

"No?" Samuels said, again with that cruel smile. "Well, I suppose you haven't yet seen Dr Page."

"You can't —" Abby began before she registered what he'd said. She felt her heart thumping in her chest.

"What..." she murmured, "what's happened to Sarah?"

"Well this is a bit awkward, isn't it?" Becker grinned as he took a seat opposite Connor.

Connor slouched in his chair, arms pinioned behind his back. It seemed to hurt him to sit up straight, so he gazed up at the man through his messy fringe.

The ARC didn't have an interrogation room, so they had commandeered the security room. A bank of television screens flicked between different views from the building's many CCTV cameras. Dirty cups and crockery nestled by the sink.

"You want a cup of tea?" Becker asked. "I could do with one myself."

"I want," Connor replied, "a lawyer."

Becker sat back in his seat and sighed. He had tried to be nice.

"And under your terms of service and the Civil Contingencies Act, you're not entitled to one."

"I haven't *done* anything," the young man insisted angrily.

"Really?" Becker said. "Nothing at all?"

"Come on!" Connor snapped. "You know I haven't!"

And really, Becker couldn't believe that Connor had been responsible for any of what had happened. But the tape was running, recording this interrogation, so he had to go through with it, carry it out properly. And some things just didn't add up.

"You disobeyed my direct order," he said, "earlier this evening."

"Oh, what?" Connor laughed. "You wouldn't listen! We found the Deinosuchus couple and we came up with how to deal with them. We did *exactly* what we're meant to. You only made things harder!"

Becker bit his lip. He'd have been quite happy to acknowledge that perhaps he should have taken their counsel more seriously, but now the accusation stood on the official record. He didn't like that one bit.

He reached over for the clear plastic bag of items they had confiscated from Connor, and withdrew something that looked like a mobile phone.

"You made this yourself?"

"What? Yeah," Connor said. "I build a lot of stuff: the ADD, the locking mechanism and all sorts of other equipment we use. You've never complained before."

"What is it?" Becker asked, turning the phone over in his hands.

"I'd rather not say as it's still at the development stage," Connor said a little more carefully. "I've learnt not to share stuff until it's properly tested or it gets rushed into the field. And then you're stuck out there with something that doesn't work properly."

"You used this to break into that shop. Where you stole the deodorants."

"Hey! You went back and paid!"

"Yes, while you were quite happy just to steal."

"Is that what this is?" Connor said incredulously. "You've arrested me for looting? We were up against two giant crocodiles. I took what we needed for the job! Come on, Becker, this is ridiculous."

"It's establishing a precedent." Becker raised the mobile phone. "You've been keeping secrets. You've been helping yourself to equipment and resources. You've disobeyed direct orders that have led to people's deaths."

Connor gaped at him. "Who died?" he said. "We just got a bit wet."

"Jamie Weavers was brought down by the raptors. Left a widow and two kids." Becker had already dispatched someone to talk to the family. If it weren't for this business, he would have gone himself.

Connor just shook his head.

"I'm sorry, I really am. He was a great bloke, but you can't pin that on me. You can't. I wasn't even there!"

Becker sighed.

"No, Connor. That's just the trouble. If you'd been with me, if I could vouch for where you'd been all night... But the very moment the ARC's broken into, you're conveniently off on your own."

"We were broken into? What? When? Is everyone okay?"

"You'd better hope so."

"I didn't have anything to do with it! I was in Maidenhead with you."

"Not at the time the break-in occurred."

"I could never have got back to London in time! You know that doesn't make sense."

"You wouldn't need to be here, Connor. You'd just need to be in contact. A phone call maybe, on a phone you've built yourself so we can't trace the call."

"If you can't trace the call it's 'cause I didn't make it. You've got to believe me, Becker. There's got to be some way I can prove it. *Please!*"

Becker couldn't look Connor in the eye.

"I'm sorry," he said. "That's the problem. You know what the security is like round here — you designed a lot of it yourself, after all. I don't like any of this either, but it can only have been an inside job. And you don't have an alibi."

Sarah sat quietly in the canteen, opposite what had once been Cutter's office and hadn't yet been fitted out for Danny. Abby and Tom Samuels stood in the doorway. Abby didn't know quite what to say. Sarah didn't have any marks on her, but she sat shivering. The tea they'd made her had slopped over the copy of *Metro* on the table, its cover a full-page shot of flood chaos in London.

"I'll leave you two together for a moment," Samuels said. Sarah responded, looking up slowly. Her dark eyes were awful to behold. Samuels swaggered off.

"Hey," Sarah said, sweeping long black hair out of her face.

"Hey," Abby replied, joining her at the table. Sarah offered the open packet of chocolate digestives, and Abby took one gratefully.

"You look soggy," Sarah said.

"It's raining outside." Abby munched her biscuit.

"That would explain it," Sarah said, nodding and fiddling nervously with a strand of hair that reached down past her jaw.

"What happened?" Abby asked her, leaning in.

Sarah smiled awkwardly.

"I don't know, exactly. I just feel so stupid. I mean, what's the point of being trained in self-defence if you just go all weak-kneed..."

"It's not your fault," Abby assured her. "You against a whole bunch of armed blokes. I would've been exactly the same."

"I should have done something."

"They could have hurt you. Do you know who they were?"

Sarah hugged her knees.

"Soldiers or something. I've given all the descriptions that I could. They injected me with something, and when I woke up they'd gone."

"Injected you? Are you all right?"

"Yeah, medical says I'm fine. Bit jumpy, though that might be all the tea that this lot made me drink. And I'm just so *furious*." She banged the palm of her hand down on the table. "I feel so stupid! I'm not cut out for this stuff, Abby. I'm a researcher. An academic."

"Don't. You were outnumbered, and you should have been safe in here, anyway. We're going to get those guys."

"Yeah?" Sarah said, doubt in her voice. "They didn't take anything, Abby."

"What?"

"They knocked me out for maybe half an hour and they had the place to themselves, but they didn't take anything. They didn't even touch the artefact."

"They could have swapped it!"

"They didn't. I've checked. I checked everything. It's like they did it as a joke, just to spook me out."

"They must have done *something*."

"No mess, nothing is missing. None of the locked computer files have been gone through, none of our secrets found out."

"They didn't even break in," Samuels said from the door, as if he'd listened to their whole conversation. He walked briskly over to the table, carrying an open laptop. "Which leads one to assume that it must have been an inside job."

Abby got to her feet.

"You can't believe Connor had anything to do with this," she said, glaring at him.

Samuels didn't even look up, he just worked away at the laptop, as if not quite familiar with its different functions.

"I really hoped you'd cooperate," he told Abby. "After all, we'll only have to assume that you were his accomplice."

Abby gaped at him, struggling to control her anger, but he continued to ignore her, busy on the keyboard.

"Connor and me —" she started.

"Aren't quite an item, no," Samuels asked. "Dr Page has already explained that much."

Sarah avoided Abby's stare.

"I did say it wasn't Connor," she protested.

"Abby, you and Connor have been cohabiting for how long now?" Samuels asked.

"Not that it's any of your business, but Connor has moved out."

"A difference of opinion?"

"No, I've got my brother staying."

"So where is Connor living now?"

Abby sighed. "I don't know."

"You haven't asked?"

"He hasn't told me. I think I hurt his pride. But he wouldn't do anything. I can vouch for him."

"I'm sure you can," Samuels said, nodding. "But perhaps you're working with him."

"This is getting ridiculous!" Abby said, red-faced with frustration. "Are we suspects now, as well? I thought Sarah was the victim, not the perpetrator."

Samuels sighed and looked up at her.

"There has been a major security breach in a top ranking government establishment that's doing vital work. We are required to proceed with all due caution. *Everyone* is a suspect. You and Dr Page will consider yourselves under house arrest until further notice."

Abby realised then that the soldier blocking the doorway was for her and Sarah's benefit.

"You can't do this," she told Samuels, her voice thick with anger.

"I am sincerely sorry for the inconvenience," he replied. "But you and Dr Page need to understand where your loyalties should lie."

He tapped a final key and twisted the laptop around so Abby and Sarah could see. The film sequence had been enlarged to fill the screen, so it looked grainy, indistinct. The time code in the bottom corner said it had been recorded a bit after four that afternoon.

They looked down on the pixellated image of Connor, hurrying up to the ADD, looking over his shoulder to make certain no one was around. His jerky movements were due to the low setting of the CCTV camera, which took only a minimal number of frames per second. He began to flutter his fingers quickly over the keyboard of the machine.

"That was 16:11," Samuels said, reading the time from the bottom of the image. "The bolts on the fire doors on Exit Three are unlocked remotely from inside the building."

They saw Connor stop, check his watch, and wait. The image twitched, and then he was busy typing again.

"At 16:12, an email is sent from the ADD duty account to an unknown gmail account. The message says, 'The circle is now complete.' Apparently it's a quotation from one of the *Star Wars* films."

Abby watched in abject horror, unable to tear her eyes from the screen. She wanted to protest, wanted to laugh at the insanity of it. Again the Connor on the screen paused to check the time on his watch, and then started typing once again.

"At 16:15..." Samuels said, and he paused for effect.

"The ADD goes off," Sarah said quietly. The image flickered, troubled by the flashing lights of the alarm. They watched Connor step back from the ADD just as Abby, Sarah and Becker came running in to join him.

"You were all going to head out to Maidenhead," Samuels began.

"No," Abby said, aghast at what they were trying to tell her.

"We were all going to go," Sarah continued coldly, meeting Abby's gaze this time.

"But you thought someone should stay behind," Samuels added, clicking off the movie and closing the laptop.

"I stayed to watch over the ADD," Sarah said, "but Connor told me not to."

FOURTEEN

Danny opened his eyes, suddenly wide-awake. It took him a moment to remember where he was, as he lay gazing up at the pale plaster ceiling of their cramped bedroom.

Lester was curled in a ball on his own bed, looking unnaturally peaceful and content.

Danny checked his watch: not quite half six in the morning, local time. Half four in the UK according to his timepiece *and* his body clock. He sighed. Surely you weren't meant to get jet-lag when you were only two hours out of your home time zone.

The timber of the lodge shifted and creaked around him. There were no sounds of human activity but Lester's breathing. The gamekeepers must have worked late into the night, and deserved to be sleeping now. He closed his eyes and tried to relax, but he couldn't lie still.

Gingerly, so as not to wake his roommate, he extracted himself from the bed and padded barefoot, in boxer shorts and t-shirt, to the shower room down the corridor.

Either the shower didn't offer hot water or he was flummoxed by the controls. He held his breath and stepped directly under the frothy cascade. The icy water zinged against his skin, slicing into him like blades. He shivered as he exhaled, his senses tingling and alert.

He counted slowly to ten, forcing himself to endure the cold. But it didn't look like his body was going to get used to it, so he scrubbed himself down quickly and efficiently and then got out of the water.

His pink skin steamed as he dabbed himself with his towel. Blinding sunlight glimmered through the shutters on the window. If it was hot in this shadowy washroom, what must it be like outside? They were likely to be out under it all day.

The towel they'd given him seemed like more of a hand cloth than the bath sheets he was used to. When he'd dried himself as best he could, it didn't quite reach all the way round his waist. He held it in place, one hand bridging the gap of his exposed thigh, and made his way back to the bedroom where his clothes were waiting. His damp feet left footprints on the tiles behind him. Just a few steps down the warm corridor and his clean skin was already prickling with sweat.

He reached for the handle on the door to his bedroom, then sensed someone behind him. Further down the corridor, in the kitchen, Sophie stood watching him.

"Hi," he said in a cheery whisper, adjusting his towel self-consciously. A droplet of water skittered down his chest.

Sophie looked clean, tanned, and healthy in a fresh black vest and camouflage trousers. She didn't say anything, just gazed at him, her eyes wide in surprise.

"I'll, uh, just put some clothes on," he told her. It broke the spell. She shook her head, running her hand through her newly washed blonde hair, and he thought he might even have glimpsed a slightly crooked smile. Then she turned from him and got on with whatever she'd been doing.

Lester still slept as Danny closed the bedroom door behind him. He found his clothes — the same jeans from yesterday, his one change of shorts, a red polo shirt, his leather jacket — and dressed as fast as he could. He wanted to get out there before Sophie put up her defences again. She'd seen him half-naked and been lost for words, which suggested progress. She was a competent, professional and *very* pretty girl. He might just stand a chance...

A mug of tea awaited him when he entered the kitchen, his leather jacket dangling from one hand. He took the tea through to the mess room, and was surprised to find it empty. The room barely showed any signs of the terrible events of the previous night. Were it not for the crude covering over what had once been a window, he could almost have believed it had never happened.

Danny made his way outside onto the raised platform overlooking the car park. Sophie's SUV stood alone in the brick-red dust. She stood beside the open hatch. He shielded his eyes from the incredible sun that shone in a vast and spotless blue sky. The colours of the dust and foliage seemed so rich and vivid, it was as if his own sense of colour had been greatly improved. He reminded himself that this landscape, this air, was what human beings had evolved to fit into. This was *their* territory, too.

He breathed in a great lungful of the warm air.

"You want to come with me?" Sophie asked, busy loading up her car. He tried to detect awkwardness, embarrassment in having been startled before, but she gave nothing away.

"Sure," Danny replied, sipping his tea. "Got nothing better to do."

"We had a delivery." She lifted one of the bags from the back of the car so that he could see. It took him a moment to recognise the package as the handheld anomaly detector they had brought from London which the South African customs officials had impounded.

"They've let us have it all back?" he asked, stepping down from the platform to join her. Lester's angry phone calls must have made an impact on someone. The sun pressed hard against his exposed face and arms. Danny had the sort of complexion that needed time to tan. So he put his tea down and pulled on his jacket. It might be over-dressing for the heat, but it would stop him from burning.

"Some of it," she said. "Not the guns or the things they thought could have been guns." That was bad news, but rather than dwell on it, he walked over to assess what they *did* have.

They'd got a handheld anomaly detector and Lester's laptop — containing Connor's purpose-built database for identifying dinosaurs and their epochs.

"Great," he said, "though the guns would have helped. The Winchester is all very well..."

"It's all we've got," Sophie said curtly, cutting him off.

"Of course," he answered quickly. "After all, what can possibly go wrong?"

Sophie slammed shut the back of the SUV.

"All done. You'd better leave a note, tell Lester where we're going."

"Oh," he said, grinning sheepishly. "Good idea."

As he made his way back to the lodge again, she called after him, "Don't want to appear too eager."

He looked back at her to make a joke, but instead caught her eye. For a moment they just held each other's gazes, then Sophie quickly looked away. Her long blonde hair fell forward, hiding her face. But not before Danny had seen that she was blushing.

"Be right back," he said instead, heading into the lodge. He fought back the urge to laugh out loud. Score one for the Quinn charm — Sophie liked him all right.

They found the remains of the theropod a short distance from the lake. Its carcass was ripped open, ribs and bones exposed. A lot of the meat had been eaten away by the night's many scavengers.

The dead creature lay in a clearing surrounded by shoulder-high grass. Danny felt vulnerable so out in the open, wilderness all around them. The weight of the sun made him move sluggishly, and his clothes felt damp with sweat. Smelly and slow and out of his depth, he thought he presented a pretty good meal.

Wrinkling his nose at the pungent stench, Danny made his way around the other side of the enormous animal, examining the multiple wounds inflicted on the creature the night before, including their own gunshots. And now they'd be going after the Postosuchus with the same Winchester Model 70.

Sophie appraised the tracks around the creature.

"It's already been visited by scavengers," she said, indicating the whorls and waves in the dust from lots of different feet. "So we don't have a trail to follow for the lizard thing."

Danny had expected this. "Not to worry," he told her. "There's something we can do first."

He worked the handheld detector, but didn't get any kind of blip. He started walking, waving the thing around him; trying to get a signal.

"These things *have* to have come through from somewhere," he said.

"You said holes in time," she answered, her voice thick with doubt.

"Yeah," Danny said, checking and rechecking the detector in his hands.

"Maybe your customs lot dropped this or something. But there's no anomaly anywhere near."

Without a solid lead to follow, they made their way back to the lodge. Along the way Danny tried asking Sophie about herself. At first she resisted, but he had been taught to interrogate witnesses by gaining their trust, and he wrung a few choice details from her. She had elderly parents who depended on the money she sent them, and she muttered angrily about the lack of welfare in the country, that decent, hard-working people could suddenly find themselves practically on the poverty line. This verdant land held such opportunity, yet everywhere money was tight.

It seemed she'd also once had a brother, who had been her parents' favourite. He'd either died or absconded, but Danny didn't want to press her to find out which. He glanced at her at regular intervals, trying not to let her see him doing it; she didn't once turn her head in his direction. At last they pulled up, and still there were no other cars in the car park.

"Thanks," he said as he got out of the SUV. "It was a lovely outing." He shut the door.

She looked up at him from behind the wheel, the engine still rumbling.

"Need some more stuff if we're going after this thing," she said. And before he could respond, she reversed smartly backwards and was bombing away down the road. Danny stood watching the dust curl in the air behind her. Then he stepped up onto the raised platform and went back into the lodge.

He found Lester in the mess room enjoying a regal breakfast. Something cooked, judging by his plate, and a rack of toast. Now he was finishing off with a dripping mango while topping up his coffee.

"Ah," he said, seeing Danny. "You want some of this?" He splashed dark coffee into a cup then waved the pot in the direction of the milk and sugar.

Danny sank onto the seat opposite him and exhaled.

"Thank you, yes," he said, wiping his forehead. "Woo, it's already hot out there."

"Mmm," Lester said. "That's why I've stayed inside. The gamekeepers have rather left us to it, which isn't especially wise given that this place was invaded last night. Once animals know they can get into somewhere, there's no holding them back." His mouth twitched with irritation. "But since there's nothing I can do about it, I just helped myself."

"I can see. Did you call Connor?" Danny splashed milk into his coffee and then took a sip. It had a strange, musty flavour, as if it had been spiced. He washed it round his gums, feeling the tannins and caffeine and whatever else igniting in his blood.

"Couldn't get hold of him. His phone seems to be switched off, and no one else at the ARC is responding either. I keep getting that automated message we use for fobbing off the public."

"Jenny at her sultry best," Danny commented. "I might ring them again, just to hear it." The message simply said that the caller had come through to a division of the Home Office, and could they leave a name and number. But the *way* Jenny said it...

Lester grunted, clearly not in the mood for jokes — when was he ever? — and continued with his mango. He'd put on a crisp new shirt and plain silk tie — not really the thing for the stultifying heat or such messy fruit, but Lester ate with deft and delicate skill. Danny assumed it was something you got taught at public school.

"I've had an odd morning," he said.

"Mmm." Lester reponded, not feigning any interest. "Thank you for the note."

"Didn't want to wake you. Unless you wanted to come with us?"

"What, play gooseberry to you and Safari Girl?"

"It's nothing like that. Well, not yet anyway," he replied, and he grinned. "I can't hold her off forever."

"She does seem mysteriously besotted with you," Lester observed dryly.

"We'll see." But the comment gave him new hope. He filled Lester in on the events of the morning, including their equipment delivery and their discovery of the grim remains of the theropod.

Lester nodded. "As the Postosuchus is from a different period, we're still looking for two anomalies."

"Sure." He held up the handheld anomaly detector. "This thing's only got a limited range, so we can go out for a longer scout around the game reserve once Sophie gets back with more supplies."

"What's she made of all this?"

Danny considered what to tell his boss. He didn't want to give away anything that Lester could use to antagonise her. He realised that he actually wanted to *protect* her.

"She's doesn't say much, though she was happy to prod about the mess that was left of the theropod, so she isn't squeamish."

Lester's eyes narrowed as he mulled over this information, as if he was unpicking all the things that Danny hadn't told him.

"She's used to animals killing each other," he mused.

"Yeah, but not to shiny great holes in time."

"So this reconnaissance... You're assuming the anomalies will both be in the game reserve."

"Not assuming, but it seems like the best place to start."

Lester leaned back in his chair and sipped his coffee.

Danny spent an agonising hour waiting for Sophie to return, fidgeting around the lodge, kicking his feet, while Lester sat demurely at the dinner table checking his BlackBerry periodically as he continued to try to reach Connor. When he wasn't doing that, he was reading a fat paperback, *The Scramble for Africa*. He seemed to have a thing for history, for military tactics. His office back at the ARC had all sorts of pretensions to the great strategists of history. Danny suspected that he saw himself as the ARC's Duke of Wellington — with everyone else as the cannon fodder.

Eventually they heard the thrum of Sophie's SUV pulling up outside, the engine purring over. Danny hurried out to meet her while Lester followed at his own pace. She poked her head out of the open window of the car and Danny found himself grinning at her. She looked back at him with eyes hard and sharp like diamonds.

"Uh," Danny said, his smile faltering.

"Get," she told them, "in the car."

He jumped down from the platform, and beat Lester to the front seat. Lester muttered something under his breath and got into the back alongside bottles of water, a box of ammunition, and a few other bits and pieces. Danny strained round in his seat to look over the provisions, then tossed Sophie another grin. She eyed him warily.

"Is something wrong?" he said, acting all innocence.

"Everything's fine," she told him. "Though *he*'s not dressed for this."

Lester smiled. "A good suit means you're ready for anything."

"Don't mind him," Danny said. "He's management."

"Indeed," Lester said. "Fieldwork isn't my usual line. So perhaps we can get on with this."

Sophie put her foot down and the car lurched backwards in an arc, throwing Danny forward. He heard Lester hit the back of his seat with a thump, and fell back into his seat as Sophie shoved the car into first gear and they bounded off along the red dust track.

"What's your plan?" Lester said calmly, once they were on their way. He ran a hand through his slicked-back hair.

"We find this creature," Sophie said, her eyes fixed on the road. "Turns out it's had quite a night. Worked its way through a lot of the wildebeest and zebra. Didn't eat them, just tore them up. If it goes on like this, we won't have a game park left. So we find it, and we bring it down." She peered at Danny beside her. "If we can, we send it home. But I'm not going to lose any sleep if we can't."

"How *are* we going to find it?" Danny asked.

Sophie smiled.

"Got something trussed up in the back that'll bring it out."

Danny twisted round, to see Lester looking over the back of his own seat into the boot of the SUV. Something bleated meekly back at him.

That could just as easily be us, he mused. And this time he didn't grin.

FIFTEEN

Connor had no idea of the time, no sense at all of how long they'd kept him in what they now called the 'interview room'.

He'd seen films where suspects were deprived of sleep and their wristwatches, putting them in a surreal and itchy-eyed state where they'd agree to just about anything. He'd also watched enough episodes of *24* to know some of the nastier things an interrogator might do so you'd say what they wanted to hear.

They'd removed his handcuffs but he'd learnt that it didn't mean he could get up from the chair. So he sat on the hard plastic, his bum passing from discomfort to sore to a weird numbness. Possibly he dozed off sporadically, but he couldn't be sure.

His best measure of time had come from counting the different interrogators. Becker had been relieved by a bloke called Adam who usually worked at the front gate. Connor and him had developed a routine where Adam rolled his eyes whenever Connor came in late. Which was — to be fair — every morning. They'd not spoken, as such, not that Connor could remember, and now here the guy was, standing over him and yelling questions. But not looking entirely comfortable with it.

He'd been left on his own for a long time, before a small man with a bunged-up sort of voice took over. After he left, it was the female security guard some of the other men called Pliers — though, he'd noticed, never to her face. A scar reached from her bottom lip to just below her jawline.

As he struggled to answer her aggressive questions, he pitied whoever had dared to cross her path.

They all asked the same things, but in different ways: where he'd been, who he'd talked to and what about, what proof he could offer to corroborate his answers. He knew they were trying to confuse him, changing the emphasis of the questions or implying he'd said something differently before. Over all, he felt he'd done okay on sticking to his story. But the more he went over the same tiny details, the less sure of them he became. It was like saying your own name out loud over and over, until it lost all sense of meaning.

He assumed they knew that anyway, that they just wanted to wear him down. They prodded and probed him, got angry or pretended to be his best friend. Connor tried to cooperate but remained defiant, indignant about the whole thing.

He needed a shave, and to wash, sleep, and eat something — and to check his email. In fact, they had him neglecting a whole routine of small tasks that helped oil the ARC machine. But they weren't very interested in that, no matter how much he tried to explain. Connor could merely sit as comfortably as the hard plastic would allow, answer their questions to the best of his ability, and wait for them to make a decision about what to do with him.

His only solace was the thought that somewhere outside this room, he knew Abby would be raising merry hell on his behalf.

Abby had tried to stay awake, really she had. She'd drunk her way through a whole plunger-thing of coffee, without even adding milk. But that had only made her even more manic and irritable, and then meant several trips to the ladies'. One of the female security guards — Sharon — had been made to accompany her.

Sharon had a scar on her chin from her days as a professional boxer. At least, that was what Abby had heard. She didn't look the sort to gossip about shoes or boyfriends — which was hardly Abby's forte, either — but it would have been obvious that Abby was working around her if she'd asked about fighting and guns. So she smiled and said thank you and allowed herself to be escorted back to the canteen.

Sarah lay curled up on the floor, her head on a rolled-up flak jacket.

Abby found a space down beside her, rather than sitting with the guards at the table. She watched Sharon unclip the chunky pistol from her hip pocket, and place it with two more already on the tabletop before she sat down and joined her colleagues and their card game.

"Raise you a night shift," she said once she'd examined her cards.

The man opposite her — Adam — considered his own position.

"Raise you a bank holiday," he responded.

Abby rested her back against the cool wall, her eyes and muscles aching. It had been an arduous day even before she and Connor had got back to the ARC, and now every new minute seemed an eternity.

In her dream, Cutter, Stephen and Connor stood together in Kensal Green Cemetery, in view of each of their graves. They didn't ask her why she'd not been to visit them, but the disappointment was plain in their eyes.

She woke with a start, sore and muzzy, spittle drooled on her chin. The security guards looked up from their card game but paid her little heed. Abby got awkwardly to her feet, yawning and rubbing at her eyes.

"What time is it?" she asked. It wasn't easy to tell from inside the ARC with its total absence of windows.

"Getting on for three in the morning," one of them told her. "You were only asleep half an hour."

Abby cursed under her breath. She'd vowed to herself that she'd stay awake, if only to show solidarity with —

"Where's Sarah?" she asked. But the guards just went on with their game.

She lay back down, wondering if she should be alarmed. *Probably not*, she mused. *Sarah's not the one they're after — it's Connor and me they want.*

Though she tried not to give in again, exhaustion triumphed, and she nodded off again, startled herself awake, then lost the battle altogether.

Abby had advised Sarah on her first day at the ARC that she should bring in a spare set of clothes and cosmetics. Sometimes, she'd said, they had to work through the night, but more often they just got a bit messy.

Sarah emerged from the ladies' feeling fresher and better, but still wishing she could have showered. Her skin felt grubby under her clean clothes, just from having slept on the floor. But there was also a deeper sense of uncleanness from the attack by the squad of soldiers.

Sarah shivered, remembering it — the way they'd broken in so easily, the way she'd been so helpless. The ARC's security agents didn't seem any the wiser about how they'd achieved it, what they'd done, or why they'd then disappeared. And that disturbed her more than anything else.

Sharon saw her back to the canteen where Abby still slept on the floor. In whispers, Sarah's guards asked her if she wanted anything to eat or drink, then bickered about which of them should fetch it. She took a seat at the end of the table, politely declining the opportunity to join the game of cards.

Adam made her some toast, and as she ate it, she became aware of Tom Samuels standing in the open doorway of the canteen. His tie hung loosely under an undone top button, his shoulders slouched.

"Good morning," she said curtly, resentful at being his prisoner. He didn't reply, just nodded his head to one side, indicating she should follow. Silently she obeyed.

He led her to the main operations room, holding the swing door open for her to pass through. Technicians beavered around the tables of equipment and two soldiers stood on duty at the five-screen ADD.

Sarah followed Samuels up the walkway to Lester's office, and gasped when she saw the disarray. Papers and files spilled over every surface and all across the floor. At first she thought the soldiers who'd attacked her must have been responsible. Then Samuels weaved through the mayhem and round the back of Lester's desk. He studiously avoided sitting in Lester's chair as if it was his, but took a seat at a distinct angle. And that was when Sarah realised the mess was of his making: he'd spent all night reading through this stuff.

She scooped up the papers that sprawled over the low, leather settee and sat herself down. He seemed busy checking over some notes, so she let her eyes wander slowly around the room at Lester's precious statues and ornaments. The lion statue looked like a Renaissance copy of an original from the late classical period. The mask of a Spartan that sat on Lester's desk didn't look like any she remembered from the British Museum. It occurred to her that it might be a genuine relic, purloined from some government collection.

Her captor continued to ignore her.

"So," she prompted, "you want to ask me some more questions."

He scratched at his closely cropped beard; she could hear the rasp of the bristles.

"Actually, I thought you might want to ask them of me." He looked up to gaze levelly at her.

"I thought I was a suspect," she replied, puzzled.

He smiled.

"I think we got off to a bad start. Really, I'm not a villain. I wouldn't even be here were Lester still around. But there's a problem, and there's no one else to sort it out, so here I am." He spread his hands.

"All right," Sarah said, still wary, "so I'm free to go home if I want?"

"Well, I'd obviously rather you didn't," Samuels replied casually. "We've got quite a lot still to get on with, but if you feel you need to go anywhere, I'm not going to stop you."

"And Abby?"

He sighed.

"That's a bit more tricky. I want to trust her, I really do. I want to trust Connor Temple as well. But what little evidence we have to hand just stacks up against them."

"What are you going to do with them?"

"I thought I'd ask you." Samuels studied her carefully as he waited for her reply.

"Well then, let them go."

He laughed.

"I'm asking you to persuade me. I'd hoped to find suitable testimony from Lester amongst all these files, but even *he* has his concerns about them. Connor seems to have illegally accessed the ARC's personnel records. Abby's keeping a —" he checked his notes — "a Coelurosauravus illegally as some kind of pet. I'm sure Lester had this all in hand, but it doesn't exactly work in their favour."

"What do you want me to do?" she asked genuinely. "What do you want me to say?"

"Tell me about them," he said. "Tell me everything you can. I hardly need tell you that this is important. Everything the ARC does is at risk if these two can't be trusted, so I need to appreciate why you're so certain that they can be."

"I..." Sarah began. "I haven't really worked here that long, you know."

Samuels leant forward, his face full of concern.

"But you know you can trust them, don't you?"

SIXTEEN

It had just gone midday when they pulled up in a wide-open space roughly the size of a football pitch. A low, tangled tree of thick branches sat at the centre of the clearing, and a few sparse shrubs broke up the rocky ground. The lack of greenery in such a teeming, verdant country made Danny immediately suspicious. This was the kind of place to which primitive man would have attributed evil spirits.

"Picnic spot?" he said to Sophie as she turned off the car's engine.

"Yeah," she said. "Salt in the earth means nothing much grows here. Help me get out the lunch."

First they unloaded the guns — two Winchester Model 70s and a much bigger, more modern rifle of a make he didn't recognise — and the other supplies. Danny checked over his rifle, the same one he'd used the night before. He was about to check the magazine when Sophie put a hand on his arm.

"All set?" she asked him.

"Just checking it's loaded," he said. "Better safe than sorry."

"Sure," she said. "But I did that before we set out."

"Good thing I trust you," he said, grinning. But Sophie didn't smile back. She looked quickly away, leaning into the back of the car to drag something bleating and mewling towards her. The creature's hooves were roped together, and it tried to prod her with its short curly horns. Danny didn't know livestock particularly well, but the thing was about the size of a goat.

"Impala," Lester observed.

Sophie fixed a rope around the animal's neck, then freed its hooves. The impala struggled to escape her, straining at its leash, but Sophie held it firm.

They followed her as she led the animal out to the twisted tree in the centre of the plain. The ground was hard and uneven — Danny stumbled more than once. Heat pressed hard against them, and the air was thick, as if they were walking through water. Even with his Ray Bans on, he had to squint.

He nodded at Lester.

"What's that they say about mad dogs and Englishmen out in the midday sun?"

"That they usually have someone else to carry their equipment," Lester replied.

They could see for miles and miles, across great plains and twisted woodland to the vast mountains beyond. But while they were out in the open, anything hidden in the tall grass and acacia bordering the space had a perfect view of them, too.

A short distance in front of the tree a wooden stake emerged from the ground. Sophie attached the impala's rope to a metal ring hanging from the stake. The animal lunged away from her as soon as she stood back, racing for the cover of the tall grass. It came to a sudden, shocking halt as it reached the end of the tether, the impact knocking it from its feet. They watched it choking, spluttering and walking a few steps one way and then the other, testing how far it could get.

Sophie ran her hand along the rope and walked out to the impala. It mewled at her miserably. She stroked its nose and forehead, calming it. Then she reached into one of the side pockets of her camouflage trousers and withdrew a small plastic bottle, a simple spray like those used for cosmetics. She sprayed the clear liquid over the impala's back. It kicked and fidgeted, trying to resist, but Sophie held onto the rope so it couldn't get away.

"What is that stuff?" Danny asked as she made her way back to them. Behind her, the impala rolled itself on the barren, hard ground, trying to scratch off whatever she'd just sprayed on it.

"A hunch," she said. "Come on."

She led them to the shadow of the tree. From close up they could see a platform built amongst its higher branches. A rope hung down, but there didn't seem to be a ladder.

"How do we —" Danny began.

Sophie ran forward, jumped high against the tree and then scrambled quickly upwards. They watched her swing a leg over the rail running round the platform. She peered quickly around it, presumably checking for snakes or poisonous spiders, then looked back down at them.

"Pass the guns up first."

"You don't seriously expect me to climb up there?" Lester said.

"No, not unless you want to," she said, and smiled sweetly, "but it's safer than being down there."

"It's not just the Postosuchus we need to worry about," Danny said. "Anything could take the bait."

"I've read John Patterson's account of hunting lions at Tsavo in 1898 —" Lester began pompously.

Sophie smiled again, but this time there was nothing sweet about it.

"You would have."

"He also staked out an animal, watched it from up a tree. But he rather neglected the fact that lions can climb trees."

"Still killed them," Sophie said. "Didn't he?"

Danny laughed. *She has you there.*

"Yes," Lester snapped irritably, "but nevertheless this strikes me as a rather dangerous game." He continued to eye the rope as if it was a snake, coiled to strike.

"You got a better idea?"

He peered up at her.

"We could look for its tracks, and follow them."

"You know how to do that?"

"Don't be ridiculous, I'm a civil servant, not a hunter. That's your job."

"The tracks aren't distinct enough, and we'd be on ground we couldn't secure. This is about the best guarantee we've got of facing this creature and surviving. Unless you know some other way we can do this, you'd better get up here."

Danny stepped forward.

"Doesn't look like there's much room up there," he called up.

“There isn’t,” Sophie informed him.

He turned to an angry looking Lester.

“Hey,” he said. “This could be fun.”

Two hours later, they were still squashed together on the platform. Danny remembered fishing trips with his dad, an uneasy attempt at male bonding in a family that had almost collapsed after they’d lost his brother Pat. They would sit watching the river, their fishing rods standing idle. He would go over in his mind all the things he might ask his dad, just to break the awful silence. But whatever he said only earned the same long-suffering expression, that sense that his father could’ve coped with losing a son if only it had been Danny.

He felt a similar sense of anger and frustration now, cooped up on the platform with Sophie and Lester, unable to speak and weighed down by the heat. He’d taken off his leather jacket and hung it from one of the branches above them, but even in just his polo shirt the sweat dripped from him in constant rivulets. At first he’d apologised when his bare arm had brushed against Sophie’s. Now they were just used to pressing against each other, sharing their skin and smell.

When he did try, Sophie ignored any effort at conversation, even if brokered in a whisper. Since she’d gone to get the supplies she’d seemed even more distant — if that was possible. *Perhaps she has a boyfriend*, he mused for the hundredth time. *Perhaps someone has teased her about running round after the two pale Englishmen.*

Perhaps she was setting them up.

Lester sat motionless, his bad mood further stifling the atmosphere between the three of them. They watched the impala circle idly round the stake, scratching at the ground, mewling, going to the toilet.

All at once Danny felt Sophie tense beside him. The impala stopped its endless circling and stood perfectly still, watching the long grass at the edge of the arid ground. Sophie reached for her field binoculars with one hand and raised her rifle with the other. This close, Danny could read the names of the thick cartridges in the clear panel of the magazine. They were .585 Nyati, a size he didn’t know. But a cartridge like that, in a gun that didn’t look more than twelve pounds, would come with quite a recoil.

He raised his own Winchester, which had enough kick as it was, and aimed it in the same general direction.

They watched and waited. The impala's legs trembled.

Then the grass parted and a long snout pushed its way through. Slowly, the crocodilian shape of the Postosuchus padded out onto the rocky, dry ground. The thick ridges of armour-plating ran down its back like the rungs of a ladder, and glistened in the sun. It took its time, occasionally rising up slightly on its hind legs, revealing its pale underbelly, sniffing the air in deep lungfuls, the length of its face and the jagged teeth giving it what looked like a crafty smile. Danny noted the long, sharp claw on each front limb, which he assumed it had used to gut the doomed Eustreptospondylus.

Suddenly it was moving, galloping fast across the ground, its long forelegs tucked underneath its body. The impala let out an awful wail of distress, but the Postosuchus barely hesitated as it snapped the thing up in its jaws. It still didn't stop; chewing goat, it charged at the tree in the centre of the clearing. The tree in which three humans were hiding. Danny raised his gun.

Sophie's gun exploded beside Danny, and he heard her grunt with pain as the butt tried to break through her shoulder. He glimpsed the trail of the bullet as it bounced off the creature's thick armour, an unlucky shot that just didn't find the right angle.

Beside him, Lester fired off two shots, and Danny aimed right into the creature's open jaws. The Postosuchus took the blasts and didn't even blink. Danny just had time to wonder if he'd even hit the thing when it crashed against the tree.

The whole platform shook, and their bottles of water rained over the back and down onto the ground.

The Postosuchus reared up on its hind legs, snarling, biting and scratching. Its huge savage jaws reaching a half metre below the platform. Danny fired again, right into its face.

This time he knew his gun was faulty — he couldn't have missed at this distance, yet his shot had had no effect at all.

Sophie struggled to aim at the creature's head as it bundled against the tree. It was moving quickly and angrily, enraged that it couldn't quite reach them. She squeezed back on the trigger and a bullet streaked down the armour plating on the creature's back. Because of the close proximity, it scored a long rent of blood behind it. The Postosuchus cried out in rage and smashed hard again into the tree.

The tree shook.

And bent.

The Postosuchus pressed itself against the trunk. Danny held on tight to the rail of the platform, his legs swinging out over the ground below. Lester and Sophie hung on beside him, Lester's gun escaped his grasp and disappeared over the edge.

"Hold on!" Danny yelled, but the tree was cracking, the platform coming apart. He flung himself forward, reaching for the higher branches, but he missed and fell back just as the platform gave way. Lester, Sophie and Danny tumbled out of the tree, the remains of the platform and twigs and leaves plummeting to the ground around them.

They hit the ground hard. Only Danny had managed to hold on to his gun; the other two lay out of reach.

The Postosuchus glared at them. On all-fours its eyes were about shoulder height, its jaws as long as Danny's arm. It watched them with beady, hungry eyes, as though deciding who to eat first.

Then Danny noticed a strange aroma hanging around them. He looked round and his quick eyes picked out the wet stain at the pocket of Sophie's trousers: the spray bottle she'd used on the tethered impala had broken in the fall. The Postosuchus sniffed through long thin nostrils, then settled its eyes on her.

Realising what was about to happen, he ran forward, firing right into the creature's face. It turned its head slowly to look at him, but was completely unaffected. An awful realisation dawned on him.

"I'm only firing blanks!" he shouted. "Someone's set us up!"

He threw the rifle, smacking the Postosuchus squarely on the nose. The creature growled at him. He took a step back, but with chaos all around him there was nowhere he could run. The creature started to lunge right at him, its ghastly jaws hanging open.

He braced himself...

And then Sophie was lunging at him, too, shouting.

"No, leave him!"

She pulled the mangled plastic bottle from her pocket. Immediately, the

Postosuchus turned from Danny and threw itself on Sophie's out-stretched arms, the full weight of its armour-plated body crashing into her. She cried out. There were a series of explosions.

Lester stood tall with Sophie's rifle in his hands, firing a quick succession of .585 cartridges into the creature's face and neck. They smashed into the soft tissues, detonating blood and bits of skull. The Postosuchus fell back under the onslaught. Lester kept shooting until the gun clicked empty, by which time the creature was very dead.

Danny ran over to where Sophie lay, spattered with blood and remains. Her right arm was mangled and, as Danny got close, he could see she had been crushed. He knelt down beside her and wiped her bloody hair out of her face.

"I'm sorry..." she croaked. "They wanted me to..."

"Don't try to talk," he told her. "We'll get you to a doctor."

"I'm sorry," she said again, the muscles in her neck straining with effort. A bead of blood appeared at one nostril and trickled backwards down her cheek.

Danny looked round at Lester, who was quickly and professionally replacing the empty magazine of the gun.

"She's dead," he said, struggling to maintain his composure.

Lester looked up, and Danny saw something terribly cold in his eyes.

"Yes," he said, glancing at the body.

"She gave us guns that didn't work," Danny said, his arms still round the broken body. "She set us up."

"Indeed."

"And then... and then she tried to save me."

"Your charm must have got through to her." He pulled at the bloody mess of his tie, discarding it on the ground. "We've been played since we first got here. This creature rather conveniently ambushed us last night. Sophie hasn't been working alone."

"What should we do?" Danny asked. He got up from the ground, a torrent of conflicting emotions coursing through him.

Lester's shirt was spattered with gore, the huge rifle nestled in his arms. Danny didn't see him as Wellington any more, but as a one-man army.

"We take her back to the lodge and we try to contact London. But our options have been curtailed very efficiently. This isn't over yet."

SEVENTEEN

"Okay," Sarah said. "This is what I've got so far."

Connor and Abby sat red-eyed but alert on the settee, a good arm's length between them at the insistence of their guards. Adam and Sharon watched over them coolly, Adam filling the doorway that led out of Lester's office, Sharon standing in a corner, her arms crossed. Samuels sat back in his chair, still at an angle to Lester's desk, still trying to suggest he was just filling in rather than taking over.

He smiled at Sarah encouragingly.

"The soldiers who broke in here didn't take anything, as far as we can tell," she continued. "One assumption is that they were disturbed, that security got wind of them before they'd got whatever it was they came for." She paused for a moment. "I don't think we can have been that lucky. They haven't made any effort to come back, though."

"I've had some security people brought in to beef up the numbers," Samuels put in. "Good people we can trust, who know what they're doing. Then again, the systems here are pretty complex, no one person understands them completely."

"I do," Connor protested dourly.

"Most of the time," Abby added.

"That fact does rather incriminate you, Mr Temple," Samuels said. "Sorry, but it does. Go on, please, Sarah."

"Right, well, imagine a policeman investigating the evidence here.

He looks at the facts, identifies suspects, matches them to motive and opportunity — we've all seen it on television — and on that basis the evidence points in one direction."

"Me," Connor said glumly.

"But why would Connor turn on us?" Abby protested.

"Maybe," Sarah said, "you're fed up with the ARC's management and handling of the anomalies, especially in light of Cutter's death. You think we could be doing things better."

"Well, we could," Connor put in, and Abby grimaced.

"There's new people on the team and your old loyalties have shifted. Even Abby threw you out on the street."

"I didn't!"

"You sort of did," Connor told her kindly. "It's okay though, I understand." He turned to Sarah. "Um, this is all really good. But aren't you meant to be clearing my name? You're kind of stacking things up against me."

"It does all sound rather convincing," Samuels agreed.

"Yes," Sarah said, "it does. A policeman might think it all slotted together just perfectly."

"Yeah," Connor sighed, and he looked more dejected than ever.

"The thing is, I'm not a policeman," Sarah said. "I don't look at things in the same way. I work with myths and legends, stories that have been handed down to us over hundreds, even thousands of years. We check and compare them against other evidence, the facts of history and archaeology. But we also analyse them as stories, and this simply doesn't work as a story."'

"You're saying he's been framed?" Abby said hopefully.

"The CCTV footage of him at the ADD has some strange jumps in it, like it's been tampered with, like it's been edited by someone."

"But the break-in wasn't a story," Connor said. "It really happened, didn't it?" He peered at her intently.

"Yes," Sarah confirmed, "those were real events, but just as with myths, events are shaped by the person telling the story. They're edited, crafted, built on, adapted. My job is to ask certain questions: Who told the story? In what context and for what purpose?"

Abby leaned forward eagerly.

"You mean, why would anyone want to frame Connor?"

"Exactly," Sarah said firmly.

"So you start by presuming he's innocent," Samuels said.

"It's sort of a principle of the legal system," Connor reminded him. "But what's so important about me?"

"You tell us," Sarah said. "If you hadn't been arrested —"

"He wasn't *arrested*," Samuels protested.

"If you hadn't been *helping security with their enquiries*," Sarah corrected herself, "what would you have been doing?"

All eyes were on Connor now. He could only shake his head.

"I don't know, nothing that special. I'd have come in, had some tea, maybe written a quick summary of our day, seen if there was any bread left for toast, checked my email and backed up the..." He stopped, a look of wonder on his face. "Oh yeah."

"Oh yeah?" Abby asked. "Is that in a good way?"

"I'd have backed up the server," he said. "I like to do it manually because I can check a few things, but if I'm not here it's set to do it anyway. If I were a bad guy and I broke in here, I'd want to copy everything off our systems, so I'd let it back up as normal — just onto my own server. I'd just change the address that it's going to, as no one is likely to spot that. Unless they're doing it manually."

Samuels leant forward and began typing quickly on his laptop, his expression stern. The others crowded around him to see the screen.

"Yes," Samuels said after a moment, "I can see it. All the logs copied over at 2.15 this morning."

"When Connor was under arrest," Abby pointed out.

"Indeed."

Connor nudged the others aside so he could see the screen properly.

"But you can't just copy the logs. They'd need the actual files, and that's going to take forever. We've got a lot of stuff."

Without asking, he swung the laptop round from Samuels and rattled his fingers over the keys. But Samuels didn't protest. Connor's eyes glinted with excitement as he worked. Sarah couldn't keep up with the huge scroll of information flicking up the screen — but evidently he could.

"Gotcha," he said at last. "They only began at 2.15. They're forty-eight per cent of the way through."

"Who?" Samuels said as Connor started typing again, his fingers blurring with speed. "We have to know *who.*" He seemed to have given up entirely on the theory that Connor was the culprit.

"Working on it," Connor told him. "There are a couple of tricky things in this code. Stuff I put in as safeguards."

They watched in anticipation as complex instructions filled the screen. Connor stuck his tongue out as he worked, and started humming to himself. Then he clapped his hands together and moved back from the laptop.

"Okay," he said easily, "who wants to tell me I'm brilliant?" The old Connor was back.

"You blocked them," Samuels said.

"Aw, that would have been dead easy. I spiked the data they were downloading. Transmitted a special message the stuff they've already got will respond to, and it'll start to corrupt. Might do their systems some permanent damage, too. Depends if they're as clever as me — which I doubt."

A column of text began to scroll again up the laptop's screen. He sat forward again, examined it, and his brow creased with concern.

"What's that?" Abby asked.

"Oh," Connor said, a smile forming on his face. "Oh! They're not *nearly* as clever as they think." He began typing again. Sarah marvelled at the speed and dexterity with which he worked the keys. "They've spotted that I'm on to them and they're trying to stop me. *Hah!* How stupid are they? They've completely missed that the data they're holding is already falling apart."

"You know who they are?" Samuels asked again.

"No," Connor replied, "but they're showing me which bits of data they think are most worth fighting for. And..." He bit his bottom lip as he concentrated on his work, "I think I can do something else."

With a flourish he finished a complex instruction and tapped his index finger on 'Enter'. The laptop screen went blank for a moment. And then a map of London W6 popped up, an arrow pointing to a particular building.

"That's them?" Samuels said.

"Number thirty-two," Connor told him proudly. "They're using a mobile receiver. Satellite picked it up."

"I'll get some people over there..." Samuels reached for the phone on Lester's desk.

Connor tutted.

"Already done that," he said. "Used your name, of course, since I'm technically still a prisoner. Told you I was brilliant."

Samuels regarded him for a moment, then smiled. He patted Connor firmly on the shoulder.

"Yes, Connor, I think you are. I can see that nothing gets past you. All right, I think you've convinced me. Hope you can understand why I had to be cautious."

"Sure," Connor said, still enjoying the adrenalin rush of victory, "no hard feelings. But it's nearly five in the morning now. If you're not going to arrest me or have me shot, can I go shower and get some sleep?"

They'd taken over an empty third floor office in Hammersmith. It had a working toilet but little else in the way of comforts. They wore official-looking uniforms, something not quite either police or fire service, with bright armbands, and explained to anyone who got close that they were part of an exercise.

"Boss..." said a freckled programmer working at their quickly constructed machine, "I think they're on their way."

"You said we'd have another forty minutes," his boss told him gruffly.

"I said I only *thought* we would."

"All right, better pack this lot up. Nothing and no one gets left behind."

They worked quickly to dismantle the wires and antenna, packing them into canvas bags that didn't look as though they'd contain a computer. The boss watched his men check around the room before they made their way out into the night.

He followed, reaching for his phone.

"Sir," he said into it, "mission accomplished."

The alarm blared through the ARC facility, and Becker knew there was no one to answer it. He ran quickly down the corridor, his boots slapping against the concrete. Soldiers and technicians wisely got out of his way.

He barrelled into the main operations room and skidded to a halt. His mouth hung open in amazement at the sight before him.

Becker had spent the morning preparing his resignation. The short letter began with the general subject of loyalty and moved swiftly onto the specifics of Connor's value to the team. He didn't want to leave the ARC, but it seemed the only bargaining chip left in his possession. Samuels had refused to listen to anything else he'd said the previous night. He had to do what was right.

All this meant he was more than a little surprised to see the subject of his letter laughing with its intended recipient. Connor and Samuels — and Abby and Sarah — stood around the ADD in the ARC's main ops room, looking like they'd always been best friends.

"I still don't trust you entirely," Samuels said wryly.

"That's all right," Connor told him magnanimously. "I'm not sure about you, either."

He'd had some sleep since Becker last saw him, and a wash and change of clothes. In fact, he looked pretty much as good as Connor ever did.

"Uh, excuse me," Becker said uncertainly as he approached them. "Good afternoon."

"Captain Becker," Samuels said genially. "I trust you're fully rested."

"Uh, yes sir. Thank you, sir."

"Good," Samuels continued. "We seem to have another anomaly. You'll go out and put it right, won't you?"

"Yes, sir." Nothing about the scene made any sense, but he decided to get the lay of the land before he made any sudden moves.

Samuels continued: "I've got some people down in Hammersmith following up on our break-in, but otherwise take all the resources that you need. And I'd like you to take your orders from our specialists here."

"He means us," Abby explained, and he detected a smugness in her voice.

"We're special," Connor added.

"You have to do what we say," Sarah said.

Well, they're entitled.

"Yes, ma'am," he told her.

"Uh," Connor said. "Should one of the specialists stay behind here?"

"Do you think there's a need?" Samuels asked him.

"Well, yeah, what happens if there's another alarm while we're out at Wapping?"

They regarded him carefully.

"You're volunteering?"

"Um, yeah, if you want. Don't all look at me like that, it's not so I can steal all the systems or whatever while you're out of the building."

"I'll stay." Sarah stepped forward.

"But last night..." Abby began.

"It's okay." Sarah hugged her arms. "There're a lot more security people here now. And I've got to get back on the horse sometime. It's fine. Go. You're meant to race off as soon as the alarm sounds!"

Abby, Connor, and Becker glanced at each other. Becker nodded, and something that resembled understanding passed between them. Then, laughing, they hared off to their new assignment.

"At least you'll be out of the rain here," Samuels said after they had gone.

"Yeah." Sarah sat down and opened up her laptop.

"You're sure you're okay now? After last night?"

"Yep, I'm fine," she said, though she still didn't quite feel it. How could she ever trust ARC security after what had happened? There were people with guns conspiring against them.

And she still didn't feel as if she knew where Samuels fitted into it all.

He continued to gaze at her with concern — at least that was how it looked. In the end he neatly changed the subject.

"Lester suggests that anomaly activity increases with bad weather."

"That was a hunch of Cutter's. I don't think there's any real proof."

"Do *you* think they're connected? We've had floods all over the country for the last couple of years. Are they a side effect of the anomalies?"

Sarah looked up at him. He was standing very close to her and she found herself looking at how his muscles filled out his suit. She couldn't decide whether it was impressive or ominous.

"We don't have sufficient evidence to really know," she told him. "I can get some of our research team looking into it. Maybe the anomalies are a side effect of the climate, rather than the other way around."

"Mmm, at least the bad weather keeps people indoors. We seem to have significantly fewer sightings of creatures while it's raining which must make the whole process much easier."

Sarah nodded.

"Jenny had a whole team just to keep it all secret. Feed the media any excuse." She recalled the notes she'd been making the previous evening, while sitting in this same seat.

"You know," she said, "I've been thinking about the future. Connor said we could do things better here, didn't he?"

"What would you like to propose?"

"Well, just on the basis of resources, maybe it would help to go public — if we presented what we know sensibly, with academic weight behind it. We're assuming people will go mad and panic, but maybe we're underestimating them."

Samuels nodded.

"You'd see yourself as the academic sell on this?"

"I suppose I'd be part of it, yes."

"It's an interesting idea. But you'll need to convince more than just me. Give me something I can show a few people higher up."

"Er, okay. I will."

He turned and made his way swiftly up the walkway to Lester's — now his — office. Sarah watched him go, surprised and impressed by the purposefulness of his stride. He was genuinely going to consider her suggestion. They might actually come out to the world.

She knew Lester would never have countenanced the idea. And realised she might actually prefer answering to Tom Samuels.

EIGHTEEN

Danny drove them back to the lodge, following the tracks they'd made in the dust on their journey out. He'd always had a pretty good sense of direction, anyway, and felt himself coming to grips with the rough layout of the park. It might be bigger than Central London, but it only had a handful of roads.

Beside him, Lester busied himself with Sophie's mobile phone, so Danny resisted bothering him with the questions charging through his brain. Nor did he say anything when he spotted a second set of vehicle tracks, weaving over the top of their own. Whatever vehicle it might have been, its axles were wider than the SUV, the heavy treads of the tyres pressing further down into the dust. He couldn't be sure they were left by the same vehicle whose tracks he'd spotted the previous night, but things were starting to fit together.

It seemed quite a coincidence that the Postosuchus had been so conveniently close by to pounce on them.

Perhaps the dinosaurs *weren't* appearing in the game park via anomalies; rather they were being transported there. Whoever was moving the creatures — and using them to try and kill Danny and Lester — must also have some kind of storage facility, because they weren't just using dinosaurs from one period. This had to be a relatively large operation.

"Hello, Ted?" Lester said into the phone. "Do you speak any English?"

He then explained in a few words what had happened, and said that they were bringing Sophie's body back to the lodge.

"Well," he said to Danny when he'd finished the call, "he should be there ahead of us."

"Okay, good."

"Not necessarily. He was her friend. I'm sure he's caught up in this, too."

"Maybe. I suppose we'll just have to deal with that when the time comes."

Lester sighed.

"You know, I've rather had my fill of this country."

"It's not exactly been a pleasure trip. You could always upgrade our tickets home to first class."

"I might upgrade mine."

"Hey!" Danny said. "I thought we were a team. Like Butch and Sundance."

"More like Laurel and Hardy. If we're such a good team, why haven't you pointed out the other tracks on the road? Which I assume to be from the same vehicle as last night. I take it your observation skills are sharp enough to pick them up — that is, after all, what we employ you for."

"Er, yeah," Danny said, surprised. "You noticed them? Didn't think tracking was your thing."

"I prefer to sit behind a large desk in an air-conditioned office *because* I'm not a complete idiot."

They came to a fork in the road. Their own tracks headed left, to the lodge. The heavily laden vehicle had gone in the other direction.

"We could follow them," Danny offered.

"Why bother? There's coffee at the lodge. And they've already made it perfectly plain that they're happy to come to us."

"Good point."

Ted and a number of other gamekeepers were waiting for them at the lodge. They came forward, saying nothing as Danny and Lester clambered out of the SUV. Danny tried to help them, but Lester stayed back, his face sombre as they withdrew Sophie's bloodied body from the back of the car. Their expressions were all set and serious. Danny at least expected some kind of rebuke from one of them, but they just seemed to want to get on with the job.

He and Lester might not have even been there.

"She saved my life," Danny tried to explain to Ted as they carried her inside. Ted regarded him balefully, then followed the others into the lodge.

Danny and Lester were last to go in. They made their way through the hallway to the mess room which had witnessed the deaths of Sophie's colleagues the night before. And they'd been losing people even before that, too, Danny knew. Perhaps that sense of resignation was what made the survivors so sober. He wanted to shout at them, to get some kind of reaction, but he kept quiet.

They lay Sophie's body on the dining table, and lifted the tablecloth up around her, wrapping her inside. A sequence of folds interlocked around her covered shoulders and ankles, creating carry handles.

It struck Danny that you learnt this kind of quick, efficient handling of the dead by having death as a constant all around you. He wondered about the keepers' lives, the hardships they had lived through. They seemed like quite a brutal lot. South Africa promised so much opportunity, but there were people here who'd lived so long without. Whatever Sophie had been mixed up in, he thought he could understand the temptation. He hoped they'd paid her well.

"They blame us," Lester told him as they watched the simple, respectful way the keepers worked.

"So do I," Danny responded. He clenched his fists together at his sides, surprised to find anger coursing through him, rather than grief. Anger at the injustice of the fact she'd died. Anger that — though she'd changed her mind — she'd also tried to kill them. Anger that he'd known her not quite twenty-four hours, and yet he seemed to be more affected by her death than any of her colleagues. How different it would be, he thought, were it the ARC team dealing with the body of one of their own.

He had seen for himself how they'd all been knocked sideways by the loss of Nick Cutter...

This stony-faced group just weren't normal. It wasn't a cultural thing or the weight of successive losses. These people, working closely and easily together, didn't behave as if Sophie had been part of their gang. He glanced around at Lester, to see him scrutinising the group in his own way, perhaps thinking along similar lines.

Sophie's wrapped body was carried back outside and laid in the back of one of the other battered cars. Danny silently said goodbye to her as the door was closed. Then the car pulled away and headed down the road. He watched until it had disappeared out of view.

One of the last gamekeepers to leave explained to Lester that he and Danny were to remain in the lodge for the night. A tall, weasel-faced man with few teeth, he said the keepers would be patrolling, looking for any more 'lizards'. It would be a shame were the two British guys to get in their way, he said; there might be some kind of accident.

Lester responded coolly.

"Quinn can't sit still for more than five minutes so if you see him where he's not meant to be, you have my blessing to shoot him."

The weasel-faced man leered.

"I'll do that," he said.

The remaining keepers packed up their things in silence and piled into their own cars. Only Ted in any way acknowledged Danny as he stood watching them.

"You will go home tomorrow," he said. He spoke slowly and carefully, with a precision that suggested he didn't know much English.

"We'd like to stay for the funeral," Danny responded. "Pay our respects."

Ted regarded him, searching over his features as if trying to make sense of what he'd just said. Perhaps his English didn't stretch to "funeral". Perhaps it was something else.

"It will be soon, because of the heat," he said finally. "Then you will go?" And Danny realised it wasn't an order; rather Ted was sounding him out.

"We were sent here to help. If that help is not wanted..."

Ted nodded.

"I'm very sorry she died," Danny said, glancing around to ensure none of the other gamekeepers remained to hear them. "But she died saving our lives. She wanted to help us."

Ted said nothing. A few minutes later he drove away.

Lester went inside armed with his laptop to set himself up as a remote office and try and get through to the ARC again.

Danny stood outside on the raised platform, watching the last of the departing cars disappear into the fading light. He knew he'd be on edge for the rest of the evening, waiting for the next thing to fall on them.

But there was nothing he could do, except maybe make dinner. He wandered back through to the mess room and into the kitchen to investigate the cupboards.

He found Ted standing there.

"Uh, hello."

The man raised one finger to his lips.

Danny took a moment to recover, then said in a whisper, "It's all right. They've all gone."

Ted remained completely still, poised and alert, listening intently. Then when he seemed to be confident that Danny had been right, he relaxed.

"Don't know about you, boss," he said with an ease that suggested he was much more comfortable with English than he'd let on before, "but I could do with a drink."

Much to Danny's surprise, Lester abandoned his laptop and proposed that he'd cook. So Danny and Ted sat down at the table to talk.

Danny soon found that he had a few more hoops to jump through before Ted would be ready to confide in him. As he sat down Ted reached into the pocket of his army-issue jacket and withdrew a clear plastic bag. It took Danny a moment to realise that it was filled with fat blue and green caterpillars. Once he caught on, he jerked back in his seat in surprise — he'd never been very good with crawly, wriggly things — but as Ted reached a hand into the bag, he saw the insects were all dead.

The gamekeeper withdrew a single specimen and laid it flat in his palm. It had the same length and thickness as one of his fingers and was covered in short, bristly spikes.

"Caterpillar of the Emperor moth *Imbrasia Belina*. Live in mopane trees. You shake the trees and they come tumbling out."

"Very nice," Danny said, trying to be polite.

"Here." Ted passed the thing over. Danny took it carefully between two fingers, its skin was thick and hard, like it had been cooked.

"Thanks. I take it I'm meant to eat it?"

"Oh, yes, a favourite of my youth. Sixty per cent protein, plus phosphorous, iron, and calcium. Makes you grow up strong. Best free food there is."

He grinned mischievously at Danny, willing him on.

"It's not going to give me weird visions or anything, is it?"

Ted's nostrils flared.

"You watch too many things on television."

Danny leant forward so he could look into the kitchen. Lester had his back to them, an apron tied round his waist, caught up in saucepans and chopping, oblivious to Danny's plight.

"All right, then." He took a deep breath and bit the front inch off the caterpillar. The surface crunched dry against his teeth, but it was horribly soft underneath. It had the texture, he thought, of an over-cooked sausage, maybe one of those vegetarian ones. In fact, as he chewed, he was a little disappointed by the bland flavour.

"Yeah, it's all right," he told Ted, and obligingly chewed the rest of it. Ted grinned, dug deep into his bag and produced several more, popping one into his own mouth.

Danny swallowed. The caterpillar left a slightly bitter aftertaste, and he failed to stop himself pulling a face.

Ted grinned broadly.

"But you want to have some more," he said, and it wasn't a question.

Danny reached forward and picked up another one. He bit the head off, and chewed it with gusto, eager to show his willingness. Ted watched him, then got up from the table. What he said next sent dread coursing through Danny's veins.

"I brought something else." With that, he went into the kitchen. Lester turned around from his cooking and took in the dead caterpillars that still lay on the table. He pulled a face like this was all he'd ever expected from Danny.

Danny lounged back in his seat, grinning broadly at Lester's discomfort, then popped the remainder of the caterpillar into his mouth and chewed with his mouth wide open. Lester just raised an eyebrow and turned back to his work.

Cockiness turned to suspicion as Ted returned, brandishing a couple of carrier bags which strained under the weight of the large cartons that had been squeezed into them. They banged heavily as he plonked them down on the table. Danny tried to read the cheaply printed inscriptions. In slightly blurred red ink, it said something about Johannesburg.

"In the old days," Ted said, heaving out the cartons, "we weren't allowed to drink the white man's beer, so we made this stuff ourselves. Jo'burg Beer. Local delicacy." He expertly worked his thumbs round the corners of one of the cartons and pulled the thing wide open.

Danny relaxed a bit. He was a lot less squeamish about beer than he was about caterpillars, and he leant forward to investigate. The contents looked frothy and pale, more like fresh milk. He got a nose full of raw, pungent yeast.

"Reminds me of the home brew my mate's dad used to make."

Ted pushed the open carton across the table to Danny.

"We drink this in the shebeens. It's like a pub, only with a dirt floor and chickens."

"Sounds like my local." Danny put both hands around the carton. He picked it up gingerly, angling the thing round so that one open corner acted as a spout. Then, trying not to spill it all down his chin, he took a hesitant sip.

He'd expected fire water, or at least something surprising. But the beer had the same texture and richness of milk, though full of crude bubbles of air. Danny washed it round the inside of his mouth before swallowing, assessing what seemed to be a low alcohol content, the texture of rich proteins and goodness. The stuff was probably better for him than any brand of fizzy drink.

"It's good," he said, and he took another drink. He offered the carton back to Ted, but Ted shook his head and reached for his own. When he had gulped back what looked like half the contents, he reached his hand out across the table.

"We've eaten and we've had beer together."

Danny took his hand and shook it, as if they'd just agreed to a cricket match. Ted shook once, then quickly changed his hand around, locking the tips of his fingers round Danny's. Then they locked thumbs. After this three-part handshake, Ted sat back in his seat.

"You're okay," he said pleasantly.

"I've passed the test?"

Ted exploded in laughter, a rich and vibrant belly-laugh that brought Lester in from the kitchen, still wearing his apron.

"Is that beer?" he said.

"It's an initiation," Danny explained, offering his carton.

"It's hospitality," Ted said. "I am being polite."

Lester warily raised Danny's carton to his lips. He took a tentative sip, then leaning back, he gulped down the whole lot and placed the empty carton back on the table.

"Not bad," he commented, turning and heading back into the kitchen.

"I like him," Ted said, staring after the retreating figure.

"You don't really know him."

Again Ted laughed. He sat quietly for a few minutes, then he fixed Danny with a serious gaze.

"Sophie liked you."

"I liked her."

"You get the animals, she said. You get that we have a duty."

"Even to these giant lizards," Danny agreed.

"Please, we have shared beer and caterpillars. There are no secrets between us. They are dinosaurs."

"They are dinosaurs."

"The two you have seen are not the first," Ted said. "My colleagues used to discuss it. There have been many strange things in the park."

"But then they stopped talking?"

Ted nodded. "Then they stopped drawing breath. Sophie, the guys who died last night, Jace and Ellie who died just a few days ago and brought you out here. But they've not all died, some simply lost their jobs. 'Cutbacks', they said. Only..."

"Only," Danny added, "they've also been recruiting."

"This new lot, they don't care for the animals. I don't know *what* they care for. I'm not the last of the old guard, but I'm the only one who'd dare speak to you like this. They've offered me money, a lot of money for a gamekeeper. And I could use it. Don't mistake me, I would have looked the other way if they had not killed Sophie."

Danny left a respectful pause before asking his next question.

"Who are they?"

Ted looked up, surprised.

"The people from your mine."

Danny blinked. "The mine?"

"The British. The oil mine. They said you were working with them."

Danny remembered the joke Sophie had made as they'd passed the mine on their way to the park. She'd said it should sport a Union Jack, and he'd picked up on the bitterness in her words. It turned out now that was because they were the ones buying her.

"They've replaced your staff with thugs," Danny said to Ted.

"Yeah. Told us you were no better. But Sophie called in this morning. Wanted my gun. Said you knew about the dinosaurs, and you only wanted to help them."

"Well, that makes a certain amount of sense," Lester said. He stood in the doorway of the kitchen and had evidently heard every word. "A British interest with government connections, who wants you and me out of the way."

"Someone we know, then," Danny suggested.

"Maybe, but not necessarily. I do have quite a reputation, you know."

Danny turned to Ted. "And you're sure it's the oil operation."

"That's where all the money is," Ted said. "They're promising every one of us will be rich. And the dinosaurs only started appearing once it had been set up, in the last month or so."

Lester frowned.

"I've got enough former colleagues and peers with an interest in my career... It could even be someone I've had lunch with in the last few days."

"That friend of yours, Christine."

"It does have her paw prints all over it. It would be just her thing to get us all the way out here, merely to bump us off and leave the ARC with no one in charge."

"She could be there now," Danny said, worry in his voice. "That's why they're not answering the phone."

"I don't think so. I've left a few instructions in case that should happen."

"You've *expected* something like this?"

"I've been in the civil service too long not to understand how it works. If I fail, then I'm out of a job. If I'm successful, everyone else wants to steal it from me."

Lester's brow creased with irritation. "Anyway, I'm not beaten yet."

"What are we going to do?" Danny asked.

"We're going to get back to London immediately. I'll call the airport now. And yes, we'll go first class..."

NINETEEN

The rain crashed down like ball bearings as they climbed out of Abby's Mini Cooper. She'd have parked at the wrong end of the huge car park, thought Connor, by the warehouse-sized pet store with the cute logo of a cat. But he had pointed out the army trucks all parked just in sight of the silver dome of Surrey Quays Tube Station. There were few other cars around, as the huge shopping centre had already been evacuated. The public had been told the flood had ruptured some pipes and a tide of raw sewage was quickly heading their way.

Abby and Connor ran through the rain to join Becker and his men sheltering in the entrance to the station, using the cover it afforded to check over their weapons.

Connor watched Becker checking over his custom H&K G36, the one with the grenade launcher added to the end and the nifty tactical sight on the top. The magazine had a clear panel so you could see how much ammunition remained. More importantly, the sight didn't fire a red tracer like you got in movies — which kind of gave you away to anyone you wanted to shoot. Instead, the hologram sat inside the sight, so only the shooter could see it. For low light conditions you could switch it from red to night-vision green.

As back-up, Becker had a pump-action Mossburg 500 on a strap across his back, with spare cartridges tucked into the loops at the breast of his flak jacket. His men sported G36s too, only without the grenade launchers.

Finished checking his rifles, Becker pulled his trusty SIG .229 from the pouch at his thigh and checked its contents and the movement of the slide.

"We're not going to war," Connor said with a grin. "It's just some big, stupid dinosaurs. Tranquillisers will be enough."

"You seen them?" Becker replied. "They're big."

"I heard the description. I think they're probably Brachiosaurus: four legs, long neck, round body — all the threat of an average cow."

Becker slipped his pistol back into its pouch,

"You say that, but you haven't seen them." He nodded at his men and led them off into the rain, making their way along the road running round the back of the station, over the gravel and mud.

Connor turned to Abby.

"Them?"

She sighed and handed him a tranquilliser rifle. They hurried after the soldiers, their progress slow as the mud sucked at their boots. Becker held open a chain-link fence that blocked their way into a building site, and they slipped and slid down a steep slope until they found themselves in a valley.

Railway lines sat in the tightly packed gravel, stretching off south further than Connor could see. Enormous four-legged dinosaurs moved mournfully about, their long necks perusing the steep grassy banks for anything they might eat. Their tails were shorter than those found on the Apatosaurus, their front legs were longer than the ones at the back — a bit like a giraffe's — and each one had a bump in the centre of its head, between the eyes. There were six of them. They looked rather unhappy with the poor quality of the grazing. They'd come all this way from prehistory just for some damp, muddy grass.

"Is the power off?" Connor asked Becker as the soldiers stepped over the rails.

"Whole line's off at the moment. They're extending it for the Olympics. Just as well, really, or this lot would disrupt the trains."

"We apologise for the short delay," Connor said, adopting his plummiest voice. "This is due to dinosaurs on the line. We hope to be moving again shortly."

He studied the huge creatures, realising as he did so that these vast specimens weren't even fully grown. He heard a terrible sad cry coming from behind them, and turned to see the head of an even larger dinosaur — a female — emerging from the railway tunnel that led into the station.

"They're not Brachiosaurus," he said, amazed. "They're Sauroposeidons — one of the biggest dinosaurs there ever was."

"Really," Becker said, standing beside him and sounding unimpressed. "What's so great about that?"

"Well, she's got all sorts of tricks for keeping her weight down just so she's able to move. Thin bones all honeycombed with pockets of air. Air sacs just like in birds."

"Looks trapped," Abby said, from where she stood on the other side of him. "Poor thing can't go back or forward." She started to walk towards the stricken creature.

"The anomaly's just behind it," Becker informed them, "but we can't get this other lot back through it while mummy's in the way."

The huge creatures seemed quite placid, but looked miserable in the rain. Connor shivered. He was pretty cold himself.

"Oh no!" Abby cried, suddenly distraught. Connor and Becker ran to join her at the mouth of the tunnel. She had got up close to the stuck Sauroposeidon, just out of reach of its slender neck.

It struggled to free itself from its entrapment, but had only done itself damage. A huge rent where its neck met its shoulder dripped thick and glistening blood. The creature looked exhausted from the pain and exertion, but couldn't even move enough to lie down.

"If we could take away some of this wall..." Becker suggested, prodding at the brickwork.

"It's too late," Abby told him sadly, inspecting the wound. "She's not going to recover from this. Oh, you poor thing." She glanced at Becker, meaningfully.

Becker nodded. "Her children aren't going to like this."

"It's the only way we can get them back home. And we need to do it quickly before they suffer too much from the cold."

"We need to do what?" Connor said. "What are we going to do?"

"Make it quick," Abby told Becker. She took Connor's hand and led him back out into the rain.

It slowly dawned on Connor. He turned back in horror to see Becker raising his G36, pointing up close to the poor creature. The female held its head still for him, as if understanding and complicit. It lowed once, mournfully, the sad note picked up by the children trapped out in the rain.

"I'm sorry," Becker said, and fired.

Connor turned quickly away. When he looked up, Abby was watching him, a steely look in her eye.

"We had to," she told him. "We couldn't do anything else."

Connor nodded, knowing she was right yet still feeling wretched.

"At least it's no longer in pain," he said.

"Um," Becker said from where he still stood in front of the huge Sauroposeidon. Abby and Connor turned to look.

They watched in dumbfounded horror as the enormous beast scraped its way out of the tunnel, destroying the masonry, and thundered towards them.

TWENTY

"I'll even go economy," Lester said testily into his mobile. Danny watched, reading from his expression that this wasn't an option, either. He finished the simple pasta meal Lester had made, wishing they'd had some garlic or chilli to spice it up.

"No seats?" he said when Lester put down the phone.

"No *flights*. All the UK airports are grounded because of the weather. They offered me something flying to Paris, but not till the end of the week — by which time God-knows-who will be running the ARC."

"What do you want to do?"

"I want to string up the airport authorities."

"What do you want to do that's practicable?"

"Oh, that's practicable. Just you wait and see." Lester took a deep breath. "Change of plan."

"The oil mine."

"I think so. If Ted were here, I'd ask him to take us there now."

"He needed to get back. Pretend he never went out."

"So we go out ourselves."

"You told them they could shoot us." Danny said, then corrected himself. "Well, you told them they could shoot *me*."

Lester blinked at him.

"Are you really going to tell me you don't want to break the rules?"

Danny grinned at that.

"Just wanted to see your face. But we need to finish up here; pour Ted's beer down the sink, finish the caterpillars."

"Must we really?"

"You heard what he said. He doesn't share stuff with the new crowd. Gets quite ratty about it. So if they see that we've helped ourselves to his stuff, they'll assume he's ratty with us. It's like a cover story. Keeps him safe."

They opened the cartons of beer and slopped them into the sink. Danny helped himself to the caterpillars, but Lester declined them with a grimace.

"Think of them as scallops," Danny told him.

"Scallops don't have spikes."

They arranged the empty cartons around their unwashed plates, presenting a tale of two British tourists drinking late into the night. They put their bags and belongings under the sheets on their beds, so that any cursory inspection would show them both sleeping. It wouldn't convince anyone if they turned on the light, but they gambled that anyone checking wouldn't want to make their presence known.

Danny suggested that there might be someone watching the main entrance to the lodge, so they sneaked out the back and made their way carefully along the raised platform. The wood creaked under their feet. They froze, listening for a sign of anyone moving in response.

The only sound came from elsewhere in the house, as the walls creaked in sympathy.

"Come on," Danny whispered, leading Lester on. He kept the sleeves of his leather jacket pulled over the backs of his hands, attempting to hide his pale skin from the moonlight. Lester had his suit jacket on, and followed the example.

They reached the corner of the lodge, and Danny peered around at the car park. Sophie's SUV stood alone in front of the door. Danny could see very little in the pale moonlight, so he listened, carefully.

The wild was alive with strange and dangerous sounds, creaking and murmuring. The tall grass shifted from side to side, as though letting monsters pass through it.

He took a step forward, his foot and lower leg exposed to anyone watching the front of the lodge. And he stopped still.

Something about Sophie's car didn't look right. He tried to keep his breathing slow, his heart hammering in his chest. Gingerly he withdrew his foot.

"Anything?" Lester asked, whispering, yet also too loud. He saw the expression on Danny's face, and bit his bottom lip.

Danny risked another look round the edge of the building. Now he saw figures crouching in the shadows on the far side of the car, maybe as many as four. And what he'd taken to be an antenna on the bonnet revealed itself to be the barrel of one of their rifles.

He waited. He had no choice. He and Lester couldn't go back inside the building, and they wouldn't last half an hour out in the wild on foot.

So he waited. And waited.

His body ached with cramp and discomfort.

Finally there was movement. The men behind the car stood up and Danny saw that there were in fact two of them, both armed with rifles. In the pale moonlight he could see they were tall, well-built and probably well-trained. One of them stayed by the car while the other made right for Danny and Lester.

Danny quickly stepped backwards, and he and Lester pressed themselves back against the wall of the lodge, trying to merge with the shadows.

The man stepped up onto the platform and they felt his eyes look over them. Danny knew they didn't stand a chance if he saw them — the intruder had a rifle in his hands and they had nothing with which to defend themselves.

The gunman waved to his companion, then continued to approach. He hadn't expected to see anyone, Danny realised. He just wanted time to slip round the back of the lodge before his compatriot went in the front way. They were here to kill them.

That made things a lot easier.

The man stepped forward, confident and sure, and Danny punched him hard right in the throat. He fell back, almost toppling off the platform. Danny grabbed him, swerving his own body around the man's gun. The man gasped at him, stunned, and tried to shout out, so Danny rammed his head hard against the hard wood of the lodge and the man dropped, unconscious. The sounds of the bush overwhelmed the sounds of their struggle.

Danny disentangled the rifle from the intruder and handed it to Lester.

Only then did he recognise the unconscious figure as one of the keepers who'd wrapped up Sophie's body. He worked quickly through the man's pockets, finding a phone and a battered Colt pistol. Stuffing the gun into the back of his trousers, he took a length of twine from the gamekeeper's utility belt and firmly tied the man's wrists to a drainpipe.

Danny peered around the corner again, and watched as the second man — confident that the first was in place — detached himself from the shadow of the vehicle, walked up the front stairs and, Danny assumed, into the cabin.

He looked up at Lester, who held the rifle ready, and nodded. They moved quietly to the front of the lodge and in through the door.

The second gunman hadn't turned on the lights. They stepped carefully through the hallway and into the mess room. Their dinner plates and empty cartons loomed in the darkness as they passed the dining table. Danny stepped into the kitchen and instinct kicked in.

He lunged forward, hurling himself at the stove as a bullet cut through the air where he'd been.

Danny turned, raising his pistol, knowing he was in plain sight. He squeezed back on the trigger, but before he released his finger two gunshots cracked loudly in quick succession. He braced himself for the pain of having been shot, and found himself struggling for breath.

Down the corridor, the second gunman toppled backwards onto the floor.

Danny let out a sigh.

Lester moved forward into the corridor, smoke curling from the end of his rifle. He made his way quickly to the man he'd just shot, checking his pulse at the neck. Then, satisfied, he turned.

"What?" he said, seeing the look on Danny's face. "We only need one of them to question."

"Unless that guy's the boss."

"Somehow I doubt that either of them is 'boss' material," he responded.

"We'll see."

Wary, ready for more assassins, they made their way back to where the second gunman was tied up. He had got to his knees but couldn't get further because of the way Danny had bound him. They watched as he strained against the drainpipe, which buckled, bit by bit, reminding Danny of the impala they had used as bait earlier in the day.

"You're not refusing our hospitality, are you?" Danny asked, nudging the man firmly in the shoulder so that he tumbled over. His body crunched against the hard wooden platform.

The gunman stared up at them, his eyes wide and fearful. He said something in the clicking language they'd heard Ted and Sophie use before.

"So long as you cooperate, we're not going to hurt you," Danny said, turning reassuring now. "Honest, we're the good guys. We're here to help."

The gunman didn't seem placated — he either didn't understand, or affected not to. He yanked hard with his arms and the rope around his wrists tore loose the ancient drainpipe. Drops of water splattered out of the jagged pipe and its lower end fell forward, pointing up at the gunman accusingly. He gazed down at his wrists, still tied to each other, but not to anything else. Then he looked up into the barrel of Danny's pistol.

"You're not going anywhere, sunshine. Not until we've had a few words."

The man glanced round at Lester, and back at Danny. He was shaking with fear, fat droplets of sweat rolling down his face.

"Now, easy..." he said, reaching forward for the man's shoulder to help him to his feet. The man flinched away, looking quickly around for any means of escape. His breathing was fast and ragged, he looked sick and terrified.

"Hey," Danny said, trying again to be the good cop. "It's all going to be fine..."

The man gazed levelly at him, then turned to face the wall of the lodge. He leant back, said something quiet in his clicking language, and then brought his head crashing down on the jagged end of the drainpipe. With a sickening, wet sound the hollow spear of plastic burst through the back of his skull.

TWENTY-ONE

The female Sauroposeidon wrenched itself from the railway tunnel and charged towards them. Her head drooped, wounded, at the end of her long and slender neck.

The creature was in a terrible state. Her huge body gleamed with dark blood where she had shredded her flesh against the brickwork. Legs as thick as tree trunks urged her onwards.

Connor guessed that when stood up straight she would be at least fifteen metres tall; he barely came up to her knee. He grabbed Abby's hand and they ran quickly up the tracks, towards the creature's massive children. The young Sauroposeidons stood watching, knowing something was wrong. Rain drizzled greyly around them and they looked miserably out of place in the London murk.

Reacting to the noise of their parent, the young dinosaurs began hurrying off down the track, the thud of their heavy footsteps echoing back towards him and Abby as they ran.

"It didn't work!" Abby wailed.

The huge rent in the creature's shoulder seeped blood and gore, but she kept coming, barrelling towards them.

Becker stood his ground, trying to line up another shot, until the creature was almost upon him and he had to withdraw or be trampled.

The creature charged on and Connor and Abby hurriedly scrambled up the grassy bank beside the railway line, out of the way. Seconds later the Sauroposeidon thundered past, knocking down utility poles, leaving a horrific trail of blood in its wake.

"The poor thing," Abby said.

"The poor thing that nearly trampled us," Connor said.

"Yeah, but it must be in so much pain."

Guiltily, Connor watched the massive creature rush towards the other, smaller Sauroposeidons, who moved away as fast as their heavy legs could carry them.

"It's scaring off the others," Becker noted, reaching them. "As soon as there's a gap in the verges, they'll scatter into the street."

"They're heading down to New Cross," Abby pointed out. "That's all residential."

Becker spoke rapidly into his earpiece.

"I need all vehicles on the railway line at the nearest access point due south. We've got creatures who can't get up the verges looking for a means of escape."

"Is that going to work?" Abby said doubtfully.

Becker shrugged. "Worth a try. We need to stop this thing quickly. Any ideas how we do that?"

Neither Abby nor Connor could help him.

Becker stepped carefully down the verge until his feet crunched on the gravel. Then he began running after the huge dinosaur, his long strides far quicker than those of the lumbering creature. What was there he could do?

But Becker had seen what Connor had not. The huge creature stumbled as it continued down the railway line. Its enormous legs were becoming slow and clumsy. It let out one long, exhausted sigh and collapsed heavily onto its side. Becker hurried up behind it, keeping a safe distance back. He circled round, to the long, wheezing head, and raised his G36.

"No!" Abby cried, running to catch up with him.

"We have to," Becker told her levelly.

"I know," Abby said. "But I'm the one in charge, remember? It should be me."

Becker considered, then handed her his gun with a nod. Abby stood in front of the enormous creature, a determined look in her eye. She pulled back on the trigger.

Then it was over. The Sauroposeidon lay still and at peace. Connor made his way over to his friends. Abby handed the gun back to Becker. In the distance they could hear the sad, panicked cries of the huge creature's children.

"They're orphans now," Connor said sadly.

Abby took his hand. "Hey," she said. "What else could we have done?"

"I know, but it's just not fair."

Becker turned to look back down the track in the direction the other Sauroposeidons had run.

"Wilcock?" he said into his earpiece. "Is that barricade in place?" He listened for a moment then said. "Only as a last resort. Ideally, we send them home safe and well. Keep me posted. Out."

"Well?" Abby asked. "Did you fence them in?"

"They've put a few cars on the line and pretty much blocked it off."

"Pretty much," Connor repeated. "That's not wholly reassuring."

"The creatures are standing their ground, just watching the barricade at the moment. Wilcock says he doesn't fancy our chances if they decide to try and break through."

Connor thought for a moment.

"Do you think we can herd them back this way?"

"Perhaps," Becker said. "These are big creatures, not used to being pushed around. Maybe we just drive slowly in their direction, and hope they retreat."

"We can't just hope," Abby said firmly. "We need to do better than that."

"I'm meant to follow your orders," Becker told her. "If you've got any ideas..."

"It's going to be like herding cats," Connor said. He looked up to see Abby smiling sweetly at him.

"What?"

"Connor," Abby said. "You've just given me an idea."

TWENTY-TWO

They hadn't turned the lights on in the lodge, but their eyes had got used to the dark. Danny found a bottle of brandy in the mess room and poured two generous measures. He handed one glass to Lester, who took it without looking up from his BlackBerry.

"Trying Yellow Pages?"

Lester smiled thinly. "A for assassins, or C for clean-up? No, I made a note of Ted's number. He seems to be our only ally."

Danny nodded as his boss held the device up to his ear.

"Hello, Ted? James Lester here. Yes, at the lodge. I'm afraid we've run out of cartons of beer. Is there any chance you could drop round some more? We'll pay for it, of course. But we're positively gasping at the moment. Yes, thank you. See you soon."

"Think that's going to help us?" Danny asked as Lester turned off the phone and took a sip of brandy.

"It might help Ted get away," Lester explained, "and if anyone was listening in, it might not implicate him."

"Good thinking."

"Better get rid of the bodies before he gets here. He might not come alone."

"What do you want to do with them?" Danny said, surprised by Lester's icy, practical tone.

"We can put them around the back of the lodge, in the tall grass where they won't be seen."

"Won't they attract scavengers? You saw how close the lions came to the lodge last night."

"That would save us a lot of additional effort in the morning." Lester drained his brandy in one swallow.

They started with the body in the corridor. Lester kicked away the man's rifle, then helped himself to the pistol in the holster on his hip. He tucked the gun into the back of his trousers, and showed no squeamishness about wrapping his arms under the corpse's armpits. Danny grabbed the ankles, and they lifted him down towards the back door.

Contrary to the concept of 'dead weight', Danny had noticed during his days as a policeman that the deceased seemed to weigh less than the living. A more credulous man might think a man's soul weighed a couple of pounds.

Lester hesitated at the door, listening to the wilderness outside. They could hear dense and vivid life out there, or at least they could imagine it. Perhaps large animals moved through the tall grass, or perhaps another assassin.

He crossed the porch and stepped down from the platform, grunting under the weight of the dead man in his arms. Danny glanced left and right as they moved into the grass. It whipped against his exposed face and forearms, as though trying to snatch the body from his grasp. Their footsteps sounded loudly as they crunched through the underbrush, obscuring any hope of hearing something that might be sneaking up on them.

Danny felt his heart pounding.

"Here, I think," Lester whispered, out of breath, and they placed the dead man down on the ground. Without further comment, he led them back to the lodge, where the second body still lay on the raised platform by the broken drainpipe. This time Lester took his ankles, Danny getting the mess of the man's bloody head all down his front.

He only had one clean shirt left.

They placed the second body beside the first, then returned to the lodge. Danny didn't know how soon it would be before the park's creatures picked up on the scent of blood, and he didn't want to be there to find out. He felt a pang of remorse for the abrupt way these men had been dealt with, the way their bodies would be picked clean. But Lester seemed resolute as he poured them another couple of brandies.

"It was them or us," he said as they chinked glasses.

"Yeah," Danny said. "Law of the jungle."

A vehicle pulled into the car park about twenty minutes later. They watched from the window as Ted emerged, looking around nervously before he approached the lodge.

Lester moved silently up to the door of the mess, waiting just behind it. Ted came in slowly, eyes wide in the darkness. And Lester raised a pistol to his head.

"Are you alone?"

"Yes, Mr Lester. Brought you that beer you wanted."

"Good — Danny, check that he's not carrying a gun."

Danny came over. Ted met his eyes and he shrugged in a *what-can-you-do* kind of way. He began to frisk the man.

Danny retrieved the gun, a chunky, much-used Colt. Ted didn't appear to have any other weapons on him. Lester seemed satisfied and lowered his own gun.

"They were right," he said. "We had company."

"Least they didn't have you." Ted smiled grimly.

"We left the bodies outside. Now we need to get out of here."

"You're going home then. That's good."

"We will when there's a flight," Danny said. "But for the moment we're stuck here, and as long as that's the case..."

"I can get you out of the game park," Ted interrupted. "But that's all."

"Fine," Lester said flatly. "Then drop us somewhere near the mine."

Ted stared at him. It took him a moment to find his voice.

"You know how many people they got there? You won't get in through the gates."

"You don't know Lester. He's very persistent," Danny assured him. "Got a natural air of authority. It's something they teach you at public school."

"Will you do it?" Lester asked brusquely, ignoring Danny's remark. He was a man on a mission.

Ted's eyes narrowed as he thought it over.

"You know what happens to me if they find out?"

Lester nodded. "I do."

"We're your only chance to stop whatever it is that's going on," Danny said.

"Yeah, and you don't stand a chance. Not if I don't help you." Ted grinned. "You finish all the brandy? If we're doing this, I'm gonna need a drink."

TWENTY-THREE

They made their way into the dark railway tunnel, following the beam of Becker's torch. The huge Sauroposeidon had smashed all the lights as it pushed its way through, and broken glass crunched underfoot. There was also a strange stink of machinery, all grit and electricity, the odour of a century of trains.

Connor stopped for a moment to put down the large cardboard box they had lugged from the pet store on the far side of the car park. Massaging his sore fingers, he admired the ancient brickwork of the tunnel. Somewhere up ahead it met up with the Thames Tunnel, running under the river from Rotherhithe to Wapping.

Connor and his old friends Tom and Duncan had once done a walking tour of the tunnel, organised by the local museum. They'd been less interested in the history than in just getting to explore the cool place, but Connor still remembered some of what their guide had told them. The tunnel had been built by Victorian engineer Isambard Kingdom Brunel — the first major project he worked on — and back then it had been for pedestrians, livestock and carts.

As most animals don't like being led into tunnels, there was a bend in it so it was impossible to see all the way through. And that same dislike was probably going to make it even more difficult to get the Sauroposeidon juveniles back through the anomaly.

He lifted the heavy box again and hurried to catch up with the others as they ventured further into the darkness. Mice scurried across the gravel in front of them, trying to keep out of the torchlight. On the walls he glimpsed crude graffiti.

A little further and they could see the anomaly, shards of orange and yellow light twisting and turning slowly around one another. Connor put down the box again and reached for his handheld detector. He shivered; something about this anomaly didn't feel quite right.

Connor tried to make sense of the readings on his detector.

"This isn't right."

"Why?" Abby asked peering over his shoulder.

"What's the problem?" Becker demanded, striding towards them.

"The readings are all wrong," Connor said.

"But we haven't done anything to it yet," Becker said, frowning.

"Could it be a new kind of anomaly?" Abby suggested. "Or the weather? The anomalies have been a bit different recently anyway. That G-rex we fought at the airport came through one that was huge."

"It's just not *right*," Connor insisted.

"It never is," Becker muttered impatiently. Then he added more loudly, "We need to get a move on or the creatures are going to try their luck with the barricade."

"And we need to get them out of the rain," Abby said. "Connor, the anomaly's working, isn't it? They'll go through okay."

Connor studied the readings again.

"Oh sure, it's working. It's just... weird."

Becker spoke into his earpiece.

"Start moving them up this way — now."

Abby tore open the box Connor had brought with them. There were smaller boxes inside, each one showing the same cartoon picture of a grinning cat. She ripped the top off one packet and wafted it round the tunnel. Tiny grey flakes trailed in the air, giving off a faint, grassy smell. Abby threw the packet down the tunnel, back the way they had come, then helped herself to another, and began moving down the tunnel, building up a trail to the anomaly. Connor's nose began to twitch as he watched her.

"But what if they don't like it?" he asked her.

Abby shrugged. "You've seen the size of their noses. Let's hope this smells weird enough for them at least to come take a look. Cats can't resist catnip."

"But these aren't cats," Connor said.

"You said they were just the same."

"No I didn't. If this doesn't work, you can't blame me. And *you* can explain to the pet shop why we helped ourselves to all their supplies."

Abby grinned at him and hurled another open packet up the tunnel behind them. Unlike the bait they had used on the crocodilians, this scent was in no danger of dissipating. Here in the stillness of the tunnel, the smell hung thickly in the air.

"Think that should be enough. Don't want to use all of it at once."

Connor picked up the box.

"We should probably get out of here, then. We don't want to be crushed in the stampede."

They made their way quickly back the way they had come, and out into the grey drizzle. It was getting late in the evening and the light was fading fast. Connor really didn't fancy messing with the giant creatures in the dark.

"Wilcock," Becker said sharply into his earpiece, "how are you getting on?"

Connor watched his face, anxiously trying to gauge the answer from his expression, and he saw Abby doing the same. Then they heard a gentle lowing coming from further down the line. They turned, and could just see the first of the enormous young Sauroposeidons coming into view.

"It's working!" Connor said breathlessly. "I think it *is* my plan."

Abby grinned back. "But you needed me to help you.."

"We're a team."

"Batman and Robin."

"Yeah," he said. Then he cocked his head at her. "Am I Batman?"

Her eyes twinkled. "Maybe, if you're good."

Becker rolled his eyes and stepped back from them. Connor decided that meant he had licence to flirt as much as he liked. But when he turned back to Abby, he found her watching the military man, her eyes open wide.

With a sinking feeling, Connor looked to see Becker staring into the dark railway tunnel. Something rumbled from within.

"Um," Connor said nervously, "that doesn't sound good."

"No, it doesn't," Becker murmured. Taking a step forward he grabbed Abby and Connor by the arms and threw himself — and them — to the side.

Connor almost dropped the box of catnip. They'd barely got clear of the tunnel entrance when two huge Sauroposeidons charged out into the evening rain.

"Oh crap," Connor said, standing on the verge as they passed. "That's something we didn't think of."

"The catnip attracted creatures from the other side of the anomaly," Becker said disgustedly.

"Oops," Connor said. "Okay, Abby, it was definitely your idea." He turned, but Abby was already on the move, running off down the verge towards the other Sauroposeidons and the army vehicles that rumbled behind them.

"Hey!" he yelled after her. "I didn't mean it! Joke!"

Sarah sat at a desk in view of the ADD, looking over the notes she'd made on her laptop. Samuels had asked the technicians and soldiers to leave her to the operations room so that she could complete her work. She felt only mildly guilty about that, glad for the silence and head space, but knowing they all had important projects of their own.

Her job was to match the creatures with the monsters in myths and legends. There'd been anachronous sightings throughout human history, but only now was the ARC making rational sense of what was happening. Slowly they were putting the jigsaw together. Every creature they encountered, required investigation and research, and that information had to be assessed and analysed. It sometimes seemed an impossible task just to keep up with each new incident. But now they might be able to share the load. She looked over what she had written on the screen.

"This proposal is divided into two sections," it said. "First, *why* we should go public concerning the anomalies and creatures. Second, *how* we break the news.

She read over the proposal again, tweaking and moving sentences around. The civil service seemed to like nothing longer than two pages: three succinct bullet points on page one and some explanation on page two. Apparently, it made it easier for them to make a decision, but it also required a lot more effort on her part to keep her argument focused. She usually needed more than two pages just for all her endnotes.

At last she was happy with a first draft of what promised to usher in a new age for the ARC. She hit the 'print' key, realising as she did so that she didn't know where the nearest printer was. She looked around and up at the balcony in front of Lester's office. From where she sat, she couldn't see inside, but she thought she could hear Samuels working at his own laptop.

No, she realised, what she could hear was her proposal printing out up there.

Sarah got to her feet, a little annoyed with herself. She'd wanted to read the pages over once again before handing them over, keenly aware of how easy it was to miss things when proofing them on screen. But Samuels would have the proposal in front of him now, might even have made a decision one way or another before she had got up there to see him.

Nothing to do about it but face the music.

So she adjusted her linen blouse and waistcoat, swept her hand through her long, dark hair, taking deep breaths to prepare herself for the task of selling her ideas. And just as she stepped away from the ADD, the alarm went off. The siren wailed loudly throughout the whole ARC building, and the lights flashed pinkish orange. The screen already showed the anomaly at Surrey Quays that Connor and Abby had gone to investigate. But now there was *another* anomaly.

She sighed and reached over the keyboard to turn off the noise. The light still flashed and swirled, reflecting off the screens. Her nimble fingers fluttered over the keys to home in on the signal.

The central of the five screens showed an aerial photograph of the south of England. It blurred, honing in on Greater London; then Central London; then a particular section of the city...

Sarah gasped.

She was staring down at the domed roof of the building she was in.

That was when she noticed that it wasn't just the pink-and-orange alarm lights that were flashing. She turned slowly around, and then arched her back to look up again at the balcony of Lester's office. As clear as day, she could see the twisting, broken-glass anomaly hovering right over his desk. Light reflected in the plate glass windows of the office, and rebounded all around the operations room.

Sarah pressed a button on the keyboard of the ADD.

"Security." A man's bored-sounding voice came from a speaker beneath the five screens.

"This is Dr Page. Send a unit to the operations room. There's an anomaly in Lester's office."

"Saves us a bit of petrol," the man replied with unexpected humour. "We'll be with you shortly."

By rights, she should wait for the soldiers to arrive — she knew better than to approach an anomaly on her own. But what about Samuels? What if he was still up there?

"Mr Samuels?" she called up to the balcony. There was no reply, but she thought she heard movement. Perhaps he was hurt.

"I'm coming up," she called to him, making her way to the walkway. As she headed up the slope she found she was shaking with a mixture of fear and excitement. She thought of turning back, of going to find a tranquilliser gun, but she had barely any experience with the things, and armed she probably risked causing more damage to herself than to anything coming out of the anomaly.

Anyway, there were trained professionals on their way.

Despite her fears, she felt a thrill run through her at having an anomaly of her own to investigate. Reaching the entrance to the office, she peered inside. The phenomenon twisted and twinkled behind Lester's desk, the papers and files scattered all around it as if it had caused a small explosion.

There was no one in the room.

"Mr Samuels?" she called again from the doorway, hesitant to actually step through. Something behind the desk stirred, it made a noise that might have been a moan.

"Tom? Are you there? Are you all right?"

There was no response. She peered over her shoulder, back down at the operations room, and wondered why the soldiers hadn't arrived yet.

Again, something moaned softly behind the desk.

She took a step forward and stopped, then took a deep breath and walked confidently over to the desk.

The moaning was coming from beneath the anomaly.

"Tom?" she said, walking slowly around. "There are soldiers on their way. Are you okay?"

And a creature leapt out at her.

TWENTY-FOUR

Abby found the best way to run across the sloping verge beside the railway line was to aim upwards. It made her a bit more sure-footed and compensated for the occasional slip and slide. It was still hard going though, and she felt pleased with herself for sticking with her kick-boxing exercise regime, however much her brother teased her about it.

To her right, the massive Sauroposeidons crowded into the valley of the railway line. The two newcomers entwined their incredibly long, slender necks round the others, in some kind of friendly greeting. They lowed at each other mournfully, as if discussing the misery of the rain — or the death of their mother. Abby felt an awful pang of guilt as she ran on, heading for the convoy of army trucks and cars that blocked them from getting any further south.

"Ma'am." Wilcock saluted as she reached his 4x4. "How can we assist you?"

"You can get out," she told him. Wilcock glanced at the soldier sitting next to him, then turned back to her.

"Sorry?"

"Get out of the car, soldier!" she snapped at him. "That's an order."

The two soldiers quickly scrambled out into the rain, and Abby decided she liked her newfound authority. She jumped up into the driving seat, adjusting the dial at her hip to bring the seat nearer to the pedals. Once she was comfortable, she smiled sweetly at Wilcock and his comrade.

"Thank you," she said, and put her foot down.

The 4x4 bucked forward, tyres scrunching on the gravel of the railway line. She honked the horn and the huge creatures turned their necks to look back at her. Abby yanked on the wheel, skidding the car hard to the left so that it bounced against the rails. The impact threw her into the air and she hit the ceiling with a *thump*. She rubbed the top of her head with one hand, and yanked the car left once more. This time she got the angle right. The vehicle bounced its left wheels over the top of the rail, then landed straddling it.

Bouncing along, Abby honked the horn again, coming up fast on the massive dinosaurs. They lowered their heads to scrutinise her as she approached. She imagined the thoughts slowly forming in their dinosaur brains as they rather resentfully shuffled themselves out of her way. She sped through, hardly able to steer around them while her 4x4 straddled the rail. Only when she'd got past them did she let out the breath she'd been holding.

"What are you doing?" Connor demanded as she pulled up in front of the mouth of the tunnel.

"Put the box in the back," she told him. "Quickly, before any more of them come through."

"Okay, okay." Connor ran round to the back of the 4x4 and struggled to open the hatch. Becker hurried to assist him.

"You need to secure the box," she shouted back at them. "Make sure it's packed in tight."

"Right," Becker said, fixing the luggage straps round the cardboard. "And then open up all the packets — right?"

"All of them," Abby acknowledged, and she nodded, straining back in her seat to check they were doing it properly. Becker tore at the cardboard packaging.

"Come on, come on," Abby said. "Wave one of them around so they pick up the scent."

Connor reached for a packet, tore off the top, then turned to face the Sauroposeidons that had massed further down the track.

"Oi!" he yelled to them. "You lot with the long necks. Get a whiff of this!" Cautiously he moved closer, holding the packet out in front of him. He blew across the top, trying to waft the scent in their direction.

Like tall trees moving in the breeze, the Sauroposeidons turned to stare at him through the gloom. Abby saw their eyes open wide as they sniffed the pungent, grassy odour. She'd learnt to make stink bombs in chemistry lessons at school, and had been given detention for gassing the boys' toilets. *Why can't you apply your talents to something useful?* her headmaster had despaired. If only he could see her now.

"They're coming!" Connor cried. The dinosaurs moved slowly at first, but with more excitement as they picked up the scent and their instincts kicked in. The young ones in particular had been without much to eat ever since they had arrived, and they followed as quickly as their bulk would allow.

"Right," Abby said, "that all the catnip?"

"We've got some more in the other truck," Becker told her. He took the open packet in Connor's hand and dropped it into the box. "But all of these are open, and I think they'll do the trick. Good luck!"

"Thanks," she said gratefully.

"But wait," Connor said, "aren't we coming —"

She put the car in gear and the 4x4 thrust forward, jarring her teeth as the car juddered over the sleepers. In her rear-view mirror, out through the still open hatch, she saw Becker dragging Connor out of the way of the Sauroposeidons, who were picking up speed as they gave chase. Like most creatures — and people — she had encountered, they were motivated mainly by their stomachs. And though they might never have smelled catnip before, it appeared they found it appealing.

She drove at speed into the tunnel, and suddenly the car engine was echoing loudly all around her, the car thrumming and bouncing over the sleepers. She glanced up at the mirror again, and saw the first Sauroposeidon ducking its head down to squeeze into the tunnel. With its neck stretched out in front of it, it continued to chase after her. She hoped the others would queue in an orderly fashion and follow on behind.

Ahead of her the anomaly twinkled and spun. She put her foot down hard again and the 4x4 sped into the light. She felt the topsy-turvy prickling as she passed through time, the uncomfortable pull as everything metal in the car strained towards the light, and then the car was bouncing over the dry earth of a vast savannah. Abby kept going for a couple of hundred metres then skidded to a halt.

As she leapt out of the car, the first Sauroposeidon emerged from the anomaly behind her.

The sun beat down hard on her damp skin and clothes, making them steam as she ran to the back of the car and heaved at the box of catnip. Her face and hands were slick with sweat, and the box remained stuck fast in its moorings. Becker had lashed it in too well. She struggled with the knots with her sweaty fingers, but to no avail. Her plan had been to dump the box then steer a wide arc round the dinosaurs and drive back into the anomaly. She had to get rid of the catnip, or the creatures would just follow her back through.

Digging her hands inside the box, she scooped out as many packets as she could manage. They jostled to escape as she turned around, and fell at her feet. She had thought she might throw them, to divert the dinosaurs from the car. But there wasn't time.

The Sauroposeidons lumbered towards her. There were seven of them, eight as another emerged from the anomaly. She couldn't remember how many there had been in London, cursing herself for not thinking to count them. She looked back at the 4x4, but it was too late, they had almost reached her. Instead, she scrambled out of the way just as the first Sauroposeidon poked its head in through the hatch, squashing the box altogether.

The other Sauroposeidons collided with the first, shoving and jostling for the strange food they could smell but not see. They nosed at the packets and the more they struggled, the more she could see their frustration. They lowed and shoved and snapped at one another. One Sauroposeidon stumbled against the 4x4 and knocked it over on its side. The others seemed to agree that the car had been at fault. They shoved it and slammed their bulky sides against it, smashing glass and crunching metal.

Abby ran back in the direction of the anomaly. She could smell the stink of the catnip on her clothes and skin, and hoped the Sauroposeidons would be too busy with the car to notice. Her boots sank into the soft brown earth, and to her weary legs it was as tiring as running through sand.

She glanced around. No, they weren't following. But they'd stopped pounding her poor car. They stood tall, long necks craning towards the horizon.

Puzzled, Abby stopped in her tracks, maybe a hundred metres from the twinkling anomaly. She followed the dinosaurs' gaze across the vast plain of pale brown earth, trees, ferns and foliage under a sweltering, clear sky.

And her jaw fell open in amazement.

They were in the Early Cretaceous, something like eighty million years before Abby's own time. Yet on the horizon stood a squalid black factory; a man-made monstrosity, belching thick smoke into the sky.

TWENTY-FIVE

They watched Ted from the hallway as he went out to his car. He took his time rearranging whatever lay inside, and then he stepped back, glancing around at the starlit darkness while he rolled a cigarette. A few moments later he turned to the lodge, nodded almost imperceptibly, and rummaged for his lighter.

Danny and Lester walked swiftly out into the night, and clambered into the back hatch of the SUV. There was hardly room for them both, even without the cartons of Jo'burg beer. They folded themselves up as tightly as they could, and Ted slammed the door behind them.

They were immersed in total darkness. Danny could hear Lester breathing right up close. Outside, he heard the crunch of gravel as Ted ambled to the front of the car. Then the engine started and they took off at some speed. The cartons of beer sloshed and jostled around them as the car bumped and bucked along.

Danny tried to lie still, but his legs protested at being folded up so tightly. He closed his eyes and tried to keep his breathing steady.

After a few minutes the car slowed to a stop. He tensed, hearing Ted leaning out the window to call to someone in his clicking isiXhosa. A couple of other men replied, laughing at some joke that Ted had made.

The laughter sounded cruel, and with a rush of panic Danny realised what a vulnerable position they had put themselves in. Had Ted just sold them out?

He heard the driver's door opening, and Ted hauling himself out of the car. His footsteps crunched on the earth again as he made his way round to the back. The two other men continued to laugh as he chatted to them.

Danny heard Lester cocking the pin back on his pistol, ready to put up a fight. But realistically, crammed in the back of an SUV, they were both sitting ducks.

The hatch creaked open, letting bright starlight flow in behind them, partly obscured by a human silhouette. As he leaned in, Ted didn't make eye contact, and ignored the pistol Lester pointed in his face. Instead he reached forward for a couple of cartons of beer, wedged them in the crook of one arm and used his free hand to slam the hatch back down.

Danny sighed as he heard Ted making his way over to the two other men, and more cruel laughter echoed as he handed out the drink. He guessed that Ted had been telling them that the two Englishmen wouldn't now be needing the beer they'd asked for.

After what seemed like an eternity, Ted returned to the car, climbed in, and they moved off again. Danny found that the cartons had acted as a useful shield for his shoulder, preventing it from hitting the side of the car, and now that they were gone, he kept bashing against the same hard, metal edge. He gritted his teeth against at the pain.

When the car finally ground to a halt for the second time, he almost cried out in frustration as Ted took his time getting out and ambling around to the back. And then the hatch was open and they scrambled out, stretching aching limbs and gasping in the cool, clean air.

He had parked up beside the tall chain-link fence that stretched off as far as they could see in both directions. Signs at regular intervals showed the same stick-man being electrocuted. The top of the fence, high above their heads, stuck out an angle, barbed wire glistening in the silvery starlight.

Danny looked back at the rough scrub and bushland of the game park, a vast expanse in the dark.

"I thought you were getting us out of here."

"Yeah, but not through the gates — they'd probably search the car. Lucky they've not missed your two friends yet."

"So we scale the fence?" Danny asked. "That might get a bit hot."

"You think?" Ted pointed at the ground. Heavy-set tyre tracks snaked back and forth under the same portion of the fence. Danny recognised the tracks they'd seen before. "You know what's in that direction?" Ted asked, indicating where the tracks disappeared off to on the far side.

"The mine, I'd guess," Danny said.

Ted nodded, then using his torch he scrutinised the marks in the ground. "Come and go most nights. Been through here twice today."

"That's because they've tried to get us eaten twice in the last twenty-four hours," Lester said. "I'm beginning to think it's personal."

"So how do we get through?" Danny avoided the temptation to simply prod the electric fence.

"Don't know." Ted scratched his chin. "Never seen them do it. Just followed their tracks."

Lester picked up a stone, bounced it in his hand as he assessed its weight, then threw it in a precise arc so that it hit the fence just above the tyre tracks. The fence clattered with noise and sparks of electricity, and the stone exploded in a plume of dust.

"Ah," Lester sighed.

Danny squinted into the pale starlight.

"Maybe there's a remote control box, something they can switch on and off without getting out of the truck."

Without getting any closer to the fence, they appraised the tall poles that were supporting it, looking for any incongruous detail. But there was nothing.

"Perhaps they just turn the electricity off at specific, pre-determined times," Lester suggested.

"It's dangerous to turn the fence off," Ted said, "since the inmates might escape." He shook his head slowly, trying to puzzle it out.

Danny paced up and down in front of the barrier, nervous about how exposed they were, and how soon the other gamekeepers would be on their trail. They had to get past this thing, and quickly.

He walked over to the fence, and stood in between the two lines of tracks. Peering through the chain-link, he could see only scrubby earth. He didn't dare get any closer for fear of ending up in very small, crisply barbecued pieces. He turned carefully around, his back to the fence, and took three careful steps away from it.

"Look," he said, pointing. Lester came over to look from his vantage point.

"Tyre tracks," he said, "leading off into the distance. I expect the top lot go back to that tree where Sophie died."

"And —" Danny prompted.

"And what?"

"Look. There's a kink in them. Just there."

Lester looked. Danny took another few steps forward and stood directly on the point where the truck had changed direction ever so slightly before passing through the fence.

"The tracks are sunk further into the ground, so they must have stopped here for a bit."

"Waiting for the electricity to be turned off," Lester said.

"Yeah, or because —" Danny turned back to face the fence, then adjusted himself so he stood beside the right-hand track, in roughly the same place as the driver would have sat while the truck had parked.

To Lester's distain and Ted's delight, he mimed rolling down a window and reaching his arm out, and the tips of his fingers nicked the needle-like thorns of an acacia. He withdrew his hand quickly, sticking his cut fingers in his mouth. They tasted of blood and dust.

Ted came over and crouched down by the acacia bush. He tentatively poked a finger in between the thorns. Something hidden inside clicked distinctly, a ticker whirred and they watched the fence, assuming it would swing open.

Nothing happened.

Lester hefted another stone and bowled it at the electric fence. It rebounded, still intact.

"A timer — we can get through as long as that thing's still whirring. How long does that give us?"

"Let's not find out," Danny said, racing for the fence. He examined it quickly and soon found a long metal pin that seemed to connect one section to the ground. He fought to release it, and then found the section of fence trying to swing away from him.

Ted fired up the engine of his SUV and drove quickly through the gap, the other two following behind on foot. They closed the fence and Lester reached his fingers through to grasp at the long metal pin that would secure it once again. His fingertips brushed against it, missed, and pushed it further out of reach. He sighed, exasperated.

"Let me," Danny said. And not waiting for a response, he pushed a stick through the chain links, tapping the pin towards its slot. The timer whirred from the far side, then went silent.

Danny gave the pin a sharp bash with the stick and it fell into place. A sudden rattle of sparks exploded in their faces. They leapt back, falling into the dirt. As they sat up, Danny raised the stick he'd been holding. Smoke trailed from the burnt-off end, just a centimetre from his fingers.

They left the car about a mile from the mine and made the rest of the journey on foot. Ted had a Winchester Model 70, and Lester and Danny the Colt pistols they'd taken from their would-be killers.

A cool night breeze brushed at them as they followed the road that went snaking through the scrubby landscape. When a car appeared further up the way, its headlights dazzling novas in the otherwise twinkling night, they dropped to the ground, lying flat in the earth where it dipped away from the road. The headlights created a long shadow over them as the car passed by. They waited a good minute after it had gone, just to be sure, then continued on their way.

The mine stood tall and imposing, a looming behemoth on the otherwise unsullied horizon. It stank of oil and industry. A fork-lift truck moved a huge drum across the forecourt to join a vast stash of the things; equivalent to the petrol needs of all the ARC's own vehicles for about a year. Danny could almost smell the money pouring from the place.

Avoiding a second tall electric fence ahead of them, they skirted around the perimeter of the complex. Ted pointed out armed guards on duty, but none of them looked their way. Danny also spotted large trucks with trailers — just the thing for transporting oversized cargo back and forth — prehistoric predators, for example.

They continued on, until they located a break in the fence, a man-sized gap guarded by a bored sentry. He was a solid black shape, back-lit by the glaring bright lights of the mine. Danny would have attempted to get past him, but Ted grabbed his arm. They hung back, in the shadows, watching as another soldier emerged through the gap. The sentry and the soldier exchanged a few words, then the soldier took a few steps further out into the open and lit a cigarette.

“You wouldn’t want to allow smoking on top of an oil mine,” Danny whispered. “Think of the insurance.”

A few minutes later the soldier stubbed out his cigarette, turned, cuffed the sentry on the elbow and made his way back into the mine.

“Okay,” Ted said, getting to his feet.

Danny touched his arm.

“You can leave us here; you’ve done more than enough.”

Ted shrugged. “I’ve come this far...” His eyes gleamed with excitement, and something else.

Danny grinned and smacked him on the back.

“Okay then, we know they’ve got their own private store of dinosaurs, but they’ve also got gaps in their fence, so the animals probably don’t roam freely round the complex. I reckon they don’t want anyone seeing them, anyway, so we just need to handle the human security.”

“We go in,” Ted said, “knock them out, and put on their uniforms. Just like in the movies.”

“Or we just go in and knock them out. Probably a similar result.”

They kept to the shadows as best they could. The silhouetted sentry seemed to be gazing out to their left, so they arced round to the right. Heart pumping, Danny sprang out from the darkness about a hundred yards from the man, who still didn’t look their way. He ran quietly, swiftly, fifty yards... twenty...

He skidded to a halt as huge searchlights blazed into life, blinding the three intruders.

“Drop your weapons,” a South African accent blared through a loudspeaker from somewhere behind the glare. “Drop your weapons, or we’ll shoot you where you stand.”

Ted laid his rifle at his feet, then took a step back. Lester and Danny snapped the magazines out of their pistols then tossed the guns onto the earth just in front of them. Soldiers rushed forward, rifles aimed towards them. Danny heard one of them — perhaps the one who’d spoken through the loudspeaker — say something into an earpiece.

“Tell the boss we’ve got them. And Ted as well.”

“He’s not with us,” Danny said. “We brought him here against his will.”

The soldier punched him hard in the chest. He collapsed down on one knee, struggling for breath.

TWENTY-SIX

Sarah dived across the desk, the massive creature just missing her legs. It collided hard with the toughened glass window that looked out over the operations room, and fell back, stunned.

She scrambled to her feet, but before she could run, the enormous long-legged crocodile had lumbered around to block her way out of the office. It stood there, shaking its long-jawed head as it began to recover its senses.

Slowly she edged around behind Lester's desk, keeping her eyes on it, wary of any sudden movement. As she stepped up close to the anomaly, the creature rocked back on its haunches, preparing to pounce again.

As it leapt, Sarah threw herself into the anomaly. She felt claws and teeth strike through her, felt them ripping her apart — she was certain of it. And then she was rolling across a metal grate in some other place.

She had not been torn in two; she'd passed through the anomaly.

Behind her, something crackled with electricity, and the creature let out a startled, angry roar. Sarah looked up to discover that it had followed her through and was struggling to break free of an electric snare that tightened around its thick armour-plated neck. Two black-uniformed soldiers wielding rifles stood looking down at her, while a third adjusted the controls of the snare.

A moment later the creature settled down, bowing its head in submission.

"Sir," one of the soldiers said into his earpiece. "We've got Dr Page."

He listened for a moment, then motioned to his colleagues, saying, "We put her with the others."

Oh God, Sarah thought, panic constricting her throat. *They've got others, too — others,* plural. *They must have taken Samuels, but who* else *could they mean?*

And then even more terrible questions occurred to her. Had someone *deliberately* opened an anomaly right inside Lester's office? If so, how? And where was she now? Sarah's mind was reeling.

The soldier with the snare directed the creature into a corner, and the other two came towards Sarah, brandishing their guns. For the second time in twenty-four hours she was captured and powerless. She bit her lip, and dug her fingernails into the palms of her hands. Tears welled up at the corners of her eyes, then trickled down her cheeks.

"Please," she said feebly. "Please don't hurt me!"

The soldiers looked at each other. One grinned cruelly back at her.

"Shut up and come on," he said as he reached forward to force her to her feet.

Sarah stood miserably, tears dribbling from her chin. The soldier held her arm, but let her go when she tried to wipe her face on her sleeve. He glanced back at his colleague, about to make a joke, and his colleague lowered his gun as he leaned in to hear it.

She knew she must look a pitiable mess.

That was the idea.

She grabbed the soldier who had helped her up, pulled him back towards her. As he stumbled, she thrust down on his shoulders, lifting herself into the air. She swung round like a gymnast towards the other soldier, who raised his rifle to shield his face. Which meant he exposed what she'd been aiming for anyway — she planted both feet hard in his groin.

He fell back with a satisfying grunt.

They were handcuffed, then marched through the gap in the fence.

Well, we made it through, Danny mused darkly.

He stumbled once, unbalanced by the handcuffs and the searing brightness of the searchlights. A soldier growled at him to keep moving, he had taken a handful more steps before he realised — the soldier had spoken with an English accent.

He knew the mine was a British concern. He knew that it mattered to the government as it offered a potential solution to the energy crisis, and that he and Lester had been sent out here to make sure nothing got in its way — not even the nuisance of an anomaly or two. So they were all meant to be on the same side, weren't they?

Except that it seemed as if they had been royally set up. Someone high up in the government really didn't like them. And that someone had access to carnivorous dinosaurs and soldiers, and was prepared to use them. Against Danny and Lester — and probably anyone else who got in their way.

Like Sophie.

So who? There was Lester's old friend Christine Johnson, who promised to be trouble. Would she — or anyone else — dare to sabotage the vital work the ARC was doing? Could you be so ambitious you'd risk unleashing the catastrophe they held back on a daily basis? It didn't make sense.

But Danny also knew just how valuable the ARC and its work could be, and he was discovering how much fighting and internal politicking that could create. As Lester had said, show some success and everyone will want a piece of it.

He looked over at Lester, who had his head bowed as he walked, his eyes glimmering with intelligence as he puzzled out their options. He was struck by the fight in the man; smart, canny and ruthless. You crossed him at your peril.

They weren't beaten yet. Not by a long shot.

The group passed through a side building full of guns and army equipment, and then through a sliding door that led into the main warehouse of the mine. After the glare of the spotlights outside, Danny took a moment to let his eyes get used to the relative gloom.

The room was completely empty. No machinery, no mining equipment, no shaft down into the depths of the earth. So where the hell were they getting the oil from?

His thought was answered by an explosion of orange-pink light, right in the centre of the room. Ted and the soldiers looked away, but Danny and Lester both stared directly at the anomaly.

A *controlled* anomaly.

"You can call them up whenever you want them," Lester said.

"Maybe we can," said one of the soldiers, shoving him forward.

"What is this thing?" Ted asked Danny, and he sounded frightened.

"Don't worry," Danny said. "It's just a doorway. Local delicacy where we come from. It's gonna be okay." He hoped he sounded confident.

Ted nodded, but didn't look convinced. The soldiers shoved them with their guns, herding them towards the twinkling portal. Lester stepped through first, his body fracturing amongst the shards of light, Ted swore under his breath, looked at Danny for reassurance, then stepped after Lester. Danny went through last.

They emerged into another building, this one a vast cathedral to industry. But for the handcuffs, Danny would have clamped his hands over his ears to protect them from the noise. Machines as big as houses clanked and growled, churning out black smoke and the stench of oil. Smoke and sparks filled the working area, scratching at their eyes, burning their throats, making them cough.

Danny doubled over, struggling to get his breath back, and only when he looked up again did he see the enormous square hole that was plunging down into the depths of the earth.

The soldiers led them off the workplace floor and into one of the side rooms. The group stepped through a door. Then while two of the soldiers remained, rifles at the ready, the third thug disappeared through a second door.

"So they *are* drilling for oil," Lester said, as the door behind them closed and they could hear again. Despite all they'd been through in the past couple of days, Danny realised he had never before seen Lester truly shocked.

"But in another time," Danny observed. "We must be in the prehistoric past now — which means they're exploiting the anomalies somehow."

Lester regained his composure.

"I suppose it makes sense to use them if we can."

"What?" Danny spluttered. "You think this is going to end well? They'll eat up the world before we've even evolved here. Remember what Cutter said — he knew the score. They'll cancel out the human race."

Lester shrugged. "Solves a lot of problems that way." He smiled at the man who stood in front of him. "Doesn't it, soldier?"

The man didn't flinch, just kept his eyes on them. Lester turned to Danny and rolled his eyes. But he rolled them in the direction of the door.

Yeah, it was getting time they made their excuses.

Danny coughed violently, bending over double and hacking up some phlegm. He hardly needed to act — his throat still burned raw from being out in the mine. One of the soldiers nudged him with the butt of his rifle, urging him to stand up. Danny moaned a little, swayed unsteadily on his feet.

Then he stood up and kicked the man across the room.

Lester got behind him as he fell, and tripped him so he impacted with the wall. Danny turned to see Ted headbutt the other soldier and knock him unconscious.

Lester crouched down with his back to the soldier who'd hit the wall, using his still-handcuffed wrists to feel his way through the man's pockets. He pulled on a chain, revealed a set of keys, then nimbly worked his way through them to select the right one. Once he'd got it, he stood up and came over to Danny. It took a bit of fumbling before their wrists met and Lester found where to place the key, but the handcuffs soon clicked open.

"You've done this before," Ted said as Danny quickly released Lester and then him.

"Once or twice," Lester responded, coolly. "Hostage training is part of my management package. Along with a private dentist and a rather handy chauffeur."

They picked up the fallen rifles and hurried to the second door. Danny eased the handle down slowly, not making any noise. He looked to Lester, who nodded, so he pushed it open a crack and squinted through into the corridor that lay beyond.

He turned back and grinned at the others.

"Told you it would be okay," he said to Ted. He pushed the door wide, and they hurried through, then rushed down the corridor, grabbing lab coats from a rail at the end.

"We won't fool anyone," Lester grumbled as he pulled the white coat on over the top of his muddy, bloodied shirt.

"Not if they're paying attention," Danny said. "But it might just help if we don't give them time to think about it."

They opened the door at the end of the corridor and stared out across a paved courtyard. Though they had left the darkness of night, here they stood under a blue sky and brilliant sunshine. A forklift truck moved huge barrels of oil around the tarmac, but there was no chain-link fence around this mine. Beyond the pavement they looked out onto a vast horizon of undulating hills.

"Where the hell are we?" Ted asked, stupified.

"Somewhere in the prehistoric past," Danny murmured. "See those trees? They were in a briefing I went to. Can't remember what they are, but they were definitely on one of the slides."

"Brilliant," Lester muttered. "That narrows it down to a few hundred million years."

"Well, if you can do better..."

"I will, when I get my hands on whoever's in charge. Come on. We need some answers." At that he stepped out into the sunshine with Danny and Ted following close behind him, brandishing their rifles. The forklift driver didn't notice them. Danny thought he was speaking to someone, then realised he had headphones on and was singing along to his music.

They made their way around the side of the huge complex, eyes peeled for anyone —or anything — that might present a threat. It took a moment to navigate the low walls of sandbags that seemed to mark out space on the concrete floor, but not in any way that made obvious sense.

While the mine didn't have an electrified fence running round it, they noted that it did have heavy artillery. What might have been anti-tank guns stood at various strategic positions, and Lester pointed out mortars and rocket launchers as they passed.

"But this stuff can't be for keeping dinosaurs at bay," Danny said.

"It's like they're expecting a war," Lester observed.

"Yeah, but only at this end of the mine. Look, there aren't any other guns about. Why just defend this corner?"

"The sandbags," Ted said. "You think they keep the oil separate from the guns?"

They looked and realised he was right. The sandbags would effectively stop any leakages from reaching around this far. Oil would be channelled away around the building, well clear of the guns. With the bare concrete in between the bags now dazzling in the sun, it looked like a dried-out river.

And then, without warning, something charged at them.

Danny fired before he'd even taken it in. A bullet spanged off the armoured scales of a Postosuchus as it bore down on him. Lester dived, grabbing Danny and knocking him out of the way. Lying on his back on the floor, Danny fired again, smacking the creature in the soft flesh where its leg met the underside of its belly. The creature let out a shriek, claws skittering round on the concrete floor as it sought to come at him again. In the blur of movement, he thought he saw some kind of dark collar around its neck, almost like a domestic cat.

Ted knelt on one knee and fired two shots in succession at the dinosaur's soft underside. The bullets slammed hard into the creature, dark blood spitting out of the single deep wound. The Postosuchus tottered forward, not quite in control of its legs. Ted fired again, but the creature lowered its head and the bullet spanged off its armoured jaws.

When it regained its balance, it had a renewed hunger in its eyes.

It lunged forward again. Danny and Ted both fired shot after shot, but the creature wouldn't be stopped. It opened its massive jaws wide and Danny watched in horror as it snapped up Ted in a single bite. He didn't even have the opportunity to cry out.

The Postosuchus chewed greedily as it turned to face Danny and Lester. Danny fired again and again, anger coursing through him, but the creature stood its ground. And then a brilliant light blazed round its neck. The beast whimpered and lay down on the ground.

Soldiers ran forward, all but one pointing guns at Danny and Lester. The last soldier handled some kind of remote control that seemed to subdue the creature. Danny put his rifle down on the ground and let them come over to cuff him.

"Oh dear, oh dear," a voice said, and they turned to see that it belonged to a man with cropped hair and beard, who appeared from behind the soldiers. His muscles bulged inside an immaculate suit. "How very unpleasant. Another death to add to your woeful record. Isn't that right, James?"

Lester regarded the newcomer with cool contempt.

"Friend of yours?" Danny asked.

"Oh yes," the man said. "We go back a long way, James and I. Name's Tom. Tom Samuels."

Lester sighed wearily. “We were at the same school, but we were never exactly friends. You were always so...” he looked up at the sky as he searched for the right word, “keen.”

Danny turned back to the suited man, to see his eyes burning with barely contained anger. The soldiers were looking back at him, too, not quite hiding smiles.

Oh, thought Danny, *this is going to be good.*

TWENTY-SEVEN

It looked as though there was a ranking system governing the way the enormous Sauroposeidons queued to squeeze themselves into the railway tunnel. Connor stood on the grassy verge in the rain, watching. He would have expected the smallest to be shoved out of the way by the bigger ones, but one of the largest creatures had taken the back of the line and seemed to be organising the others.

Behind the huge dinosaurs a number of army vehicles filled the valley. Soldiers leant out of windows or poked through the sunroofs to watch the incredible spectacle. These men had probably all seen combat before, even with other dinosaur species, but the Sauroposeidons were probably the largest that even Connor had dealt with. They moved with such careful grace, such consideration for each other, he could easily forget the cold and the rain falling on him just watching them.

Then at last the herd were all through and the traffic-warden dinosaur squeezed itself in after them.

That was when Connor and Becker dared to slip down the slope behind it, lugging the locking mechanism and its tripod between them. Connor stood in the tunnel entrance, watching the creature's tail slip into the darkness.

The tunnel stank of sweaty, wet dinosaur and the tang of the catnip they had been pursuing. The military man shone his torch and they could just make out the tail tip of the last Sauroposeidon some way up ahead. Slowly, keeping their distance, they followed on behind. They had to lock the anomaly once the creatures were all through, to ensure they didn't come back.

"Nothing to this one," Becker said cheerily as they reached the glinting shards of light that indicated the anomaly.

"Don't jinx it!" Connor insisted as he worked on setting up the locking mechanism. "We haven't got Abby back yet."

"You know, you may want to give her some space," Becker told him.

Connor looked up at him. "What?"

"I said she probably needs some space."

"Hey, me and Abby, we're just mates, that's all. And we work together. And we used to share a flat. Anything else makes things all complicated."

Becker nodded, an infuriating smile on his face. He didn't seem to want to leave it alone.

"Actually, I meant you need to leave some space around the anomaly so Abby doesn't run you over. She is in a car."

"Oh, yeah. Good point." Connor stepped back so that he was leaning against the chipped, ancient brick wall of the tunnel as he calibrated the locking mechanism.

"So you and Abby..." Becker began.

"What about me and Abby?"

"There's nothing going on there?"

Connor sighed. "No, there's nothing going on there."

"But you'd like there to be?..."

"There's nothing going on between us," Connor repeated, his tone exasperated.

"Right, so you wouldn't mind if I asked her out?"

"What?" Connor gaped in horror.

"Well, if there's nothing going on between you two, maybe I could ask her out."

"No!" Connor snapped. "It would never work. You and her aren't suited!"

Becker shrugged. "Why not? I've got great prospects. I'm good looking, talented, experienced. And I'm an officer, too... You know what they say about girls and the uniform."

Connor stared at him, appalled.

"Abby's not like that," he said quietly. "She doesn't want a soldier boy. She wants... Well, she'd probably rather have... I don't know," he shrugged defeated. "Maybe you *should* ask her out."

Becker slapped Connor on the arm.

"Don't be daft," he said, grinning broadly. "Everyone can see she's only got eyes for you."

Connor took a moment to digest this.

"Really? Everyone?"

"What are you stalling for, Connor? Go on, ask her out."

"I will! Just, you know, in my own time," he tailed off.

Becker laughed. "One thing I've learnt on this job, Connor: there's no time like the present."

They gazed at the glinting, twisting anomaly.

"All right. As soon as she comes back through, I'm going to ask Abby if she wants —"

He tailed off. Something moved inside the anomaly, a dark shape that was twisting and turning. Becker readied his rifle. Connor aimed the locking mechanism. They stood ready as the shape coalesced... and Abby staggered out of the light.

"You're," she said, gasping for breath, "you're gonna ask me if I want what?"

Connor grinned sheepishly. "It can wait. Are you okay?"

"Sure, but we've got a slight problem."

"More dinosaurs on their way?" Becker asked, and he turned a wary eye to the anomaly. "Maybe we'd better close it up."

"No, worse. We need all your men up here, right now."

The soldier lay curled up in a foetal position, his hands between his legs, moaning in agony. Sarah grabbed his rifle and turned to face the other one, who was getting to his feet and fumbling for the pistol at his hip.

"Drop it," she told him. He let the gun slip from his fingers and it clattered on the metal grating as he raised his hands.

The third soldier, the man with the remote control, stood watching them. Sarah waved her rifle at him.

"Over here." She tried to sound calm, but her hands were shaking as they gripped the heavy gun.

The man knelt down beside the other soldier. Sarah reached for the remote control in his hand, but before she could grab it, he quickly jabbed one of the buttons. She grabbed for it again, but as he snatched it away all she managed to do was knock it out of his fingers.

"No, wait!" Sarah cried.

The control box spun through the air and shattered across the grating. They all turned to watch as the blaze of energy around the creature's neck disappeared. For an instant it didn't seem to realise what had happened. Then it leapt towards them.

The kneeling soldier lunged for the pistol, but Sarah instinctively kicked it across the room before he could reach it. So the man grabbed her ankle and heaved her leg out from under her. She fell back hard onto the grating, but managed to keep her grip on her gun, and slapped him in the face with the rifle.

Sarah rolled, looking up at the creature's hungry jaws as it closed in on her. There was only one option. She pulled back hard on the trigger of her rifle, unleashing a volley of bullets that smacked into the underside of its long, gnashing head and neck. Appalled at what she was doing, she kept on firing, gritting her teeth against the pain of the recoil as the gun bounced in her arms and bashed into her shoulder.

More by luck than judgement, she managed to fire into the creature's soft underbelly. It cried out, blood leaking from a series of deep wounds. She kept firing as it leapt to her right, landing its huge claws and teeth on the soldier who was still clutching his groin.

Sarah turned away as the creature tore the man apart. The soldier with the pistol was on his feet now, firing into the creature's long face in an effort to save his comrade. The third soldier cowered behind him, desperately trying to put the broken pieces of the control box back into some kind of working order.

Sick with panic and fear, Sarah got to her feet and ran for the door. It had two long metal handles and a complex-looking safety lock. She slung the rifle on her back to free both her hands, and lifted the upper handle while pulling back on the lower. The heavy door heaved open just enough for her to squeeze through.

She glanced back at the two soldiers. The crocodile-like creature had finished with their friend and was advancing on them. Sarah watched in horror as the man with the gun stood his ground. He fired a shot right at the creature. It roared with pain, then took another step towards him. He fired again.

The gun clicked, the magazine empty.

The creature charged.

Sarah ran through the door — right into more soldiers. They stared at her in amazement.

"Quick!" she shouted, pointing behind her urgently, and they hurried through the door, firing a volley of bullets at the dinosaur that was feasting on their comrades.

She paused for a moment to catch her breath, then hefted the rifle from her shoulder and started running.

They emerged from the anomaly onto undulating plains of soft brown earth, the brilliant sunshine sparkling off their vehicles. Across the plain, the herd of enormous Sauroposeidons continued to trash the car Abby had driven through, nosing with long, slender necks at the broken metal and glass.

"Yeah, definitely Early Cretaceous," Connor said, scrutinising the landscape for the tell-tale conifer ferns. "Aptian or Albian epoch. I need a bit more time to be sure."

"We might have more pressing concerns," Becker told him as the small fleet of army cars and trucks continued to emerge from the anomaly. Anything that could fit into the railway tunnel had been ordered back in time. Connor knew Becker's soldiers were competent, hand-picked men who would have followed their captain anywhere. But he had seen the excitement that rippled through them at the chance of a tour back some 110 million years. As one they seemed to be thinking, *Yeah, this could be a pretty good gig.*

As he waited until all the vehicles had come through, he set to work on the locking mechanism, now set up in the back of one truck. At last they were ready, and Connor fired the locking mechanism, fixing the anomaly as a floating, solid sphere. The hope was that it then wouldn't close and trap them all there. The cars and trucks parked up around them, the soldiers assembling to hear their orders. They gazed around the incredible, alien scenery, not cracking the usual crass jokes or teasing one another. Instead they stood in silence, struck dumb with awe and wonder. The vast, cloudless sky, the scrubby alien world.

But their eyes were inevitably drawn to the ugly canker on the virgin landscape, the squat mine belching black smoke into the otherwise perfect sky.

Becker, though, was quickly giving orders, getting the trucks and guns aligned in a defensive formation, a ring like a wagon train expecting trouble from the Injuns. *Becker always likes to play things safe*, Connor thought. He, on the other hand, was anxious to get moving. This mine demanded their attention. Why bother hanging around up on the slope?

"So, what's the plan?" Connor asked Becker. "We just go down there and knock on the door. 'Hi, we're new to the area...' What then?"

"They're ready for a fight," Becker said, using binoculars to survey the factory. "I can see a Starstreak HVM system, like we used in Iraq."

"Oh, yeah, one of those." Connor scrutinised the front of the factory, but all he could see was a long wall of barrels and a few cumbersome machines.

"Is that some kind of rocket launcher?" Abby asked, pointing.

"Short-range surface-to-air missiles," Becker explained. "For shooting down enemy aircraft. They've got howitzers, too, and some things I don't recognise. Well, not the specific models, anyway. The gist of it is that they could pound us into the ground without really thinking about it."

"They're flying the Union Jack, though." Connor pointed at the rather tawdry rectangle flapping in the breeze. "So they've got to be on our side. Stands to reason. Right?"

"Only one way to find out. Wilcock!"

"Sir."

"We're going to take a car down there. Nice and slow. Show them we all want to be friends."

Wilcock saluted. "Sir."

Becker followed him to one of their SUVs. As he clambered into the front seat, Abby and Connor hurried after him.

"Don't worry," he said, "I did diplomacy at Sandhurst. Piece of cake."

"But we should come with you!" Connor insisted.

"No, you should stay up here by the anomaly and the dinosaurs.

That's your speciality, isn't it? And this is mine — I'll take care of it. Everything will be fine."

"Hang on," Abby said, "you're meant to take orders from us."

Becker smiled at her.

"I'm head of security, so this is my area. It's not dinosaurs, but men with a barrage of anti-tank weapons. Soldier stuff. It's fine."

"The more you keep saying that..." Connor responded, knowing it just couldn't be right. If there were British people back in time, why hadn't the ARC been informed? The only reason he could think of was that these people weren't *wholly* on their side.

"Yes, I know," Becker said, and he nodded, seeming to read Connor's thoughts. "So keep your fingers crossed."

And with that the car started forward, making its way gingerly down the slope towards the heavily fortified facility.

"Keep it slow," Becker told Wilcock as they trundled down towards the mine. He withdrew the SIG .229 from the pouch at his thigh and checked the magazine.

"We're not expecting fireworks, are we, sir?" Wilcock said.

"You got something to be rushing home to, have you?"

Wilcock shrugged. "Game against Arsenal tomorrow, I suppose. But don't fancy our chances much. Or with the football, either."

Becker smiled, slotting the pistol back into the pouch.

"You know what they used to tell us at Sandhurst?"

"It's not the winning that matters..."

"It's the money and pretty girls."

They continued on. Ahead of them a group of soldiers emerged from the mine, alert and carrying rifles.

"Um, sir," Wilcock said, "aren't they wearing uniforms like ours?"

The soldiers carried H&K G36s and wore exactly the same black body armour as Becker and his men. Their boots, the guns in their hip pockets... They were definitely the same issue.

"Well, that makes things easier," Becker said, somewhat reassured. "Guess they *are* on our side."

Wilcock continued to drive slowly down towards the soldiers, anxious not to cause them any undue concern. The soldiers continued to gather around the front of the mine, grouped in formation, showing that they had been well drilled. Men stood by the anti-tank and anti-aircraft stations. More soldiers appeared, wielding the kind of handheld rocket launchers and mortars Becker hadn't used since he'd been seconded from the regular army.

"I expect that's some kind of hero's welcome," Wilcock said nervously. "Rather than, you know, a show of force."

"Keep going," Becker told him, though he, too, didn't like the look of this. Surely the two of them in this one ordinary SUV wouldn't present any kind of threat. Anyway, there were rules of engagement. They were meant to parlay first.

Something rocketed up into the air from in front of the mine, a dark blur, moving almost too fast for Becker to follow with his eye. A half-second later he heard the crump of the mortar that had fired it.

"Wilcock!" he yelled, but the man was already reacting, swinging the car around sharply and putting his foot down. They sped away as the mortar smacked hard into the brown earth behind them, only yards from where they'd been. The explosion slapped against the back of their car.

Wilcock zigzagged, trying to present less of an easy target. But as they sped back up the way they had come, Becker realised they were in serious trouble. A single car, exposed out in the open, and none of the other vehicles higher up on the plain had anything like the resources they would need for this sort of fight.

"Retreat," he told his earpiece. "Everyone back to London. *Now.*"

A second mortar exploded ten metres to their right. Wilcock swerved, swearing under his breath.

Seconds later, a third mortar crashed down so close behind them it shattered the back window.

Connor gaped at the missiles as they rained down on Becker's tiny car. Abby cried out.

"What are they doing? We come in peace!"

"Sir," said a female soldier nearby. A moment later Connor realised she was talking to him. He turned to face the serious-looking woman who was saluting him.

"Yes, um," he said, "er, sorry, what's your name?"

"Goldman, sir. Captain Becker has radioed to say we're to retreat back to London."

"Right, thank you Goldman, good plan. I'd better unlock the anomaly, then."

"Yes, sir."

Connor followed her over to the truck where they had stowed the locking mechanism. Vaguely enjoying the way the soldiers demurred to him, Connor worked the controls with a flourish, and a few moments later the locking mechanism powered down.

Yet the anomaly remained locked, a solid sphere floating serenely in the air.

"Oh," Connor said, "that shouldn't happen."

An explosion sounded only a few metres down the hill from them. Mud pattered down onto his head.

Abby ran over to him.

"Come on, Connor. They're almost on us!"

"Yeah," Connor said, frantically working the controls, "but this thing isn't working." He twiddled a dial and bashed at it with his fist, then stared down the end of the machine. A terrible thought struck him.

"It's not this, it's *them*. They must be locking the anomaly from somewhere in the factory. They've trapped us all here."

TWENTY-EIGHT

Sarah tiptoed to a junction in the corridor and checked around the corner for soldiers, her rifle at the ready. The floors, walls and ceiling were covered with large, plain-coloured tiles. The sound of her steps echoed down the hallway, so she was moving as lightly as she could. Her nose itched from a familiar greasy tang in the air, though it took her a moment to place the sensation. The place smelt like the forecourt of a petrol station. Whatever industry they carried out here, it needed lots of petrol and, judging by the tiles, it was a dirty job.

She had no idea where she was going. It occurred to her that if she was lucky, the creature would have killed the soldiers so they couldn't raise the alarm that she'd escaped. Then she felt awful for thinking that, and the fact that her best bet was to have a prehistoric monster on the loose behind her.

She tried to keep calm, to focus on her goals. Her immediate priorities were not to get caught and to find out where she was. The fact that this was some kind of industrial complex suggested that the anomaly had brought her into the future, not the past. Yet the soldiers and their equipment didn't look especially futuristic... She passed a drinks dispenser. The cans of Coke and Fanta were all £1. She thought that sounded a bit expensive — a price from the future, maybe. But then she couldn't remember when she'd last used a machine like this herself, or how much the cans had been.

What she needed was a look outside. The anomaly had appeared right inside Lester's office, which meant — she assumed — that perhaps these people could control them. Perhaps she'd not been transported in time at all.

She heard footsteps in front of her, and dashing back the way she'd come, she hid herself around the back of the drinks machine, hugging the rifle to her body.

I'll be okay, she thought, *so long as they walk on past; so long as they don't want to use the machine.*

Seconds later, two soldiers strode past her, the thick soles of their boots slapping on the tiles, the noise echoing loudly down the corridor.

"Be over before dinner break," said one. "Sitting ducks out there."

The other soldier nodded.

"It's not a fight, just target practice."

Their footsteps faded as they walked on down the corridor together.

Sarah let out a long breath, listened carefully for a moment, then swept her long dark hair out of her face and continued on her way.

Moments later, she came to another junction. She sighed with frustration, if she could only calm down and get her bearings... She seemed to have followed a route around a central space. The soldiers' conversation suggested they were engaged in some kind of battle, which they were winning. It could be a fight against future creatures, though what they'd said seemed to imply they were fighting humans.

She picked a corridor at random and found herself approaching double doors. She could see bright sunlight through a panel of glass set in the upper part of the doors. Fearful of someone passing on the other side, she pressed herself against the wall as she approached.

Sarah peered through the windows, her arms shaking as she held onto the heavy rifle. She looked out across a forecourt filled with soldiers, all dressed in the same black uniforms as Becker's men. These soldiers were in the thick of a battle, running around, manning large guns and loading rocket launchers.

Suddenly the rockets were going off. She squinted through the bustle and smoke, but couldn't see what they were firing at. It looked like something high up on the muddy plain ahead, obscured by the weight of explosions. But nothing seemed to be firing back.

People were coming. Sarah flattened herself back against the wall. She heard a solider outside swipe something, and the doors beeped, opening automatically.

She found herself bombarded by noise: the boom and crash of heavy artillery, the whoosh of missiles blasting off.

The door swung fast towards her.

Sarah thought for a moment that she might be crushed; the door opened right up to the wall, leaving her squeezed into a tiny triangle of space. Through the slender window she watched a large party of soldiers passing through.

"Don't underestimate them," she heard someone say, a voice she thought for a moment she recognised. "The longer they're up there, the more time they've got to come up with ideas."

Some of the soldiers ran back out into the fighting, and the doors closed slowly behind them. Sarah remained pinned against the wall, paralysed with fear.

A platoon of about twenty soldiers had their backs to her as they marched away into the complex. To her horror she saw that they had prisoners: Danny, Lester and Samuels were being led off under heavy guard. And only Sarah and her one little rifle had any chance of rescuing them.

They were thrown off their feet as an army truck exploded, struck dead-on by a mortar. Deafened and dazed, Connor helped Abby up, and they ran with the soldiers, all covered in mud and blood, retreating up the slope away from the onslaught. The floating ball of the anomaly glimmered tantalisingly in front of them, still firmly locked. Connor's locking — and unlocking — mechanism lay in pieces amongst the burning vehicles.

A missile smacked into the anomaly and burst into pink flame. They paused to watch as the phenomenon absorbed most of the blast. Connor made a mental note to investigate that when they got back home.

He turned to Abby, and reaching over, wiped some of the dirt from her face with the back of his sleeve. Then they continued running up the plain, following the few vehicles that were still in one piece. They wanted to keep as near to the locked anomaly as possible, but that just made them easy targets.

The ground sloped upwards ahead of them for about a mile. Further up the slope in front of them cantered the herd of Sauroposeidons, lowing with distress at the ongoing barrage.

"You okay?" Connor asked Abby, not sure if he was shouting.

She nodded.

"It's weird," she said, panting slightly, "we've been trapped and knocked out, and dragged off by dinosaurs. But being shot at by British soldiers is a new experience."

"Yeah, gotta love this job," he said wearily. "Every day it's different."

"Get back!" a soldier yelled as he ran towards them.

Connor looked up to see that something had just *thunk*ed into the earth behind him. They both turned quickly, ran a few steps and were blown through the air by the explosion.

Connor lay in the soft earth, and his whole body felt like one great bruise. Someone grabbed his arms and tried to drag him to his feet. Soon he found himself behind an upturned truck — cover from the barrage of explosions. He just let them take charge, too stunned to think for himself.

"Connor." It was Becker's voice. His lip was bleeding slightly and he looked wild-eyed, his usually perfect hair dishevelled and his face spattered with blood and dirt. "We need to fight back."

"Yeah," Connor said, trying to blink the dizziness away, "Good plan. Why aren't you firing?"

"We can't — our rifles don't have the range."

"And that's not much good anyway," Abby said, appearing behind Becker, "rifles against what these guys have got." As if to make the point, a mortar smashed down not far from where they stood, the impact reverberating up their legs. Mud drizzled down on them.

Funny, Connor thought, *how you almost get used to it after a while.*

"But you were firing," he said to Becker. "I saw you."

"Yeah, we had this idea we could hit their oil barrels. Knock them over, set them on fire. Anything just to kick back."

"What did you have in mind?"

"We've not got a lot of equipment with us, just whatever was in the back of the trucks. Some planks and bits of pipe, a few good lengths of rope."

"We could build a fence," Abby suggested.

"I was thinking of a trebuchet," Becker said.

Abby and Connor stopped to stare at him. For just an instant the noise of the battleground faded out.

"A what?" Connor said.

"A trebuchet," Becker repeated. "You know, a big catapult. Like they used for storming castles."

"Yeah, I know, I'm a genius, remember. I know a thing or two about castles."

"And *Star Wars* and coding and really weird films," Abby put in.

Connor stuck his tongue out at her. "Just the good ones."

"So," Becker said, interrupting their exchange, "what do you reckon? If we stand still too long, they're going to hit us. So we'd have to do it quickly."

Connor scratched his chin, then ducked round the truck they were hiding behind to look back down the ravaged, muddy plain to the huge factory far below. The anti-tank rockets flashed and thudded. *Oh yeah*, he thought. They could take all that out with a few bits of wood and some string. He turned to the others to say so. And found them watching him eagerly, waiting on him to save them.

"Yeah, I think we could do something..." he said. "Abby, we'll need something for the trebuchet to throw. Rocks or explosives or —"

A terrible sound came from further up the hill. The Sauroposeidons were keening loudly. One of them had been battered in the blast of an explosion, shrapnel in the form of wood and twisted metal protruded from its side. It persevered for a moment, taking a few faltering steps forward, its bulky, tree-trunk legs struggling in the churned up earth. And then it simply stopped and fell over on its side.

The Sauroposeidons cried out again, their long slender necks reaching high into the smoky sky. The vast, placid creatures filled their throats with bassline, a growl of sound Connor could feel deep in his guts.

"You wouldn't like them when they're angry," he murmured.

"No," Becker agreed, spitting blood. "Damn it," he said. "They're attacking defenceless creatures."

Connor had never known him swear before. He turned to Abby, and she had that serious, bright look in her eyes which meant she'd had an idea.

"Oh no, what?" he asked her.

"Have some faith," she told him. "You're gonna *love* this one."

TWENTY-NINE

"Let me guess," Lester said, squinting in the bright sunshine as the soldiers stripped him of the lab coat he had purloined, "you're working with Christine Johnson."

Samuels looked puzzled.

"Christine? Haven't thought of her in years. Is she even still alive?" Behind him, a soldier hurried over from the anti-tank artillery.

"Oh, yes," Lester said, grimly. "Very much so."

The soldier spoke to Samuels in a low voice and received an order in response. He saluted and ran back to his post. Samuels then addressed the armed men who surrounded them. "Let's take them inside."

The soldiers crowded close to Danny and Lester, cocooning them as they made their way around the side of the building. Behind them, more soldiers readied the huge anti-tank guns. Danny glanced up the plain rising high into the distance, and could just make out a series of small vehicles. They didn't look like much of an adversary, more like target practice.

What's going on?

The tethered Postosuchus sat chewing on what remained of Ted. When Danny looked around again, he found Samuels watching him.

"You could have stopped your guard dog before it killed him," Danny growled.

"Yes," Samuels admitted, "but it proved a useful point. You noticed how James hid behind you and the unfortunate zoo keeper?"

"We were the ones with guns."

"How convenient. No, James did what he always does, protected himself at the expense of everyone else. You should remember that."

"Of course, that's what this is all about," Lester said, managing to smirk despite their unfortunate position. He turned in Danny's direction. "Once upon a time, Tom worked with me in planning civil contingencies. You know the sort of thing —what the government would do in the case of an attack from outer space. And I made the awful *faux pas* of having him fired. It's aged you, Tom."

"See, Danny, that's the kind of man you're working for. He will try to ruin your career, just as he tried to destroy mine." Samuels said coolly.

"No, *you* tried to ruin *me*," Lester insisted, equally cool. "You went over my head to the Minister. He had the good sense to ask for my response and I merely suggested some of the weak spots in your plan. If you'd had any grasp of military history..."

"It was a set up, as well you know."

"As I said, if you'd had any grasp of military history, you wouldn't have blundered in. But they didn't throw you out because of what I said. It's what you did yourself. They just didn't like how you behaved. And they still won't."

"You will pay for what you did to me," Samuels threatened darkly.

"So it seems. I suppose I should be flattered that you've had to go to all this effort."

They reached a set of double doors that led into the complex, and a soldier stepped forward to swipe his pass card. Danny and Lester looked back as they waited, and saw the anti-tank gun being readied. Seconds later, it boomed, and they saw a missile streak out across the sky, heading right for the lone vehicle far off up the plain.

Samuels followed their gaze.

"There's a better view inside," he said, "and I think you'll want to take advantage of it."

The door sighed open, and Danny and Lester were escorted down tiled corridors, the air tangy with the stink of oil. Danny's eyes darted left and right, picking over the details. Perhaps he would spot an opportunity for escape, should their troop of armed guards suddenly all look the other way. But then, as much as he wanted to escape, he was also curious to hear what Samuels had to say for himself. So he contented himself with memorising the route back to the exit.

They felt the reverberation as the massive guns outside fired and fired again.

"So," he said to Samuels, "you going to tell us what's going on?"

Lester sighed. "I'd have thought it was obvious, Quinn."

"You lured us out here to kill us," Danny said, "so, what, you could take Lester's job?"

"And there's this place, as well," Lester added.

Tom Samuels turned to regard him.

"Oh, you think you've got it all figured out, do you?"

"You've built a mine in the past to pump oil out to the twenty-first century," Lester said, rolling his eyes as if the whole thing rather bored him. "It's more than a little reckless, don't you think? You endanger the very fabric of our existence just to fuel the world's SUVs and make the oil barons rich. Leave the past to the experts."

"Experts?" Samuels crowed. "Nick Cutter was a madman — you say so in your own reports. You refer to him as 'unhinged' and 'obstinate'."

They turned off the main corridor and marched along a passageway that Danny felt he almost recognised. He looked around at Lester, who raised an eyebrow and nodded towards the swing doors ahead of them. Yes, thought Danny, there was something tantalisingly familiar about all this.

"You've got a very simplistic understanding of the work we've done," Lester said, "the kinds of issue that are involved. Perhaps you should leave it alone until you've caught up on the reading."

Samuels scoffed at him.

"You don't know the first thing about what we're doing here, or the evidence that backs it up. But let me show you."

With that he pushed through the swing doors at the end of the corridor, and led them into the main operations room of the ARC.

Sarah stayed hidden behind the door until it had closed and the soldiers escorting Danny, Lester and Samuels had turned a corner. She remained motionless, willing them not to see her.

All sorts of questions buzzed through her mind as she ventured cautiously after them. How had Danny and Lester got here when they were meant to be in South Africa? Who was being shoot at outside — did Danny and Lester have allies? Had they been spirited through an anomaly, just as Samuels had?

She reached the corner they'd turned down, and stopped to listen for their footsteps. Hearing nothing, she poked her head around the corner. The corridor was empty. Rooms branched off on either side, and there was another pair of swing doors at the end. Light glimmered behind the blue-glass windows set high into the doors, suggesting activity beyond.

Still clutching her rifle, she headed towards the swing doors, which looked a lot like the ones that led into the ARC's operations room. These people, whoever they were, also wore the same uniforms as the guards back home. They had lots of equipment and staff, and seemed able to control the anomalies.

Perhaps this was the ARC, but a few years ahead of her own time? Previous anomalies had always linked to the distant past or the far future, but there was no evidence to suggest that they couldn't link to a more recent time.

She made her way carefully to the doors, standing on tiptoes to look through the panels of blue glass.

Danny, Lester and Samuels were surrounded by armed soldiers in what looked like the operations room of the ARC. Sarah's heart beat hard in her chest as she gripped her rifle and lowered herself back down, looking back the way she had come. The rooms leading off the corridor might well have once been the labs and canteen back on the other side of the anomaly. It was as if someone had extended their building and tiled its interior.

It appeared she'd turned up in the future.

But what should she do next?

Danny stared, trying to make sense of what had just happened. Gradually he realised this wasn't the operations room he knew, just somewhere very like it. The lighting was slightly different, more pinkish than pale blue and grey. A squat, heavy computer bank ran alongside another ADD, coloured lights winking. But what really made it different was the empty space at the centre of the room.

Without Connor and Sarah's high tables piled with complex bits of machinery that they hadn't quite got working, it felt empty and bereft, like a house after all the people had moved out.

The soldiers kept tightly around Lester and Danny as they passed through the room. They made their way to the ADD, a perfect copy but for the sixth large screen. Danny thought for a moment it showed news footage, but it soon dawned on him that he was watching the battle that was taking place just outside. Missiles smacked down into the brown earth beside a glinting anomaly. The scene played out in silence, a strangely distancing effect. Even when he recognised the tiny figures running through the mud between the scant bits of cover, it took a moment to sink in.

"That's Abby and Connor," he said quietly. He turned on Samuels, shouting now: "You're firing on Abby and Connor!"

Samuels ignored him to focus on Lester.

"Don't worry, we'll make it quick."

"You can't!" Danny said, taking a step forward. The soldiers jabbed their guns into his chest and neck. He backed up, arms raised in surrender. "For God's sake, they don't stand a chance."

He watched in mounting horror as projectiles rained down on his friends. The ARC team seemed to be far enough away to make accurate bombing difficult, and they were constantly moving, making them even more challenging targets. He saw Becker, blood and muck all over him, help Connor to his feet. He watched them talking quickly, with lots of hand movements. Even against impossible odds, he could see them struggling to find an answer.

If only he could help them. A distraction, a moment's grace — anything.

One of the other screens showed the coordinates of an anomaly, the word 'Locked' flashing beside it. It must mean the floating ball of the locked anomaly he could see in the other screen; otherwise surely his friends could escape back home. He tried to move closer to check, but a soldier prodded him back into place. Danny shook with frustration at being unable to save his friends.

Samuels casually leant an elbow on the large computer bank.

"This is just the start. Think of me as a new broom, sweeping out the old regime."

Lester didn't respond. When Danny looked over at him, he thought he saw something over his shoulder. Through the narrow window in the double doors — it was the ghost of a silhouette, the top of someone's head. Then it disappeared.

That looked like...

No, he thought, *it couldn't be.* Based on the height of the windows, he made a guess at how tall the person would have been, reckoning about five foot five.

Yeah, that's about right.

He turned to Samuels. *Now, how to stall for time...*

"Like what you've done with the place," he said genially. "Much tidier all round."

He punched the soldier next to him with a mean right hook, sending him toppling into the ADD.

A second soldier came forward to take a swing at him and Danny dodged under his fist. Catching it, he tugged the man off balance and kneed him in the chest.

Lester lashed out at a soldier who was raising his gun, and Danny kicked out at a fourth. Someone clubbed him in the back with a rifle. He ignored the sudden pain in order to twist round and kick out. Another soldier kicked him in the back of the knee, sending pain flaring right through his leg. He stumbled and they kicked at him again.

Danny smacked hard into the floor, his whole body aflame.

He tried to rise and they kicked him back down. He twisted his head to see Lester pinioned between two soldiers.

"Well," Samuels said grimly, straightening his tie, "I think you've outstayed your welcome, Mr Quinn." He turned to one of the soldiers and gestured. "Take him outside and —"

But the order died in his throat.

Lying on the cold, hard floor, Danny struggled to look around and see why. Samuels was staring at the swing doors where Sarah stood, wielding a rifle. There was a terrible, haunted look in her eyes. A look that dared suggest she might use the gun in her hands.

"Let them go," she told the soldiers as she walked slowly forward.

THIRTY

Danny lay on the floor, soldiers training their rifles on him. Lester stood, but was held tight by two more soldiers. And Samuels was trapped up against the computer bank running next to the ADD. Soldiers surrounded him, and were aiming their rifles at Sarah.

"Sarah," Samuels said warmly, "how good of you to join us."

"Get out of here!" Danny yelled at her. "Save —" A soldier kicked him in the ribs, cutting him off.

"Sarah understands what has to be done," Samuels said confidently. To her surprise and confusion, he nudged around the soldiers and walked slowly out towards her. "Sarah understands about the future. She's convinced me that we need to open up the ARC, go public with what we've discovered about the anomalies and creatures. There's several million years of untapped potential just waiting for us to exploit it."

She didn't understand why the soldiers didn't stop him. Was he working with them? She raised the gun, aimed it right at his chest — but she knew she would never pull the trigger.

So did Samuels; he reached Sarah and plucked the rifle from her hands.

"Everything is going to be all right," he told her, taking her by the arm. Sarah allowed him to lead her back to the soldiers, eyes flicking to Danny and Lester, trying to make sense of it all. What was going on?

Then the truth began to dawn on her. She realised Samuels had never been interested in her ideas, had never thought she was right to go public.

To him, she was just another way to get back at Lester.

"I thought you were smarter than this," Lester said to her coldly.

"Sorry to have disappointed you," she said.

"Samuels, let her go," Danny said. "She doesn't need to be a part of this."

"But she already is," Samuels replied, still holding her arm. "Aren't you, Sarah?"

What could she say? She suddenly remembered the soldiers who'd died, fighting the crocodile-like creature when she'd arrived here. Did Samuels know about them yet?

"I got it wrong," she told him. "Some of the soldiers died. I came to give myself up."

Samuels patted her hand.

"I'm sure we can put right whatever it is. You and me together."

Slowly, she nodded. Yes, she had to put this right.

"You see?" Samuels said to Lester. "Of her own volition, Sarah and I are going to preside over a new era of the ARC."

"You're insane," Danny spat. The soldier kicked him again. He grunted, and Sarah flinched.

"Insane?" Samuels laughed. "Contrary to what James may think, I simply understand history. I've studied the facts. I know what's *meant* to be."

"But Cutter —" Lester began. Samuels cut him dead with a wave of his hand.

"The late-lamented Cutter," he sneered, "devoted his entire life to discrepancies in the fossil record, dinosaurs turning up in the wrong periods. Yet he thought the anomalies were a new phenomenon and that they threaten time itself. They've *always* been here, James. It's how it's always been, creatures moving through history when and where they can. Even human history spells it out, through our myths and legends."

He put an arm around Sarah's shoulder. She managed not to flinch. He thought she was part of his grand scheme, and maybe she could use that. Besides, the academic in her wanted to hear what he had to say, and to understand how the myths all fitted in.

"Cutter," Lester countered, "saw history change. That's what drove him. He could see it unravelling in front of his own eyes."

"Really?" Tom snorted. "I've read the files about Jenny and this Claudia Brown. What do you think is more likely — that he saw history change around that one particular person, or that he concocted the whole thing to make sense of his love life?"

Lester smiled thinly, but remained silent.

"I can *prove* the truth," Tom continued, releasing Sarah so that he could gesture grandly. "This *mine* is proof. It's very existence here explains one of the great scientific mysteries."

"What would that be?" Danny scoffed. "Why there's an industrial complex in the fossil record? You're right, of course — I remember that from all of the college textbooks."

Danny got up on to his knees. He did so warily, moving slowly lest he invite another kick. The soldiers kept their guns on him and wouldn't let him move any further.

"That would be fun, wouldn't it?" Samuels said. "It's the oil itself that provides the answer. Science has never been able to explain how oil is created. Oh, we understand the source — it's the pulp of decayed woodland. But it's the *process* that's confusing. Under biogenic theory, it's always been assumed that the vast majority of oil was biodegraded by oil-eating bacteria. Yet a whole forest should produce many times the amount of oil we find in the seams."

"And you have another idea," Lester said dryly.

"The reason there's not more oil is that this mine has mined it out," Danny said.

"Clever boy — it's the oil from this mine and the ones we've yet to build that create the gap. We've only just begun to explore the vast reserves sitting untapped in the different periods. But the geologic record proves that we succeed. Simply put, there's no other explanation."

"None that you can think of," Lester corrected. "Your *wanting* it to be true doesn't make it fact. These things need to be investigated — *properly*."

"What you mean to say is that mankind is at risk unless you remain in charge," Samuels replied.

"Well, I would have put it a little more modestly."

"The anomalies can be exploited," Samuels continued. "We've got a duty to do so. And it's not going to happen on your watch."

"Oh yes, I'd forgotten, you're not doing this for yourself at all — it's all from a sense of *duty*." Lester looked as if he'd just found something distasteful on the bottom of his shoe.

"Why so cynical?" Samuels asked him. "You were meant to be a public servant, as well."

"And you'll note that I haven't set up a project designed just to line my own pockets," Lester replied.

Samuels chuckled.

"Poor James. When push came to shove, you ended up on the wrong side of history. This time I'll get my way. I'm afraid, Sarah, we need to say goodbye to your former colleagues." He put his arm back around her shoulder. "We won't be seeing them again."

She saw her moment.

"Let me do it."

Samuels removed his arm and regarded her carefully.

"You mean that?"

She nodded, and managed to hold his gaze. At that, a smile edged its way slowly across Samuels's face. She remembered how keen he'd been to show his trust before, when he'd urged her to vindicate Connor.

"I want to believe you're on my side," he told her.

"I'm not on anyone's side," she told him. "It's about doing what's right. Making the difficult decisions."

She scowled at Danny, and saw a sparkle in his eye. Yes, he knew what she was trying to do. He knew he needed to play along.

"I've said it before," Danny muttered to Lester. "She's never really been one of the team."

"It seems not," Lester said, gently. His evident disappointment, though like knife twisting through Sarah's gut, seemed to convince Samuels about her.

He handed her back the rifle.

"Take them out the back. We've an entire menagerie of creatures. Choose whichever one you like, but leave enough to be identified."

It was the ultimate test of her loyalty to him. She nodded. "Sir."

Samuels turned to Lester.

"You see? Sarah understands that this is all already written in history."

Lester said nothing.

Sarah spun round and kicked Samuels in the groin. He fell back with a howl of pain, crashing onto the floor. She jabbed the barrel into his neck.

The soldiers ran forward but Sarah stood firm.

"Don't," she said. "I'll shoot him."

"Keep back," Samuels said through gritted teeth. He was fuming. "Don't make her do anything stupid." He glared at Sarah. "You've made the wrong choice," he told her. "I *am* doing what's right, making the difficult decisions."

"I almost believed you," she said. "I thought you offered us something better. But it just didn't add up."

Again the soldiers took a step forward, eager to help their boss. Sarah, her hands shaking, released the safety on the shotgun. Samuels held up a hand to stop them.

"No, it has to be like this," he answered in a strangled voice, his face pale, almost green. "The fossil record is proof."

"It is proof," Sarah agreed. "But the first indication that your conclusion is wrong is when it says what you *want* to hear. Yeah, history suggests there have been anomalies dotted all through time. But it also shows us the terrible cost they inflicted: mankind beset by monsters."

"But we have the technology to combat those things. It's what the ARC is already doing. I'm just showing you how the anomalies can also be used to our advantage."

"No, you want us to become the monsters, pillaging through time. I thought you were offering us a future, but you just want to burn the past."

Samuels started to get to his feet.

"Don't," Sarah told him. "I *will* shoot you." She glared at the soldiers to emphasise her point.

Samuels looked at her, fear slowly being replaced with contempt.

"You? You're not a killer."

"I just killed two men," she said, unflinching.

He hesitated then, teetering on one knee.

"Shoot him," Lester told her. And for a moment she thought that she might.

"We've got to stop them," Danny said desperately. "We've got to stop them from firing at Abby and Connor."

She glanced at the sixth screen, and saw Connor and Becker in the midst of the barrage, building some kind of contraption out of rope and planks of wood. A missile landed somewhere close, and she lost sight of them in the explosion.

She stared, horrified.

Had they just been killed?

Samuels reached forward and grabbed the rifle from her once more. Then smacked her with it.

Sarah collapsed onto the ground, sobbing. Danny tried to run to her, but the soldiers holding him struck him with their rifles, knocking him to the floor again.

"She's made her decision," Samuels said. "Take her and Quinn outside, and let one of the creatures have them."

"I'm sorry," Sarah told Danny as they were dragged to their feet.

His lip was bleeding and he was covered in dust, blood, and bruises.

"It's okay. You're better than this lot."

"No, she's weaker," Samuels retorted. "And soon she won't even be that."

"Better," Danny insisted. "You might have an army and this mine, but Sarah says you're wrong, and you're too stupid to hear her."

Samuels stepped forward and punched him in the chest. Danny doubled over; he would have collapsed had the soldiers not held onto him.

Lester spoke up.

"At the risk of sounding like a cliché, you're not going to get away with this, Samuels. Questions are always asked. Every politician who thinks they can cover something up gets ruined in the end."

"I can see it now," Danny said, gasping in pain. "'Murder and scandal involving a dreary civil servant.' It'll make all of the papers."

Samuels smiled icily at them.

"Very amusing." He held his hand up, gesturing to the soldiers leading them out. "Wait a moment." He tapped the sixth screen of the ADD. "Your friends are being picked off on the hill outside. When you're all dead, we'll continue to deal with the creatures, and we'll exploit the oil, which *will* mean an end to the energy crisis. Do you really think anyone is going to ask questions when we start delivering what they need?"

"They'll catch up with you," Lester said. "It might take time, but they will."

"But they'll have to find me first. There's nothing that leads to this place but the anomalies — no paper trail, no records. I'm invisible to the twenty-first century, except when I choose to be seen. And with this —" he patted the computer bank running beside the ADD "— I can pop up whenever and wherever I like. They can't touch me. But they'll want my oil."

"You can control the anomalies," Danny said flatly.

"Didn't I say? While Lester insists on finding ways of controlling what you've found, I've been working on *exploiting* your discoveries. The government won't keep on doling out millions of pounds to you without expecting to see some kind of return."

"And so you've got plenty of investors," Lester said. "People willing to help you, in return for a share in your success. Like the game park."

"The game park needs money and political backing, which I can provide. Some of the keepers objected to the regime change, but when the ones we couldn't buy off met with unfortunate ends, it was amazing how quickly the rest came round. It's a dangerous job, working with big game, as you're about to find out. Killed in the line of duty, I'm afraid. You just ran out of luck."

He nodded to one of the soldiers.

"Take him out with the other two. I've had enough of him now."

Lester was escorted by two armed soldiers to join Danny and Sarah at the swing doors. He walked easily, as if out for an afternoon stroll. They had no plan, no way of escape, no chance against so many soldiers, but his eyes burned with anger and defiance.

Danny reached out to take Sarah's hand, but the soldiers jostled them apart as they led them out. Sarah looked around at Danny and smiled. Whatever happened, they were in this together.

And then a huge explosion threw them off their feet.

THIRTY-ONE

Another missile crashed down into the already churned up earth. Mud and stones burst up into the air, raining down hard on the team as they worked frantically.

Two soldiers held onto the contraption of wood and ropes, their eyes on the missiles and mortars as they soared across the sky towards them. They hoped to be able to move should anything come too near, but the more they stood out in the open, the more the odds stacked against them.

Connor and Becker needed to finish this fast.

They had bodged together an A-shaped frame, with a long plank pivoting over the top of it. At one end of the plank they'd nailed a bucket, which now sat up high in the smoky sky. A line of rope snaked down from the bucket, swinging at shoulder height. Becker was busy trying to fix a busted car engine to the other end of the plank where it rested on the ground. Connor looked over, appraising his efforts.

"We need more tension. If we can weight the end of the plank down..."

"Too much weight and it'll snap," Becker responded, muttering at the exertion, his face shiny with sweat.

"We've only got one chance at this. We've got to make it count."

"Yeah, but we don't want it to come down on top of us."

"Haven't you two finished yet?" Abby demanded, lugging over a large cardboard box that had seen better days.

"Getting there," Connor replied. Another mortar burst further up the slope and they flinched as more mud pattered down on their heads.

"They're getting closer," Becker said, not looking up. "If we're lucky, they need three more shots before they hit us."

"Well, come on then! Let's do it now." Connor ran to the rope that was hanging from the bucket on the high end of the plank and tugged on it. Even lifting his feet off the ground, the plank refused to budge.

"The engine's too heavy!" Connor exclaimed, his feet swinging in the air.

Becker and one of the other soldiers rushed over to help, and between the three of them they hauled the plank down, the far end with the engine attached to it heaving up into the sky.

"Quick, Abby!" Connor yelped, his whole body straining to keep hold of the rope.

She reached into the battered box she was holding and with a knife began hacking at the contents. Then Connor and the others were met with the rich stink of catnip. Grey-green dust sparkled in the air. Satisfied, Abby wedged the whole box into the bucket as they held it for her.

"We should test it first," Becker said, teeth clenched with exertion.

Connor shook his head.

"No time. And I don't think this thing will manage a second go."

Abby finished filling the bucket with open, seeping packets of catnip and stepped back.

"All right," she shouted over to them.

"On three," Becker said. "One... Two... Three!"

The rope wrenched away from them as Connor, Becker and the soldier let go. The weight of the engine brought the far end of the plank hurtling back down into the ground, where it thwacked into the earth so hard the last third of the plank snapped. The bucket on the other end heaved up and over, hurling the open packets out into the sky, high over the top of the plain.

They scattered wide as they arced up through the smoke and contrails of the missiles, streaming their own trail of dust behind them. They began to descend slowly, heading towards the mine. Connor thought he saw one bounce off the wall of oil barrels, and another fall in among the anti-tank guns. The rest must have landed nearby.

"Damn," Becker said, watching through binoculars. "That will have to do."

Connor turned to say something, but was silenced by a rumble of thunder. Abby grabbed him by the shoulder.

"We need to get out of the way," she said urgently.

Connor looked up to see the herd of Sauroposeidons racing down the plain towards them. They lowed and grunted with excitement, hunger gleaming in their eyes, having picked up again on the scent of catnip. Nothing would get in their way.

Connor, Abby and the soldiers threw themselves out of the path of the herd. The missiles and mortars kept coming, sailing over the tops of the dinosaurs' long, slender necks and thudding down near the humans.

At first motivated by simple hunger for the weird-smelling stuff, now the dinosaurs were gripped by panic. They raced away from the explosions, faster than before, dragging their legs through the thick mud.

"Down!" Becker yelled and they threw themselves over the lip of a missile crater.

Behind them their makeshift catapult took a direct hit, scattering sharp, burning splinters. Connor held Abby close, trying to protect her. He looked up to see Becker checking on his men. He hadn't made it into the crater in time, and his body armour was bristling with spikes, the shrapnel from the blast. For a moment Connor thought he had been terribly wounded. But while the splinters had got through the fabric of his flak jacket, they hadn't pierced the armour underneath.

From down the plain they heard the rattle of gunfire. They poked their heads over the lip of the crater to gaze down on the mine. The Sauroposeidons were charging towards it, the ground shaking beneath their feet. Soldiers had broken ranks to fire at them with rifles and machine guns, but the creatures weren't going to be stopped.

They smashed into the mine, through the men and machines, and the huge wall of oil barrels quivered under the impact. Then the top line of barrels slowly cascaded backwards. Even from such a distance, Connor was blinded by the brilliant orange light. As he fell back, his face raw with heat, he heard the *whumpf* of the explosion.

Danny stopped Sarah from getting to her feet, instead gesturing to her to follow as he crawled ahead underneath the smoke that had filled the room. The tiles were thick with dust and debris, hot against their hands and knees. Soldiers ran past and over them, screaming orders.

Danny found Lester lying on his back, eyes closed, and leaned over to check for signs of life. He bent his head over Lester's face, using the sensitive skin on his cheek to feel if the man was still breathing.

"Get off me," Lester said, his voice cracked. "I'm not that way inclined."

In spite of everything, Danny smiled.

"We're getting out of here. You want to come?" Lester rolled over, propping himself up on his hands and knees.

They crawled unsteadily down the corridor, the smoke burning at their lungs. Soldiers lay dead on the floor just in front of them.

Danny led the way, moving quickly over and around the bodies, Sarah and Lester following behind.

At the turning in the corridor, Danny made to go right — the direction he and Lester had been brought — but smoke filled the corridor, thick and acrid, occasional flames visible deep within it.

"No," Sarah said hoarsely, tugging at his sleeve, "this way."

She took the lead, crawling around to the left, and as they continued the air seemed to be clearing.

Either that, Danny mused, *or I'm becoming light-headed.*

Their hands and knees protested as they continued on. Eventually, Sarah stopped at a half-open door, the space just wide enough for someone to squeeze through. A soldier lay on his back in the doorway, orange light playing over the deep scars on his face.

"There might be a nasty creature in there," Sarah said, and as Danny looked he could see dents in the half-open door, where something had tried to escape.

"Oh, good," Lester said. "I can see why you brought us here."

"There's also an anomaly, that could take us back to your office in London."

"Ah."

"So we run for it?" Danny said. "One of us might get through."

"But what's to stop that thing following us?"

"I am *not* a thing."

That wasn't Lester's voice. Danny turned to see Tom Samuels, on his feet and pointing a gun at them.

"We thought we'd just slip off," Lester said. "Didn't want the tearful goodbye."

Samuels leered at him. The sleeves of his once immaculate suit were torn and he was covered in dust and muck. Blood oozed from grazes on his face.

"It's over," he said. "I have a back door to your office: all I have to do is step through and lock the anomaly, so you'll all be trapped here. That's revenge enough for me." He wagged the gun at them. "Step back from the door."

Danny was about to lunge at the man when a hand reached out to grasp his shoulder.

"No heroics," Lester said quietly. "Let him go."

Samuels nodded as they backed away from the door.

"Very wise, James. Where there's life there's hope — except when you're trapped a hundred million years out of time. You can't survive, you know; it would change history."

He glanced quickly through the doorway, then backed into it, keeping the gun on them.

"I could shoot you anyway, of course," he said, and Danny moved forward, putting himself in front of Sarah.

Samuels smiled. "Sweet." He stepped back again towards the anomaly.

Danny started towards him.

"You're not going to stop me," Samuels told him.

Danny kept expecting the creature to appear, but it didn't materialise. *Lucky bastard*, he thought.

He decided to stall for time. "One thing before you go: how do you control the anomalies?" he demanded.

With his free hand Tom pulled a small control box from his suit pocket. He held it up. "With this."

"And where did you get that? You've copied everything else from us."

Tom's eyes twinkled.

"Not everything. You're not the only ones researching in this field."

"Who else?" Lester asked casually, but Danny could see the keen urge to know reflected in his eyes. "Was it one of Leek's projects? It makes no difference now, after all..."

"That's true, but won't it drive you mad not to know?"

He turned and leapt into the anomaly. Danny ran forward, squeezing himself through the gap in the doorway. But the portal flickered and winked out before he could reach it.

Danny heaved himself back out into the corridor, battered and exhausted. The smoke filled his lungs, and made him gag for breath.

Peering at him, Sarah's eyes filled with concern.

"We've got to find another way out," she said urgently. Danny nodded, unable to speak. Meanwhile, Lester held his ground, gazing in curiously through the half-open door to where the anomaly had been.

"What?" Sarah said, pulling his arm. "We've got to get out of here."

"Mmm," Lester murmured, "but a creature, you said?" A smile flickered across his face.

Then he followed Danny and Sarah as they raced away down the corridor.

Tom Samuels stood behind the desk in Lester's office — *former* office. Papers were strewn across the floor and the Spartan mask statue lay face down.

Like a king in chess, Samuels thought, *signalling surrender.*

He put the pistol down on the desk and regarded the remote control in his hand. *How best to pass off this gadget to the rest of the ARC's staff?* He'd just slip it into the mess that was Connor's workbench. Then, while they were mourning his death, they'd go through his effects and find it there. The ARC team would have to recruit a new technical wizard, and their first job would be sussing out what this thing did. And then they could rebuild the computer bank, and give him back his mastery over time. It would all seem legitimate and above board; no awkward questions need bother him.

He leaned over to the phone and clicked the topmost button. After a moment a female voice replied.

"Hello there." Samuels couldn't recall the names of the staff who worked the night shift. He'd make sure to learn the names of everyone under his command.

"I wonder if I could prevail upon you to rustle me up some breakfast."

"Uh, sure, Mr Samuels," said the female voice at the other end of the line. "Sorry, but where are you at the moment?"

He frowned at the telephone.

"I'm in my office. *Lester*'s office. You know what I mean."

"What?" the voice cried out. "But Mr Samuels, get out of there! I'm calling security now!"

The phone clicked off, and he stared at it. Surely they couldn't have found him out. No, that just didn't make sense. He walked around the side of the desk, through the adjoining office and towards the door that led onto the balcony overlooking the operations room.

The door wouldn't open.

He looked left and right for a door-release button, but couldn't see one. Soldiers burst through the operations room below him, negotiating the high tables of equipment to get onto the walkway. Samuels sighed. He'd soon get this nonsense sorted out.

He turned to walk back to the desk, ready to look the picture of innocence, but the remote control for the anomalies was still clutched in his hand. He looked around quickly for a good place to hide it. Only then did he catch sight of the blood on the floor.

A heavy trail of it led from his desk out into the secretary's office, where it curled around behind her desk. His heart beating fast, he followed the trail. Something large and thick-scaled lay motionless on the floor.

Samuels gazed down in horror at the creature he recognised as a Postosuchus. But it didn't move. He saw the horrific wounds in its soft belly, and let out a sigh of relief.

Behind him, the security men reached the door of the office. They carried G36s and shotguns. One of them struggled to unlock the door, while the other men waved at him urgently.

"It's perfectly fine," he told them, tapping the creature's snout with his foot. "This thing's dead as a —"

The Postosuchus opened its eyes. The soldiers shouted behind him, but didn't open the door. The Postosuchus raised itself up on its long legs, its breathing slow and ragged.

Samuels took a step back, stabbing at the remote control in his hand.

An anomaly swirled into existence behind him, and he felt its warmth on his back. He took a step towards it.

The Postosuchus launched itself at him.

He turned to run, but before he could take another step the creature's enormous jaws wrapped themselves around his body. His fingers twitched on the remote control he still held tight, but it was too late. Long teeth eased through his flesh as the thing carried him into the light.

The anomaly closed neatly behind them.

THIRTY-TWO

The corridor was still clogged with dark smoke. Coughing, eyes streaming, Danny led Sarah and Lester quickly through the chaos, with no idea where he was headed.

They heard explosions blossom behind them, and all around the ominous *clank* and *crunk* as incredible heat warped through the building.

Any moment now it would collapse.

Up ahead they heard a squawking. Danny glanced at the others. They had little choice but to carry on. The squawking continued, a terrible mêlée of voices. Danny went first, pushing through the thick and twisting haze.

He emerged into a wide bay full of giant creatures. Grey and yellow striped concrete posts marked the boundaries of the force fields containing each of the different species. Danny recognised a family of Postosuchus, snarling and slashing at their invisible cage as the smoke enveloped them. There were two distinct types of theropod, a number of other creatures he couldn't name, and an angry-looking Triceratops.

They stopped and stared at the enormous prehistoric menagerie. After a few moments, Lester spoke up.

"It's just like Leek's facility, the technology is exactly the same."

"I'm not sure," Sarah said, "but I don't think this is right. They're all from different periods, aren't they? And from all around the world."

Lester nodded. "It looks like he's been able to pick and chose his specimens. Something for every occasion."

The animals continued to screech and howl in desperation.

"We've got to save them!" Sarah cried. Danny and Lester exchanged glances.

"We can't help them," Danny told her gently.

"What?" she responded defiantly. "How can you *say* that?"

"We'd never be able to control them all — they'd just eat us."

"But they just want to get away."

"Yes," Lester said, "escaping off into whichever period we're in. A whole collection of creatures from different times. You know what would happen, Sarah."

"You think they'd breed with other creatures?"

"Or they'd just run amok. We can't risk the damage to history."

"But you can't prove they'll do any damage! They might be the very reason that some species evolved like they did!"

Danny put his hand on her shoulder.

"Sarah," he said carefully, "you were the one who told Samuels it doesn't work like that. He claimed to have scientific proof, just because it supported what he wanted. We can't allow ourselves to make the same mistake."

She gazed up into his eyes. Finally, she simply deflated, and he saw her holding back tears.

"I know," she said.

"We have to go."

She glanced around at the enormous creatures wailing in their pens and nodded, allowing herself to be led away through the facility, looking for an exit.

The smokestacks split as they tumbled into the fiery mess of the mine, a great cloud of soot hurling up into the already dirty sky. Away up the hill, Connor looked around from trying to fix his anomaly locking mechanism and thought: *This is what happens when humans invade the past.* The air stank of oil and industry, the great plain blackened by the muck raining down from the sky. Up the hill from them the anomaly remained studiously locked. If Connor couldn't find some way to reverse the effect, they were all going to be trapped.

Soldiers streamed from the mine, heading up the hill towards them. They had their hands raised as they ran, showing that they'd abandoned their weapons. They were accompanied by a large group of civilian workers, who must have run the facility, looking even more panicked than the soldiers.

"They're surrendering?" Abby said, relief in her voice.

"They want the anomaly," Becker pointed out. "It must be the only way home. How are you doing, Connor?"

Connor banged a loose wire back into position. The anomaly still remained a solid sphere hanging in the air; nothing like a doorway through which they could escape.

"Fine," he told Becker. "With you in a minute."

Becker patted him on the shoulder. Then he turned.

"I think we need to round everyone up. Wilcock!"

Wilcock hurried over.

"Sir?"

"See if you can gather a squad that will keep those soldiers together — when we get back to our time, we'll need to place them under arrest. It doesn't make sense to try anything now, as we don't have the resources to handle such a large group. We'll need some of our lot on the other side of the anomaly first, once Connor gets it open, and we'll need enough transport for them all.

"Get everyone else on their feet, as well. I think we're done here now."

Wilcock saluted and rushed off. Becker looked back to Connor.

"Any time now would be good."

Connor took careful aim at the anomaly. He fired up the locking mechanism and waited, but nothing happened. He smacked it with the palm of his hand and it began to emit a beam of energy that plunged into the floating ball of the anomaly.

But still nothing happened.

"Come on, come on," Connor told the machine. He reset the mechanism's programming and the beam of light built in intensity.

"It's not working," Becker observed, his voice tinged with anxiety.

"Yeah," Connor said testily, "I noticed. I think these guys are causing some kind of interference which the locking mechanism doesn't like. If I can recalibrate it or something..."

He worked as fast as he could, fingers moving frantically.

"Any time you like," Becker said.

"He's doing his best," Abby snapped.

There was a legion of soldiers assembled in front of the anomaly, though since they all wore the same black uniforms, and were equally covered in blood and mud, Connor couldn't decide who was who.

"The problem's with the firing piston," he said, reaching his hand out to grasp it. "It would probably work fine if I just held it here."

"Then why don't you?" Becker said.

"Hey," Abby said. "That thing gets pretty hot."

"No," Connor said. "Becker's right. There's nothing else we can do."

And before they could stop him he fired the locking mechanism again, this time with his hand held tight round the firing piston.

He kept his eyes on the anomaly, watching the energy hit the floating sphere.

The piston began to burn his fingers. He could actually see steam rising from them.

Slowly, one-by-one, shards of light began to spring out from the sphere.

"Ow, *ow, ow*," Connor said, grimacing, but he refused to move his hand. Gradually, he began to think the piston might have burnt through to the bone. Tears of agony ran down his face, making it difficult for him to see what was happening. He couldn't hold onto the locking mechanism much longer.

And then the sphere was gone, opened out into glinting shards of the twisting, glimmering anomaly. Connor dropped the locking mechanism and it fell out of the truck into the soft mud.

Becker ran forward.

"Right, everybody out of here."

Abby helped Connor up from the ground. They inspected the dark red burns on his palm and fingers.

"Oh, Connor," she said.

"Nah, it's all right," he told her, tears in his eyes. She leant forward and kissed his cheek.

"Come on," she said, reaching down and grasping the locking mechanism. "Let's get going." She handed the mechanism to a passing soldier.

Becker's men kept the other soldiers under close watch as they filed into the anomaly, two by two.

"Well, don't thank me," Connor said to him. "I only saved us all." He turned to Abby for help.

But Abby ignored him. Instead, she was gazing down the plain at the mine. Her eyes narrowed and she reached over to Becker, who was shouting orders, and plucked the field binoculars from his pocket.

"On the double!" Becker yelled to his men. The soldiers began to run, moving into the portal at increased speed.

"You, too," he said to Abby and Connor. "Time we got you home."

"Sure," Connor said. "Back to the London sunshine."

"I need a car," Abby said quietly as she peered through the binoculars.

"What?" Connor tried to find with his naked eye whatever she had seen. Thick smoke still billowed from the ruins of the mine. The herd of Sauroposeidons cantered off in the distance, nursing their wounds and generally displeased with how the afternoon had gone. What had Abby seen?

"We need to go now," Becker said firmly. "The anomaly is fading."

"He's right, Abby." Connor took the binoculars out of her hands. "We can't wait any longer. I broke the locking mechanism."

Abby shrugged him off and turned to Becker.

"Not without the others," she told him.

"Who?"

"Look," she said, pointing down the hill. Connor and Becker both looked on in amazement.

THIRTY-THREE

Danny, Lester and Sarah emerged into the open, though it took them a moment to realise it. The smoke still swirled thickly around them and they could barely see a few feet ahead, let alone the sky. But the tiles under their feet gave way to concrete, and the sounds around them changed; thick explosions masked the terrible cries of the creatures they'd left behind.

They struggled on, sticking close together for fear of getting lost. Danny could barely breathe or see, his lungs ached with the effort and his body ached from the blows of Samuels' soldiers. They stepped over bodies, their flesh scorched and pink. The terrible smell of burning flesh clogged his nose.

A few moments later they were running on earth rather than concrete, the ground soft under their feet, the smoke clearing with every step they took. They could hear creatures lowing in the distance, and Danny found himself staring at a herd of huge Brachiosaurus. His eyes seemed to be playing tricks on him, or perhaps it was the smoke, but the creatures seemed far too big, their great long necks too slender.

The three of them kept going, their legs getting heavier, their steps ever diminishing, until they collapsed into the mud, exhausted.

Drawing breath in short, painful gasps, Danny looked around. The mud plain stretched out as far as he could see, and smoke tainted an otherwise pure blue sky. A battered SUV bumped and bucked over the mud as it sped down towards them. Danny took a few steps forward.

"That's Becker," he said, amazed and relieved, "and Abby."

"Well," Lester observed dryly, "it's the least they could do." He tugged at his battered, muddy cuffs. Danny watched him pat his hair into place, as though annoyed not to have a comb with him.

The SUV skidded to a halt in front of them.

"Good afternoon," Danny said, and smiled weakly.

"Get in!" Abby shouted, her face streaked with mud and sweat. "The anomaly's about to close!"

They didn't need to be told twice. Lester and Sarah piled into the car, Danny clambering in behind them. Becker had already put his foot down before he closed the door, and Danny had to cling onto the headrest in front of him so as not to fall out.

The car thumped up the plain. Danny finally got the door closed and then banged his head on the ceiling as the SUV bounced over the lip of a crater. Mud spattered against the windscreen and Becker had to flick on the wipers. Ahead of them an anomaly flickered dimly.

"What on earth are you doing here?" Abby asked, looking back at the three of them.

"Short version," Danny said, hanging on to his seatbelt, "old mate of Lester's."

"It was Samuels!" Sarah said. "He tried to kill us."

Abby stared at her. "What? Why?"

Danny smiled wryly.

"I think Lester bullied him at school."

"He should have been grateful," Lester said. "It builds character."

The car lurched over another crater and Becker swore under his breath. They were pressed back into their seats as he pushed the accelerator flat on the floor. The sky showed blue through the anomaly. Danny held his breath.

Suddenly they were through the rucked-up ground, the car speeding forward over the level plain. The anomaly flickered, the centre of light puckering like the last gasp of a candle flame. And they plunged right into it.

In an instant the sky had switched off and they were in darkness. Becker stood on the brake and the car skidded to a halt. Danny smacked hard into the seat in front of him.

He sat back, rubbing at his bruised nose.

Steam hissed from the car's knackered engine. And just beyond the end of the hood stood Connor, eyes and mouth open wide in horror.

"You almost hit me," he protested to Becker as they climbed out of the car.

"Yeah," Becker said, "but I didn't."

Connor made to say something else, then he noticed Danny, Lester and Sarah emerging from the back.

"Hey, where'd *you* come from?"

"South Africa," Danny replied with a wink. "Found a short cut."

THIRTY-FOUR

The office was empty now, cleared of the mess of papers and broken ornaments. A faint trail of blood on the carpet hadn't quite been scrubbed away. Papers stood stacked in neat piles on Lester's desk, in the process of being put back in their files. And a small number of pages lay face down in the tray of Lester's printer. Sarah hurried over, scooping up her two-page proposal and crumpling it into a ball. It was late at night and Sarah was exhausted, but she wanted this all to be gone before the others got in the next morning.

When she turned back round, Lester was barring her way, his arms folded.

"It's just something Samuels asked me to do," she said nervously.

"But you agreed with the idea? Very well argued, I thought."

She blushed.

"I'm sorry. I would have brought it to you if you'd been here."

"Of course you would have. But you know what I'm going to say."

"That we can't risk telling people about what we do."

"Stephen felt like you did. I think Cutter might even have considered it for a while."

Sarah shivered. "And look what happened to them."

"But before they died they'd agreed to keep the anomalies secret — until we knew more about them."

"But perhaps we'd know more about them if we shared the information."

Lester shook his head sadly.

"It won't work like that. We've got enough interested parties muscling in as it is. Imagine what it would be like if we gave private enterprise a chance. There'd have to be a press conference every time we sneezed, and there'd be all the correspondence to answer. Do you know how much time gets eaten up by school groups writing in to the Home Office?"

"How much?"

"Well, I don't have the figures to hand. But the fewer people know about what we do here, the fewer people get hurt."

"Then that's your final answer?"

"I'm afraid so."

She nodded slowly.

"All right, I can understand the reasons. It's just..."

"You think we could do better."

"Yes."

"So do I. I need you on this team, Sarah. I need you to make sense of what we're doing, write your reports, analyse anything you like, but bring your insights to me."

"You might not like what I come up with."

"But I'll consider anything you bring me."

Sarah thought for a moment.

"And if the truth ever gets out anyway? Can I publish my findings then?"

Lester sighed. "I think you'll have to ask whoever is in charge." She frowned at him and he leant forward to whisper in her ear.

"The public only find out about this over *my dead body*."

"...in Maidenhead is that police are allowing people back into their homes. We also hear reports of the army helping clear the tunnel at Rotherhithe, which had filled up with raw sewage. Not a pleasant job for anyone, that!

"Apparently the methane it gave off caused problems for the locals. One woman I spoke to said she thought she'd seen monsters with enormous long necks peering over her garden wall! But anyway, the monsters seem to have vanished back into thin air this morning.

"Back to the studio."

Lester switched off the screen and turned to regard his team. Abby and Connor sat together on the leather sofa. Sarah sat down beside them, squeezing up next to Connor. Danny stood framed in the doorway.

"Job done," he said. "Jenny left a good team behind her."

Lester perched on his desk.

"I trust we're all fully rested after last night's fun and games?" The team murmured their assent. "Good. We seem to be back on our feet just now, but we need to raise our game."

"Don't tell me," Connor said. "You want us all working 110 per cent."

"I'd be disappointed if you weren't doing that already, but we're going to prioritise a few things. It's no good just waiting for the alarm to sound so we can start chasing our tails. Connor, Sarah, get back to work on the artefact."

He turned to Danny.

"You and Becker —" Lester began. Then he looked round. "Where is Becker?"

"Gone to see the family of the soldier who got killed in Maidenhead," Connor said. "He had a wife and kids. Then I think he's got some more visits as a result of our trip into the past."

"Ah, well, when he's back, he and Danny are going to shore up our security here. I'm a little fed up with having just any old riff raff coming through our doors."

"Gotcha," Danny said. "I've an idea how we can do that..."

"Good. Well, that seems to be that. Go on, then. You all have work to do."

Connor shook his head. Then he spoke up.

"But hang on — is that *really* it?"

"Not in the slightest," Lester said, sitting back in his seat. "The South African authorities will go into the mine at any moment and find there's nothing there. All those people who thought they had a share in this miraculous new oil field are going to realise they've been cheated. The British government, of course, denies any involvement in the debacle, but there's going to be some serious questions asked. It might well mean someone's job."

"And then there's the game reserve," Danny pointed out.

"We're not quite sure at what level it was involved," Lester said. "But there are some unpleasant rumours. It seems the management have gone into a free-fall now that they know they won't get their money. Perhaps some of the old keepers they fired can be brought in to put things right. But it's not really our concern."

"That's it?" Danny said, appalled.

"What else can I offer you?" Lester inquired impatiently.

"Well, what about Samuels?"

"Trust me," Lester said, smiling, "you won't make yourself popular mentioning that name in senior circles."

"But he can't have been working alone. They must have needed money to set something like that up. Just the wages for all those soldiers..."

"His men have been dealt with," Lester said. "They're going to spend a long time in jail. And the money is traceable: there's a lot of investors when you promise a new source of oil."

"But who was Samuels working for?" Danny insisted. "Surely he wasn't alone."

Lester looked round the team.

"All right, fine," he sighed. "We have to assume that what we do here interests other people. Samuels — and Leek before him — had their own ideas about how we go about our work. However, no one in government admits they know anything about any of it. In fact, they're falling over themselves to deny it."

Connor leaned forward eagerly.

"Which means it has to be a cover-up."

"Or that they don't know anything about it," Lester said. "What we do is still a reasonably well-kept secret."

"What about Helen Cutter?" Abby put in. "She knows much more about the anomalies than she's let on. He could have been working with her."

"Or your friend Christine," Sarah put in.

"We can't link either of them to Samuels," Lester said. "We can't prove anything. And I don't like conspiracies. So unless you bring me some solid evidence, we have to leave things as they are."

"We can't do anything about them, anyway," Danny said. "Can we?"

"We do what we always do," Lester responded. "We carry on. We investigate the anomalies, put things right where we can, and we wait for whoever might be working against us to make the next move."

The team stared back at him, but no one had anything to add.

"Well then," he said. "If there are no more questions, you're not being paid to sit on my sofa all day."

"Yes, sir," they barked, struggling from their seats to file out in mocking formation.

Lester watched them go. Then he walked slowly round to the chair behind his desk and sank back into it, a king returned to his throne. But the papers stacked up in front of him would not sort themselves.

Sighing, he leant forward and got on with his work.

From inside the ventilation grate just off to his left, a tiny camera watched him.

THE END

ACKNOWLEDGEMENTS

This book had a lot of help along the way. Adam Newell and Sharon Gosling thought of me in the first place, and Cath Trechman, my beleaguered editor at Titan, supplied me handsomely with books and scripts and answers.

As luck would have it, a week before I met Cath to discuss what I might write, my Aunt Sal and Uncle Richard took me to Pilansberg National Park, two hours drive from Johannesburg. It's an awesome, beautiful place stretching 55,000 hectares, and entirely undeserving of the mangled, corrupted and despicable version here. Thanks also to my cousins Georgina and Natalie for pestering a waiter.

Tim Haines and Adrian Hodges spared time from busy schedules to let me rabbit at them down the phone. They suggested many neat fixes to problems with my plot and I'm extremely grateful for their care and patience.

Nancia Leggett at Impossible Pictures let me visit the set twice during filming of series three (I got to watch the recording of episode two, scene 16 and episode five, scenes 89 and 91). The cast and crew could not have been nicer or more forthcoming, and this book is full of details scrounged from those days out.

Paul Cornell and James Moran shared insights from writing for the TV series while Steve Savile and Dan Abnett advised me on the books. Thanks also to Martin Day for his words of wisdom.

Debbie Challis and Joseph Lidster battled through my clunky prose, red-penning the more awful bits. Anna Kodicek's expertise should make her an honorary member of the ARC. Thank you to them all.

ALSO AVAILABLE FROM TITAN BOOKS

PRIMEVAL

SHADOW OF THE JAGUAR

STEVEN SAVILE

A delirious backpacker crawls out of the dense Peruvian jungle muttering about the impossible things he has seen... A local ranger reports seeing extraordinary animal tracks and bones — fresh ones — that he cannot explain...

Cutter and the team are plunged into the hostile environment of the Peruvian rainforest, where they endure a perilous journey leading them to a confrontation with something more terrifying than they could possibly have imagined...

PRIMEVAL
SHADOW OF THE JAGUAR
STEVEN SAVILE

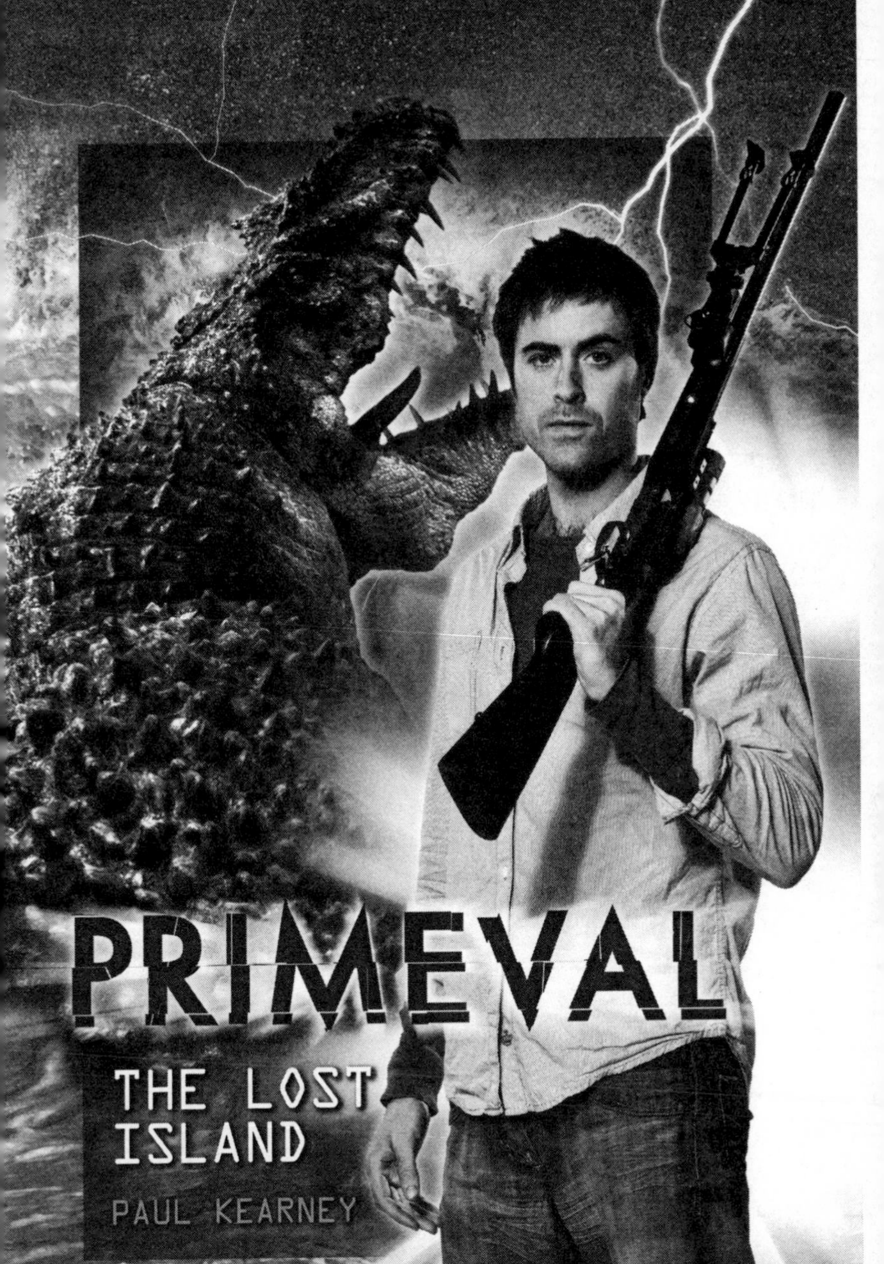
PRIMEVAL
THE LOST ISLAND
PAUL KEARNEY

PRIMEVAL
EXTINCTION
EVENT
DAN ABNETT